PRAISE FOR AMANDA LAMB

"Amanda Lamb has crafted a compelling story... Maddie is definitely not dead last but out front, unearthing clues to the unfolding mystery. Keep digging, Maddie. Keep writing, Amanda!"

–Scott Mason, author and Emmy-award-winning journalist

"Amanda has a gift of taking the reader on a journey of intrigue, laughter, and insight into what can be the wonderful and troubling world of journalism. She opens the mind with a laser beam shot of reality and we are better for it."

–David Crabtree, award-winning television anchor and journalist.

"I love the way Amanda Lamb plunges into a powerful plot and takes readers for a riveting ride! The writing is crisp and clean. The story is compelling. There's an authenticity in Amanda's prose thanks, in part, to the author's background as a top-notch television journalist covering crime stories. What an awesome debut as a novelist!"

–Bill Leslie, former news anchor for NBC affiliate WRAL-TV

"Amanda Lamb weaves together an intriguing mystery with a behind-the-scenes look at TV news. With 25 years of crime reporting, Lamb spins an authentic, compelling story about a reporter who finds herself in the midst of solving a murder. Readers will love the colorful characters & personal insights that make this mystery a must-read."

–Sharon O'Donnell, author and award-winning columnist

NO WAKE ZONE

A MADDIE ARNETTE NOVEL

NO WAKE ZONE

A MADDIE ARNETTE NOVEL

AMANDA LAMB

Light Messages

Durham, NC

Published 2022, by Light Messages
www.lightmessages.com
Durham, NC 27713 USA
SAN: 920-9298

Paperback ISBN: 978-1-61153-425-2
Ebook ISBN: 978-1-61153-426-9
Library of Congress Control Number: 2022933215

To my husband, Grif,
for sharing his love of the sea and boating with me,
and for being my safe harbor in every storm.

PROLOGUE

THERE WAS SOMETHING ABOUT THE WAY my paddle broke through the water like it was slicing through a layer of glass. I could see my reflection on the smooth surface as the sun rose in the distance casting a reddish, orange glow on the horizon. All around me plump amber jellyfish swirled and bobbed, their long white amorphous tentacles trailing behind them down into the murkiness just below the surface.

Paddling on the Intracoastal Waterway was calm and safe. Docks jutted out within reach in front of the massive waterfront homes. This was comforting in case I ran into trouble and needed to get out of the storms that often came up quickly in this part of North Carolina. Even in the early morning, recreational boaters heading out to sea for a day of fishing traveled slowly in the well-posted "No Wake Zone."

After the boats passed and their motors were just a distant whir, the only sound was my paddle pulling back the water with a tiny *woosh* and then brushing against my board with a shallow scraping sound. Boats tied up at the docks along the waterway rose and fell as I passed, straining against their lines, greeting me with their subtle groans.

I looked up as I saw my favorite gray pelican perched in a nest atop a channel marker, looking down at me like she was smiling. I didn't know for sure if she was the same bird that I saw every morning or even if she was, in fact a she, but I made up stories about her and her travels along the coast. She nodded as I passed, bidding me good morning. Sometimes, I pretended she was my mother, Patty, long dead, reincarnated as this magnificent bird to watch over me. In that vein, I often spoke to her—giving her an update on my current life situation.

"Top of the morning, Mom. Vacation is going great. Yes, I'm still doing a little work, a little writing, but getting away from the fray has been good for me."

The *fray* was an incredible understatement. I had ended up with a gun to my head while investigating my last murder case. Because of this, my boss had encouraged me to take a little break, which I agreed to do. I assumed that if my mother had the tenacity to come back as a bird, she already knew all this. I didn't need to explain it to her.

To my left, the tide was low, and the marshes with their black oyster beds were uncovered, looking naked and unkempt with masses of green grass sprouting from the dark, mucky mounds. One step into their lushness would end in a severe cut to the foot as pieces of sharp shells littered the black sand.

Occasionally, I would see a blue heron in the marsh, standing at attention, looking royal, perched on a sandbar. At the slight sound of my oar breaking through the water, the heron would take off, its massive blue wings just skimming the surface as it ascended into the sky in a powerful display of nature's untouchable and unpredictable beauty.

All felt right in the world when I was on my paddleboard. I had left the troubles of the previous months behind me. I was healing both physically and emotionally. I was feeling strong again. While my kids were not with me, they were safe and having fun at summer camp— a new experience for all of us, this independence that felt at once decadent and long overdue.

It was the beginning of a new season in my life— an intrepid news reporter who had traded crime for stories that made people smile, a widow and a single mother determined to be strong for my family. I certainly didn't have everything I wanted and needed, but stability was coming into focus; it was within my grasp. I just had to paddle a little harder.

When my paddle caught on something in the water, I thought it might be a tangle of seagrass. I had seen huge piles of the stuff floating like barges down the waterway over the years. I also knew that while seagrass might snag my paddle, it wouldn't feel like I was hitting something solid. This was different; this was *not* seagrass.

Slowly, I pulled my oar backward to turn the board around so I could retreat and look at what I had hit. I knew it could be a dolphin or a shark, so I quickly scanned the surface of the water for a fin. A shark fin moves back and forth; a dolphin's fin goes up and down. I had learned this early on when I began paddleboarding. If you were lucky enough to see a dolphin, you followed it and watched its graceful dance arcing out of the water into the air and then down again. If you saw a shark, you quickly got yourself to the dock.

It also wasn't uncommon to see the occasional stingray lounging in shallow water near the marsh, tipping one small part of its pointed body upwards, breaking the surface like a fin. Sometimes they even jumped sideways out of the water and careened majestically through the air with a trail of water cascading behind them.

Today, I saw no fins in the water. As I cautiously approached the spot where I had felt the thud, I saw *something.* I saw red and white flashes of material fluttering just beneath the surface. As I got closer, I realized it was clothing—red shorts and a white shirt, probably something someone had dropped off a boat by accident. Four strokes, and I landed right next to it.

I looked down into the water and realized it was not a pile of discarded clothing after all. It was a discarded person. The body of what appeared to be a young man on his back floated just beneath the surface, arms and legs flailed out like a starfish, his dark eyes wide open, staring back at me, begging me to help him. I had clearly arrived too late for help. His face was slack, sallow, and marred only by a single brown mole on his right cheek.

Suddenly, I heard a loud scream slice through the air and bounce off the sides of the houses along the seawall reverberating back across the water to me. I looked around to see where it might be coming from. Then, I realized it was coming from *me.*

1

FIRST CALL

"APPARENTLY HE WAS MISSING. They had been looking for him for several days. He jumped off a party boat to go for a swim, probably drunk, and his friends couldn't find him," I told my best friend Louise over the phone, the words tumbling out of my mouth like I was running out of time. I was sitting in the front seat of a patrol car wrapped in a blanket waiting for an officer to come and take my statement. My husband, Adam, had always been my first call when I was in crisis. After he died due to complications from a malignant brain tumor in 2016, I discovered I had no one to call. Eventually, Louise became my first call—she never left my side even when I tried to push her away as hard as I could.

"Honey, I can't imagine finding a dead body in the water. What did he look like? Was he real bloated, was he blue?" Louise asked without shame.

"Louise," I said with a combination of real and mock horror. "I didn't examine him. He was just a man, a young man, floating in the water with his eyes open. It was so creepy."

"I bet," Louise said in a voice that begged me to tell her more gory details.

"Even though I've seen so many autopsy photos and crime scene photos, it's not the same as seeing a dead person up close."

"I can't imagine, honey, and after everything you've been through, that crazy person chasing you through the woods with a gun, you deserve a break."

I was supposed to be on a break. Back in the spring, while I was investigating a murder case in my hometown of Oak City, I had gotten in too deep. Now, I was supposed to be on a well-deserved sabbatical at the beach working on a true-crime podcast that I had always wanted to write.

My boss at Channel 8 News, Dex, while surly and stoic, had uncharacteristically embraced me in the hospital after the attack, albeit awkwardly, and told me to take as much time as I needed to fully recover. I got my doctor to sign off on three months of Family Medical Leave. I immediately started searching for an Airbnb I could rent for the summer along the coast and chose a small apartment overlooking the Intracoastal Waterway in the quaint town of Cape Mayson.

My 12-year-old twins Miranda and Blake had begged me to let them go camping in Maine for the summer, which solidified my plan for a peaceful, relaxing getaway *until now*.

"I'm coming," Louise said.

"What?" I replied in a daze as I watched the officers rope off an area at the water's edge with yellow crime scene tape. The sun was high in the sky now, blazing down on the surface, causing it to shimmer. The kaleidoscope effect felt all wrong given that this was now a crime scene, a dead man's watery grave. A small crowd was starting to form just outside the tape—mostly people out for a morning run or a bike ride who had stopped to see what was going on.

"I'm coming to Cape Mayson. You shouldn't be alone right now. Plus, the boys are driving me nutty. I feel like I live in the car, taking them from one sports camp to another. I can't get any work done. It's time for Scott to handle their complicated schedules for a few days and maybe get a little understanding of what I have to juggle every single day of my life."

Louise juggled roles as a successful event planner and the mother of three very active boys—Aaron, Alex, and Avery. Her husband,

Scott, worked as an attorney; he was smart and kind but not always clued into the fact that Louise's business was a *career,* not just a hobby.

"Ok, well, you don't have to. But you know I would love to see you. I don't want to take you away from your work."

"Girl, I can work anywhere there's internet and cell service. I assume your cute little condo has all those modern-day amenities?"

"Yes, of course. Where do you think I'm living on the moon?"

"Pretty sure even astronauts have Netflix," Louise quipped.

"Mrs. Arnette, we're ready for you now," a man's voice bellowed from behind me.

The officer who interviewed me was young despite his husky voice. I sluffed the blanket, which now seemed silly as the temperature had quickly risen into the mid-seventies. I stood up and leaned against the patrol car and told him everything I remembered about finding the body.

"I hit something with my paddle, snagged something. I assumed it was just debris floating in the water, a tangle of seagrass, an old board, or tire, something like that. I really didn't know. But then I looked down and saw *him.*"

My words drifted off to a place where I couldn't find them. I realized I was staring down at my bare feet now, and the officer was staring at me.

"Mrs. Arnette, if you would rather do this later, you could come down to the station in a few hours after you've had a little break, a chance to process all of this," the young officer said, putting a hand on my shoulder. While he was just a rookie, he had the makings of a good policeman with his compassionate demeanor. I pulled myself out of the dark hole and looked up at him again.

"No, that's okay. There's not much more. I turned around to see what I had hit, and I saw clothing fluttering near the surface of the water. And then I saw him. His eyes were open. It was like he was

6

looking at me. It was pretty shocking. Do you know how old he was? He looked young."

"No, Ma'am. Not off-hand. I'm just a patrol officer. I know we had our investigators looking into a missing person's report that might be connected. It could be him. We won't know for sure until we get a positive I.D. A young woman, a friend of the missing man, has offered to come to the coroner's office at the request of his family to see if it is him. Hopefully, we'll know something soon."

"You mean the guy missing from the party boat; the one presumed drowned?"

"How did you know about that?" The young officer said with more angst than I had expected.

"I've been sitting here for two hours listening to the officers who set up the perimeter around the scene. I'm a journalist, a television reporter in Oak City, so naturally, I'm curious. It was kind of hard not to hear what they were talking about."

The young officer bristled a little when I said "journalist," as if a chill had just passed through his body on this balmy summer morning. But then he seemed to snap out of it and returned to his professional demeanor.

"Understood. Well, again, nothing is for sure until we confirm the man's identity and cause of death."

"Of course. I know how it works. I used to be a crime reporter. Gave it up for feature reporting after my husband died. I cover animal stories, actually, but I do miss the streets a little. Used to be in the middle of the fire; now I can't even see the smoke."

The officer closed his notebook, a sign that he was done with me and had no interest in hearing about my tragic life. He gave me his card and told me to give him a call if I remembered anything else. Part of me wanted to say that he might want my card, that he might want to stay in touch with me because, as a good investigator, he should be following up with the witness.

My gut told me to let it go. I'd had enough trauma in my life with my recent assault, Adam's death, and my dysfunctional childhood. I was here on this island to heal, not to open old wounds by inserting myself into a death investigation. But I had never found a dead body before. I couldn't stop thinking about the man's eyes—or were they the eyes of a boy? It was hard to tell. Man or boy, his eyes bore right through me. They were begging me for help. I knew in my heart that they were not something I could walk away from any time soon.

2

RIPPLE

I LET THE HOT WATER PRACTICALLY scald me as I stood directly beneath the showerhead, trying to wash death off my body. As a television reporter, I had been to many crime scenes that left me feeling dirty, but there was something about staring death in the face that made me feel hopelessly unclean.

After about twenty minutes, the water started to run cold. The apartment's small water heater was no match for my penchant for long hot showers. I pushed the linen shower curtain aside and reached for a fluffy white towel on the vanity. I was impressed with all the small touches this Airbnb included, like comfortable towels. They would be getting five stars at the end of my stay.

The apartment was perfect for one person. It was a small, tidy two-bedroom unit in a high rise right on the Intracoastal Waterway. The simple decorations gave the feeling of being in a large hotel suite rather than in someone's home. Everything was white and a soothing tone of light blue—beachy without being tacky. Over the mantle in the den hung a brooding painting of the ocean with dark skies and an angry sea. I found myself staring at it and wishing I could jump into the scene and walk along the edge of the churning surf.

When I sat in one of the large wooden lounge chairs on the patio

9

with its comfy padding and throw pillows all around me, it almost felt like I was on a ship sitting right on top of the water. The edge of the sixth-floor balcony seemed to spill into the waterway like an infinity pool. It was an illusion, of course, but one that kept me on the balcony from morning until nighttime, tapping away on my computer—a steaming cup of coffee by my side in the morning and a cold glass of wine in the evening.

I was working on a podcast about three brothers, gangsters, who stole farm equipment in Pennsylvania in the mid-seventies and then laundered the money through bowling alleys, hair salons, and bars. They would back up trucks to the farms in the middle of the night and drive the tractors right onto the flatbeds like they were mere Tonka Toys and then drive off with them.

Like most illegal activity, things eventually began to go south when the brothers couldn't decide who was in charge and how things should be run. When one of them introduced drugs into the mix, things got violent. People started getting murdered. That's when the story turned from folklore into something much darker; that's when I got interested.

I was working as a freelancer and writing the podcast for a true-crime network that had a show called *Bad Blood* about family members engaged in criminal enterprises together. The show had reached out to me after my near brush with death had garnered me my fifteen minutes of national fame. I didn't really care why they tapped me for the project; I was excited about it.

I had done most of the interviews on my laptop with headphones and an external microphone; now, I was simply listening to the recordings, researching, and writing the show's first episodes. Once I finished the scripts, I would send them to my producer, Kai, and he would finesse them until they were ready for me to voice. I had already rented space at an audio booth in Cape Mayson so that I could record my narrative and complete the entire project without ever leaving my little slice of paradise.

But right now, I wasn't thinking about the Jones brothers or their life of crime; I was thinking about *those eyes*, the eyes of the man staring back at me from just beneath the surface of the water. I kept replaying the moment over and over in my mind. One minute everything was calm, peaceful, and serene; the next minute, it was like being in a horror movie. *Cue the screaming woman.*

I decided I would call Kojak to calm my nerves. Kojak was a detective who handled homicide cases in Oak City. He was a tough-talking, irreverent old-school cop who gave me great under-the-radar information about the cases I was covering. But more importantly, over the years that I had known him, he had become like the father I never had since my real father, Roger, had been in prison most of my life. Kojak felt like the closest thing to a dad that I could imagine; he supported me, advised me, worried about me, scolded me, praised me, and generally had my back in every situation.

"So, kid must have been one hell of a morning for you. I swear, you just know how to find trouble, don't you? Just rolled on in with the tide and right up to your feet, *literally.*"

"Nice, making fun of the dead guy."

"Just trying to lighten the mood, trying to make you crack a smile. I can hear it in your voice. I'm making a dent."

Kojak always knew how to cheer me up. He listened to me when I needed to rant about my tragic childhood and my convicted felon father. He understood exactly how my mother's murder had affected me, and he also knew never to bring it up, that it was my pain to share when I was ready. It was nobody else's business.

"Spoke to one of my buddies in Cape Mayson. Says the guy drowned, was on some sort of a charter, a party boat. Some girl's birthday party. Guess he had too much to drink and maybe some recreational drugs, who knows. Just slipped under, and apparently no one could get there in time to help him."

"Yes, pretty much what I overheard from the officers at the scene. It's just so weird that no one jumped in to save him."

"They were probably *wasted.*"

"Still, it's really sad. Got a name from your buddy?"

"Nope, didn't get into all that. Said the boat belonged to a local hotel magnate who owns a string of fancy boutique hotels. Luxury cruising yacht, forty-eight feet. *Sweet ride.* But he rents it out mostly as an investment. Has a captain who runs it, takes care of it, and lives on it, I think. Didn't give me anybody's name, but he did tell me the name of the boat."

"And?"

"Full name is 'Ripple in Still Water'; most people just know it as 'Ripple.'"

"That's intriguing. Where do I know that phrase from?"

"It's a line from a Grateful Dead song. Guy must have been a Dead Head. He's the right age for that flower power hippie-dippy stuff, in his sixties."

"Got it."

"It's part of the chorus; the next lines are: *When there is no pebble tossed, nor wind to blow.*"

Suddenly, I pictured the man going overboard, his body sinking swiftly in the water, like a rock, leaving an almost imperceptible ripple across the surface beneath the moonlight, a ripple no one even noticed.

When I hung up with Kojak, I started searching for the name of the boat, trying to glean any information I could. Right away, several media reports from the local newspaper and television stations popped up with headlines like:

MAN DROWNS AFTER FALLING OFF PARTY BOAT.

The articles identified the owner of the charter boat as Mark Maron. Apparently, he had little to do with the day-to-day operations of it. Maron went back and forth between his luxury homes in Oak City and Cape Mayson. He had his own large fishing boat that he used for himself, his family, and friends, not to mention assorted small recreational motorboats. He let his captain, Perry Spotz, rent out Ripple to groups for parties, and Spotz managed the events. According to the news reports, this particular get-together had been a thirtieth birthday party for a local woman named Stella Avery and about twenty of her friends.

I immediately looked up Stella Avery on social media. There was a smiling photo of an attractive young woman wearing blue scrubs and a stethoscope around her neck. She had a round face framed by shoulder-length brown wavy hair, a wide, genuine smile, and large brown eyes. Her hands were on her hips as she gave the camera a slightly coy sideways glance. The brief information in her profile said she was a physician's assistant for a family medical practice in Oak City but that she was originally from Cape Mayson. That meant the partygoers were likely a combination of people she grew up with and maybe a few friends from the city. She listed herself as "single," interested in "men," and in the religion category, she had the word "searching."

I quickly tapped on her photos and started scrolling through them. She had dozens of pictures of herself at the beach with large groups of friends, arm-in-arm standing on the white sand, squinting into the sunlight as the blue ocean twinkled behind them. I was about ready to give up my online stalking for the day when I suddenly stopped and scrolled back to see a photo that had grabbed my attention. It was a picture of Stella sitting on the bow of a small motorboat with a man next to her. His left arm casually draped over her shoulders, and he had a beer in his right hand angled at the camera in a mock toasting motion. They both beamed. Boyfriend? Hard to tell. I zoomed in and examined him more closely. He resembled the man I saw floating in the waterway, with similar features, same color hair, same approximate age, but I couldn't tell for sure if it was him or not because the photo became so blurry when I blew it up. I was starting to realize there were a lot of things about this situation that were blurry, things I desperately wanted to bring into focus.

3

NO PLAYBOOK

I AWOKE TO THE INCESSANT RINGING of my doorbell. I must have fallen asleep on my lounge chair. I had the sliding door open and was letting the breeze drift through the screen door. I was still wrapped in my robe from the shower, my wet hair now dry and crinkled in odd, twisted lumps around my face. My laptop was resting on the chair next to me, and the sun was just beginning to set over the water. Pink and orange hues filled the sky, blending like a watercolor painting.

"Hello, anybody in there?" I heard Louise's cheerful voice through the door. I rubbed my tired eyes and looked through the peephole. There she was in all her glory, standing in the hallway, her perky blonde self, a big smile amidst a smattering of freckles. She was weighted down with various tote bags and holding up a bottle of Prosecco for me to see.

"Coming," I said groggily as I undid the chain and unbolted the door. I stepped aside to let her and her energy sail past me.

"Oh my God, this is so cute. How in the world did you score this?" Louise dropped her bags in the hallway and started darting around, poking her head into each small room. Then through the sliding door in the den, she noticed the sunset. "Get out of here. Is that for real? I would seriously live on this porch," she exclaimed, skipping outside. She grabbed the Prosecco and yelled for me to get two glasses and hurry.

I didn't feel much like celebrating as it had only been a little more than twelve hours since I stumbled upon a dead body, but then I realized there was no real playbook for what I was going through. Finding a dead body on your daily morning paddleboarding excursion wasn't exactly something anyone expected or knew how to absorb. Maybe a little bubbly would help my spirits. I was pretty sure Louise was not going to take no for an answer. I grabbed two plastic champagne flutes from a cabinet in the kitchen and headed outside to meet her on the balcony.

"Plastic? What the hell? Okay, I guess they will have to do," Louise said, flippantly rolling her eyes in a dramatic gesture. She unscrewed the bottle, and I held up the two glasses while she poured. I was silently praising the owner for only having cups made of plastic so there would be no chance of renters breaking anything. It made total sense to me. We both sat down silently on one lounge chair, side by side, and surveyed the last breathtaking moments of the setting sun.

"How are you?" Louise asked with uncharacteristic solemnity, draping her free arm over my shoulders as she continued to focus on the orange orb melting into the horizon beyond the water's edge.

"I don't know. I slept most of the afternoon. Passed out, literally passed out right here on this chair. *That's not like me.*"

"True, but you've just been through something very traumatic. I'm no shrink, but I'm pretty sure emotional exhaustion can lead to physical exhaustion. Any more information on the guy, on what happened to him?"

I resisted the temptation to pick up my laptop and see if there were any updates on the story on the local news websites. I just shook my head and ran my free hand through my angry hair.

"I called Kojak. He actually had a little bit of information. Not much. Confirmed what I had overheard at the scene, that the guy was at a birthday party on this boat and either jumped off or fell off and drowned. It was a charter owned by some rich hotel guy. But he wasn't there at the time. He's hands-off, lets his captain manage the rentals."

15

"So, no one saw him go under? No one jumped in to save him?"

"I know, it's weird. But who knows exactly what happened? Everyone was drinking. You know how that is. Not a good combination, alcohol and water. Anyway, pretty sure it was just a tragic accident, but it's really sad."

"Yes, yes, it is," Louise squeezed my shoulders a little tighter. "On another topic, how's Zack?"

She caught me off-guard, as Louise always had a tendency of doing. She was like that person in the Jenga game who always looked like she was pulling the piece that would make the whole tower fall, but then it was you who made the tower fall. This element of surprise was her gift.

"Why do you ask?"

"You know why. He's the first person you've expressed even a mild passing interest in since Adam died."

Zack Brumson was a state police officer in Pennsylvania that Kojak had asked to take another look at my father, Roger's, case for me. I had recently learned some information that put Roger's guilt in question. Just thinking about the situation had turned my life upside down. So, I didn't like to think about it. Adam died in the fall of 2016, barely two and a half years ago. I didn't know what the official mourning period was before it was okay for me to date, but I was pretty sure I wasn't there yet.

"True, but he lives in Pennsylvania, and I live in North Carolina."

"Details," Louise said, clinking our plastic glasses together making a predictable little *clack* sound. "So unsatisfying, the sound of plastic."

We both laughed then. I could barely see her as the sun had set and darkness had taken over, but I knew she was smiling. I was smiling too and crying. I felt a tear roll down my face and fall onto the lapel of my robe. I wished I had a playbook for so many things in my life.

We sat at the restaurant bar because we were informed by the tan, blonde, lanky hostess with a monotone voice that it would be a one-hour-and-twenty-minute wait for a table. That's how it was at the beach in the summertime; they packed people in, and everyone was surprisingly willing to wait forever for their fried shrimp tacos and spicy margaritas.

"So, how are you? How are Scott and the boys?" I asked Louise, trying to turn the focus away from me. I was done talking about myself.

"Everyone is good. You know the courts slow down a little in the summer because all the judges go on vacation. Not a lot of trials. That's why I knew I could leave the boys with Scott. His schedule is not that busy right now, and the kids are in like a million sports camps. It's really frigging insane trying to get them everywhere they're supposed to be all day long. I needed a break."

Louise's three boys—Aaron, Alex, and Avery—were fifteen, thirteen, and ten, respectively. They were what she loosely referred to as "active" boys, not a calm bone in their little live-wire bodies. They were in perpetual motion; therefore, so was Louise. It was exhausting to watch her parent. My twelve-year-old son Blake was the opposite of Louise's brood. He was anxious and quiet. He enjoyed solitary activities like playing piano and reading. Sometimes, I wished he had a little more bravado, more armor to protect him from the cruel world, but I knew his sensitivity would eventually lead him to be a great man like his father was, full of compassion and kindness.

"Well, please thank Scott for giving you up for a few days away," I said with a grin, dipping another tortilla chip into the delicious dish of steaming queso on the bar in front of us.

"Duly noted, but he *needs* to be without me sometimes to realize how lucky he is."

Louise was right. Scott was lucky. She ran a very successful event-planning business *and* ran their household. Scott pretty much just worked and took Louise's orders. For the most part, their lives ran seamlessly, thanks to her.

"And work, how's business?"

"Pretty good, you know, not too many weddings planned in the heart of the summer in North Carolina. Too hot. So, end of May into mid-June is super busy, and then it falls off until September. Plus, Chloe is more than capable of handling everything when I'm gone. She practically runs the show now. I just bring in the business and create the overall themes and ideas, and Chloe implements them, down to the last detail."

"That's great. That must be a big relief after doing everything on your own for so many years."

"It is. In the same way, Scott is lucky to have me; I'm so lucky to have Chloe. She's a godsend. And the clients love her too, a breath of fresh air that girl is. Lovely inside and out. She's breezy; that's how I would describe her. She breezes into a room and makes everything feel a little lighter and more pleasant."

No one would ever accuse Louise or me of being breezy. Acerbic, irreverent, tough, a little crazy—these were the words most people would use to describe us.

"Bartender," Louise said loudly over the surfer-themed music playing from a speaker just above our heads that accompanied a video of surfers shredding on a big screen television above the bar. "Can we get another round?"

I licked the last little bit of salt off the rim of my glass and took a final sip which turned out to be margarita-flavored ice. I wasn't a big fan of liquor, but like with the Prosecco, I knew that Louise wasn't taking no for an answer on this one.

"Do you think it's possible for someone to fall off a boat into the water and for no one to notice?" I turned and said to Louise out of the blue. It was a thought that had been bouncing around in my head for hours. I knew saying it aloud meant that I was descending into another rabbit hole. It meant that I would not stop until I found the answer. I was afraid of my own tenacity—it often overpowered my common sense. I was here to get away from the news business for a while, to write my podcast, and to focus on rebuilding my sanity, not to do something that could potentially torpedo the whole process.

"No, I don't," Louise said to me with surprising frankness. "I think something is fishy about this."

I giggled at the word "fishy." Not that there was anything funny about someone drowning. The margarita made me do it.

The waitress with a short, dark pixie haircut and curly purple bangs had just put our drinks down in front of us and was wiping the chip crumbs off the bar. Her face was tilted, and I could tell she was pretending not to listen but that she *was* listening to us intently. Her head was cocked with her left ear in our direction. She wore a tight black tank top exposing her tattooed arms that bore zero hint of a tan. I wondered silently if she might be a vampire. How could you live in Cape Mayson and not have the least little bit of color from the sun?

"Ladies, the tacos are on the way. More chips?"

"Not for me," I answered quickly, lest Louise challenge me. I had no discipline with tortilla chips, and we had already devoured an entire basket and practically licked the queso bowl clean.

The waitress smiled and turned to walk away, carrying her wet rag in one hand and the empty chip bowl in the other hand. Then, she abruptly turned around again.

"I agree with you, by the way," she said, putting the towel and bowl back down on the bar, leaning in close to us, trying to whisper over the surf jam music screaming above our heads.

"With what?" Louise said with more curiosity than criticism.

"About drowning. You're talking about that guy who fell off the party boat, right?"

Louise and I turned to look at each other, the margarita fog having clouded our judgment in how loudly we had been talking.

"Yes," Louise said without hesitating, now looking directly at the pixie-haired waitress with great interest.

"I think something happened on that boat. How could all those people not see anything? And if they did, how could they just leave him? That's *unconscionable*."

For some reason, I was surprised by the pixie-haired waitress's use of the word "unconscionable." It reminded me once again not to judge people by their outward appearance.

"So true!" Louise said conspiratorially, raising her margarita glass into the air triumphantly to cheer with an invisible drink that the waitress wasn't holding.

"I have a friend who busses tables at another restaurant down the road. He has a friend who was on the boat. Guy who pumps gas at one of the marinas. He told me that the guy told him that the captain, Perry, knew exactly what was going on, and he left the guy in the water. I mean, I wasn't there, so I don't know for sure. But it just sounds kind of *off* to me."

Suddenly, the expression on the waitress's face changed. Her eyes went cold, and she nervously gripped her rag in both hands and turned away from us quickly. Obviously, she felt like she had said too much. She probably had. On one hand, I was glad she did. She had reinforced my feelings that something wasn't right about the situation, but on the other hand, she had raised major red flags that I couldn't ignore now, even if I wanted to.

"Uh oh," Louise said knowingly as she caught the expression on my face.

4

SWIMMING LESSONS

THE NEXT MORNING AS I SAT ON THE PATIO looking out over the water in every direction, the impossibly radiant blue skies just beyond the balcony's railing convinced me that I was overreacting. How could such evil happen in a place as stunning as this? The white fluffy clouds played tricks on my brain—first, there was a mermaid, then a bunny, then my mother's smiling face looking down at me, a tiny speck on a comfortable lounge chair in a great big world.

I didn't know my mother as an adult. She had died when I was three. So, any guidance I attributed to her was pure speculation. But from what I had pieced together from my grandmother over the years and the few photographs I had of her, I wanted to imagine that she would have been an incredible mother—patient and kind, firm and strong, loving and supportive, but also someone who pushed me to do my very best. In a way, not having her most of my life gave me the opportunity to create a memory of the mother *I wanted* instead of the mother I had. I listened to my friends complain about their mothers endlessly. They said they were passive-aggressive, critical of everything they did, and that nothing was good enough for their mothers. I always suspected the truth fell somewhat shy of their extreme descriptions and that, in reality, most of them would not trade their mothers for anything in the world. I silently thanked

God that my imaginary mother would always be perfect in my mind.

As I sipped my coffee, I watched the early morning boaters zip by too fast for the No Wake Zone. They were mostly recreational boaters and fishermen who knew the sheriff's boats wouldn't be patrolling the water until well after nine.

I decided I was going to let this one go; I was not going to investigate this man's drowning, as sad as it was. I would leave it up to the local police to handle it while I did what I had come here to do: to get my life together.

Against my better judgment, while Louise was still sleeping, I Googled the drowning story when I got back from a three-mile run. I told myself I would only read one news article, the first one that popped up, and that would be it. I would drop it after that.

The first article that appeared was from a local television station. It identified the drowned man as 28-year-old Max Prince. The information on Max was minimal. The article said he had grown up in Cape Mayson and that he was a lifeguard on the beach in-season and an elementary physical education teacher and soccer coach during the school year. It said that the family had declined an autopsy to determine the cause of death, but they had agreed to a toxicology screen to see if he had alcohol or drugs in his system. My guess was, based on what I had heard about the party, alcohol was most likely going to be a factor. According to the article, the body had been released to the family, and they were planning a wake and service with the help of the Windstream Funeral Home.

The photos of Max in the article were pretty blurry. They looked like candid shots lifted directly from Facebook. I tried to pull up his page, but it appeared it had already been taken down. Understandably, family members probably didn't want to field a million inquiries and sentiments from his friends on social media. Then I went back to Stella's account and found the photo of her with the man I had looked at the day before. I screenshotted it and used a photo app to put it in a double box next to Max's photo from the newspaper article. Based on the hair and the general shape of their heads, they looked like the same person. But was it the man I found floating in the water? *It had to be.* Yet, something about my memory of that traumatic moment wasn't gelling with the photos in front of me. There was a detail that I couldn't put my finger on.

The fact that Max had been a lifeguard stopped me cold—*a lifeguard drowned?* It didn't make any sense. I knew that beach lifeguards went through rigorous physical training to prevent themselves and others from succumbing to the power of the ocean. Sure, even the strongest swimmers could drown, but it seemed like lifeguards had the best chance of survival given their skillset.

Still, investigators told the reporter who wrote the story that they believed Max's death was simply a tragic accident and that in the absence of any other information pointing to foul play, they expected to close the case soon.

I couldn't wait to tell Louise these details when she finally woke up from her beauty sleep. I had peeked into the second room and saw that she had fallen asleep on top of the comforter, snuggled around an army of throw pillows. At least she had taken the time to change from her sundress into a t-shirt and sweatpants. I imagined that the joy of sleeping in without being interrupted by three raucous boys could not be overstated.

The news about the police preparing to close the investigation so quickly didn't sit well with my brain based on what the pixie-haired waitress had told Louise and me the night before. I tried to shove her words out of my crowded head and instead focus on the brilliant sunshine that was now twinkling across the surface of the water and casting a diamond-shaped pattern on the white stucco ceiling above my balcony. Just as I closed my eyes to take in the stillness of the moment, my phone rang. I fumbled in the pile of throw pillows at my side, trying to locate it.

"Maddie Arnette," I said in my professional television reporter voice. I only had one phone, so I always erred on the side of caution and expected it to be a work call. I didn't bother looking at the screen to see who it was.

"Maddie, it's Zack; how are you?"

I lost my breath for a moment.

"Zack, what a surprise. I'm good. I'm actually taking a little time off work. Spending the summer at the coast, working on a freelance writing project." I tried to sound casual as if I had been expecting his out-of-the-blue call.

"Yes, Kojak filled me in on what happened with that crazy guy with the gun. Very scary situation. So glad you're okay. You should be dubbed an honorary detective. If it weren't for you and your courage, they may never have solved that case."

I blushed at his mention of my bravery. What was happening here? Was I a 14-year-old girl or a 42-year-old woman?

"I'm good, I mean okay. Better now, much better. This place was exactly what the doctor ordered," I blabbered. What was I saying? *Just what the doctor ordered.* Who talked like that?

"I sent you a card and some flowers when you were in the hospital. Not sure if you got them or not."

"I did, thank you. I'm so sorry I didn't acknowledge them. Everything was just so overwhelming."

"I know, I'm sorry. Didn't mean to say it like that. I just wanted you to know I was thinking about you. Whenever you're ready, we can talk about Roger's case, but there's no rush. Well, actually, there might be a little bit of a rush. His lawyer filed an M.A.R. appeal, which stands for Motion for Appropriate Relief. He may be getting a hearing soon."

I got quiet at the mention of my father, Roger. Suddenly, my girlish excitement over hearing Zack's voice morphed into a dark cloud that hung over me whenever Roger became part of the conversation. Kojak had asked Zack on my behalf to investigate the possibility that another man named Clifton had killed my mother. I had visited Roger in prison in the spring after not speaking to him for thirty years, and he had played with my emotions, making me want his paternal love, a love that I had ignored for decades, just like I had ignored his letters for years. I had hundreds of them in a big plastic bin in my walk-in closet. I only recently read parts of them. In his most recent letter, he told me that he did not kill my mother but that he was responsible for her death just the same. I didn't know what this meant, and I wasn't sure I wanted to know. At Kojak's request, Zack, who was a friend of his from the police academy, had reviewed the old files and discovered something. That "something" was contained in a manila envelope that Kojak had given me before I left for my sabbatical. But I told him I wasn't ready to look at it yet, that I would hold onto it until the time was right. Now, I felt like Zack was forcing my hand, that he wasn't giving me time to digest whatever his investigation revealed at my own pace. He was essentially opening the manila envelope for me.

"Wow. That's pretty unbelievable." I was sure he could hear the deflation in my voice.

"Anyway, let's not talk about this over the phone. I am going to Cape Mayson on vacation. I heard the surfing is pretty good there. I'd love to get together and talk about the case *or not*. We don't have to talk about anything that you don't want to talk about."

My heart skipped a beat. Roger was pushed back into the recesses of my brain again. I could only think of Zack, sitting on a deck with me overlooking the water, sharing a meal, not a care in the world. I didn't even stop to ponder the coincidence of his coming on vacation here, to the place where I just happened to be living for the summer. Maybe it wasn't a coincidence. *Kojak.* He had obviously told Zack I was here. I was flattered and anxious at the same time.

"Okay, sure, I mean yes. Let's get together, definitely. When will you be here?"

"Tomorrow. I'm staying on the beach at a small hotel, nothing fancy, just an efficiency with a little kitchen and den. But right on the beach. Pretty sweet for a land-locked Pennsylvania dweller."

"Sounds perfect," I replied, my words devoid of any real excitement. Suddenly, I was questioning his motives, wondering why he would plan a vacation here of all places? After all, New Jersey and Delaware had nice beaches that were much closer to Pennsylvania. Then just as quickly as the skeptical thoughts entered my head, I shooed them away. Why was I always so suspicious of everyone? I guess it was one of the burdens that came with being a journalist.

"So, it's yes?"

"What's yes?" I asked, momentarily confused.

"Yes, to getting together."

"Oh, right, absolutely."

"Great, so I'll call you."

"Sounds good."

And it was good, the thought of seeing Zack. This surprised me, and I wasn't a person who was easily surprised.

"So, he just called out of the blue?" Louise said as she threw a handful of wet cut-up fruit from the colander into a bowl full of Greek yogurt and granola.

"Yep, it was a total surprise."

"Fabulous. I'm feeling pretty good about this," Louise said as she shoveled a big spoonful of her breakfast concoction into her mouth and nodded for me to follow her to the balcony, where we settled into opposite chaise lounges like an old married couple in a well-worn routine.

"Me, too. I guess."

"What do you mean, *you guess*?" Louise said, swatting me with her napkin across the small space between the chairs.

"I don't know. I just don't know if I'm ready for this."

"What's *this* anyway? It's just a meal. It's not like you're giving him a lung or anything."

"I know, but it seems too soon."

"Too soon?" she said, almost spitting yogurt out of her full mouth. "It's been almost three bloody years, for God's sake. Are you planning on becoming a nun or something? Adam certainly wouldn't expect you to be alone for the rest of your life."

"No, he wouldn't. You're right. It's just a meal. I don't know why I'm so weirded out by it. I guess it's just been a long time. And don't give me some crap about *it's like riding a bike.*"

"I wouldn't dream of it! It's like swimming. You don't suddenly forget how to do it. You might be a little rusty, need to warm up a little, maybe stretch, but in no time, you'll be doing the breaststroke across the bay."

It was me who hit her with the napkin this time. Quietly, I wondered where I might be able to get some swimming lessons.

5

RABBIT HOLE

WHEN I TOLD LOUISE WHAT I HAD LEARNED about Max Prince, she agreed that something wasn't right. She said *there is no way a lifeguard drowned in calm waters.* I couldn't disagree with her. Yet, I didn't know what I was going to do about it. I wondered if I could find the pixie-haired waitress's busboy friend. I could go back to the restaurant where she worked and ask her to connect us. But based on the abrupt way she had stopped talking to us that night after she unloaded her information, it seemed unlikely she would cooperate.

My other option was to locate Stella Avery and see if she would talk to me. After all, it was her party, *and* I had seen her getting cozy with a man who could be Max in one of her Facebook photos. She might not have been dating the man in the photo, but they were at least close enough to take an affectionate picture together. My gut told me Stella would not be forthcoming with me. She had likely already spent a lot of time speaking with the police about the incident and probably felt guilty that someone had died at her party, even if she had nothing to do with it. At the very least, she was friends with Max and was grieving his death. I could feel myself slipping down a rabbit hole again, looking at all the angles of a case like I did when I was a crime reporter. It was impossible just to turn it off.

I was waiting for Louise to get dressed, and we were going to head to the beach for a little while. I had already packed a cooler with water, fruit, cheese, and crackers. The apartment came equipped with beach chairs and a little rolling cart to carry our gear for the five-block walk to the beach. I was busy trying to figure out how to strap everything down when my phone rang.

"Maddie Arnette," I answered, quickly slipping my AirPods in my ears so that I could continue what I was doing.

"Maddie, it's Janie! It's so good to hear your voice. I miss you so much. It's just not the same without you here, for real. How are you? Are you relaxing? You deserve it. I don't know how we're getting by without you. It's crazy. I mean you of all people, you know how it is!"

Janie's words tumbled out of her mouth like a freight train barreling down the tracks. Janie and I had worked together for five years. She was nothing if not enthusiastic about every story she pitched to me. I admired her positive attitude in the face of an industry full of cantankerous skeptics. When I stepped back from crime reporting after Adam's death to do animal stories dubbed "Amazing Animal Tales," Janie scoured social media for me, looking for mentions of runaway emus and lifesaving dogs.

"Miss you too, girl. But I don't miss the stress. I'm enjoying this new pace. What's up?"

I knew for sure that Janie's call was not a social call. They never were. She needed something from me, and she would gracefully back into her real reason for calling.

"Well, see, the thing is, we need to get a camera into the courtroom for a first appearance today. I called the judge's office and left a message, but no one is calling me back. Can you text Judge Baron and ask him if we can have a camera inside? I would do it, but he probably won't respond to me. I *know* he will respond to *you*."

"No problem," I said after a moment of silence. I knew this would not be the last call from the newsroom during my sabbatical. News never took a day off, and I had built up an army of contacts and knowledge over the years on the crime beat that couldn't be replicated by new reporters still getting their bearings. Building relationships and trust with sources took years, and most up-and-coming reporters didn't stay in a local television market long enough anymore to do this. They were on to a bigger market within three to four years. I was the unicorn. I had stayed in Oak City for nearly fifteen years because this was where Adam and I had chosen to raise our family. I knew it had been the right choice, but at the moment, I felt so unmoored that I wondered if a fresh start somewhere else might just be the answer.

"Thanks so much! You're *amazing*," Janie gushed.

"For you, anything."

"I'm sure we'll be talking again. I really don't want to interrupt your sabbatical. I will try not to take advantage of you too much."

"No worries."

I was about to hang up when, after a brief moment of silence, Janie spoke abruptly like the rubber sole of a sneaker catching on a linoleum floor.

"There's one more thing," she said with something bordering on panic in her voice.

"What?"

"So, you know the guy they found dead at the beach?"

Police had thankfully not released my name publicly, so neither Janie nor anyone else other than the handful of people I had told knew that *I* was the one who had found Max Prince floating in the water. The news reports simply said *a woman paddleboarding came across the body*. Technically, if the news outlets pushed the issue, they could argue that my name was public record because I was a witness in a death investigation, but in a small news market like Cape Mayson, no one was going to challenge the police on this point, especially when everyone believed the death was an accident. It was basically old news now that the body had been found; the media would move on to the next big story.

"Yes, of course, I am aware of it. It happened right around the corner from where I'm staying," I said, trying not to sound like I knew too much but not outright lying in the process.

"Well, I have some inside information about it," she said, making it clear that she was about to let me in on what she thought was a major secret.

Suddenly, I was paying close attention, something I had to admit I didn't always do when Janie talked. My mind was racing. How in the world would Janie have a connection to a group of people on a fancy charter boat in Cape Mayson?

"Damien, you know, my boyfriend," she said tutorially even though I had met Damien at least half a dozen times at company holiday parties, summer picnics, and other functions.

"Yes, of course, I know Damien," I replied, trying to sound casual. Frankly, I didn't like Damien. I didn't think he was good enough for Janie. He seemed like a freeloader to me. He was always "in-between jobs." He'd been in some trouble in the past, nothing major. Janie had told me about his record over drinks one night after work. He had been arrested for having a small amount of marijuana in his car during a traffic stop, for not paying child support on time, and for failing to show up for court a few times. The charges were all dismissed or pled down to minor offenses where he had to pay a fine and do community service. She told me he was taking classes at the local community college and that he was *getting his life together,* which as a journalist, I learned was usually a euphemism for people who did not have their lives together. In short, I didn't think he was worth her time, but she was my friend, and I didn't feel like I had the right to butt in because she really did seem happy with him.

"Well, he has a friend who was on the boat that night, and he says his friend thinks something shady went down."

"Really? Shady in what way?" I responded, again trying to sound much more disinterested than I was.

"I'll let him tell you. I don't want to get in the middle of it. But it sounds like they took off and left that poor guy to drown."

"That's horrible," I said with sincere disgust, even though it was something I already suspected.

"I know, right? Who does that?"

"Horrible people."

"Exactly."

"So, will he talk to me? Will Damien talk to me?"

"Yes, if you keep his identity confidential. He thinks if what he heard gets out, there are going to be some pretty angry people who have the power and inclination to do him harm."

"Yes, I will keep his name out of it. You know you can trust me. Give him my number."

"Will do. Oh, and Maddie, one last thing—"

"What is it?"

"I'm counting the days until you come back."

"Thanks, Janie. I miss you too," and I meant it.

It amazed me how Louise could sleep anywhere—in a car, on a plane, and now on the beach in the stifling North Carolina afternoon summer heat under an umbrella with random kids running and screaming and jumping into the waves just feet from where we were set up. I had promised her we would have a beach day, and then tomorrow, I would need to get back to work on my podcast. She said she understood, not to worry about her, that she was perfectly capable of entertaining herself and was just thrilled to be here with me. I chuckled to myself as I heard her snore loudly beneath the straw hat she had placed over her face as she lay perfectly still on a massive blanket in the shade. *This* was her idea of spending time together.

Secretly, I was happy for the quiet moment to think about everything that had happened in a little more than twenty-four hours. It was hard to believe I had found Max's body yesterday morning, and now, here I was, sitting on the beach with my best friend, looking out at the mesmerizing blue water, trying to forget what had happened. The problem was that I *couldn't* forget. When I closed my eyes, I could still see his dark eyes staring back at me from just beneath the surface of the water as the sun rose, casting a dusty pink hue over my memory.

The twins had sent me letters from camp, and I shoved them in my beach bag, hoping I would have a moment to read them. I knew they would be a good distraction from what was going on in my life. Camp Pinetops didn't allow the campers access to electronics or to speak to their parents by phone until after the second week of the session because they wanted them to push through the homesickness, but they were allowed to write letters. This was new to them, the snail mail thing. The only type of mail they had ever received or sent were birthday cards and thank you notes.

I had bought a stack of postcards from Cape Mayson and was trying to send them each one every other day. We had never been apart before, and after their father died, we had become a tight little threesome. Even though I knew the separation was healthy for all of us, it left me feeling down some days that I could not hug them or hear their sweet little voices.

I had given each of them a stack of envelopes with my Airbnb address on them, complete with stamps. They were flabbergasted that they could simply drop a letter in a blue metal post office box in Maine, and somehow, it would magically appear in my mailbox in North Carolina. For kids who had grown up emailing and texting, I knew this letter-writing thing was going to be a challenge.

I read Miranda's letter first. It was very straightforward, all business.

> We went canoeing.
>
> We did the ropes course.
>
> The food is okay.
>
> I like my counselor.

It was clear that she was writing to me out of obligation because I had given her eight stamped self-addressed envelopes. She was not a child to waste even one of the stamps by failing to send me two letters per week. But her letters, like Miranda herself, were devoid of emotion. Of course, she did have feelings; she just wasn't the type of person who was comfortable sharing them with others. I had hired a psychologist to work with the twins after Adam died. Dr. Jacobs told me that it was natural for Miranda to keep her emotions to herself. She was angry about her father's death and was still trying to come up with coping strategies to deal with that anger. While I agreed, in part, with his assessment, I also knew that this was part of the reality of Miranda's personality, a trait that made itself known way before Adam ever got sick.

Blake's letter, on the other hand, contained details that let me know how he was feeling. He told me that, at first, he had been scared to do the zipline, but then said:

> Mom, I overcame my fear. I think you would be
> pretty proud of me.

"Proud" was underlined twice in bold black magic marker. He told me he had made a friend named Benji and that they liked a lot of the same things, including archery and the all-natural chunky peanut butter that the camp served as an alternative to any meal a picky eater might not like. He told me he was *considering* staying for the eight-week session. I had signed them up for the four-week session and told them it was up to them to decide whether they wanted to stay longer. I figured if he bailed, he could just come stay with me in Cape Mayson.

Adam had attended Pinetops as a child and considered it one of the most important formative experiences of his young life. He had talked about it to the kids ever since they were little, preparing them for the time when we would ship them North for the summer. Miranda had always been intrigued by his bygone era stories of pie-eating contests and sneaking out in the canoe at night to cross the lake to the girls' bunks. Blake was, not surprisingly, terrified by the thought of being away from home for a night, let alone an entire summer, but he was emboldened by the thought of continuing Adam's legacy there.

I missed them, but I knew this was what we all needed. They needed to have independent experiences without me, with kids their own age; that's what summer was all about. And I needed that, too. But most of all, I needed to get my life together once and for all, for my sake and theirs.

Louise finally stirred; we had some snacks that I had packed, went for a swim, and then decided to call it a day. We were both getting burned despite how much sunblock we slathered on our pale winter skin. I knew at my age that more sun ultimately equaled more wrinkles. While I loved the way I looked with a tan, I always fast-forwarded the clock and pictured myself as a tanned, weathered old lady someday, like the character Magda in the movie *Something About Mary*.

"Where did it happen?" Louise asked me as we sluggishly rolled our cart along the sidewalk from the beach back to the condo. We were zapped from the sun and the heat. I paused for a moment to try and understand what she was talking about. Louise was famous for non sequiturs.

"Where did *what* happen?"

"The drowning. Where did the guy fall off the boat?"

I thought about it for a minute, trying to remember what I had read in the news articles. I had bookmarked one from a local television station. I stopped and pulled it up on my phone and squinted to see it beneath the brim of my baseball cap.

"Looks like it was on the other side of the island, in a pretty calm area, not far from some condos and a sandbar where people like to party. It's not far from where we are right now. We're going to pass it."

"Let's go," Louise said, tugging at my free arm that was not rolling the cart. Back in the day, before kids, Louise had been a budding journalist. She had done a short stint as a television reporter at a cable station in DC; that's how we met. But when the boys came along, she decided to be a stay-at-home mom. And she was good at it, *very good at it*. She was heavily invested in all her sons' sports, taking them to games, cheering for them, making meals for the teams, but a few years ago, she decided she needed to feed her brain again, and that's when she started her company, "Elegant Event Planning." Secretly, I knew she had never completely let go of the journalist part of her brain. Here it was again, peeking out.

"Why? What could we possibly learn by doing that? Nothing the police don't already know."

"You'd be surprised."

Louise snatched the phone out of my hand and hit the GPS walking directions to the location. An Australian voice emanated from the phone, telling us we were just seven minutes away. I didn't want to lug all our stuff with us, so I convinced Louise to let me at least stop for a moment and park the cart near the entrance to my building. I was pretty sure no one would touch it, and I didn't intend for this little field trip to take more than a few minutes.

After we dumped the cart, we crossed the busy road in front of the high-rise and headed to the other side of the narrow island. A long row of beige townhouses with docks jutting out into the waterway lined a thin grassy area. Across from the townhouse was a large sandbar. Small boats were pulled up all around it, anchored in the shallow water near the thin strip of sand. Competing music was playing from the boats' stereos as people swam, floated near their boats on inner tubes, and drank from red Solo cups. On the sandbar, which you could barely call an island, groups of young people stood around chatting. One man was throwing a tennis ball to his dog, who was running wildly back and forth across the thin strip of land to retrieve it. I had stopped here a few times to have a sip of water during my early morning paddleboarding excursions, but I had never been here during the partying hours.

Louise stood at the water's edge with her hands on her hips, surveying the scene.

"Well, I'm sure *this* wasn't going on at night when the man fell into the water."

I could see the rusty reporter wheels churning in her head as she scanned the area.

"Doubt it. I think it was close to high tide when this happened. The sandbar would have been covered with water. They were probably just anchored out here because it's pretty calm water. It's part of the No Wake Zone."

Louise started taking pictures with her iPhone of the area like she was a crime scene photographer mapping out the scene. I grabbed her arm.

"Louise, what are you doing?"

"I don't know; I just think we should document this spot in case something comes up later, and we need to refer to the photos for any reason.

She ignored the annoyed look on my face and my exasperated eye roll and kept on snapping. I knew the water was pretty shallow here based on my paddleboarding experiences, maybe six feet at the most. I also knew it was possible to drown in shallow water. But the fact that it had happened *here,* in this calm spot, made me wonder once again if Max could have been saved by someone on that boat if they had just paused and taken a moment to help. Why didn't someone jump in to help him? I wasn't buying the excuse that no one saw him go in. So why didn't they do anything?

I decided it was time to get some answers. Reluctantly, I realized that I probably needed to reach out to the Cape Mayson Police before they closed the case forever.

6

TRUST EXERCISE

I DIDN'T HAVE ANY CONTACTS with the Cape Mayson Police Department, and I certainly wasn't going to reach out to the patrol officer who took my statement. He was green, and while compassionate, he ultimately seemed pretty disinterested in what I had to say. I couldn't imagine that he would suddenly want to hear from me now.

Then I remembered that our new crime reporter at Channel 8, Keri Hue, had started her television career in Cape Mayson and might have some contacts here. I shot her a quick text, and within a minute, she got back to me with a name.

> You need to talk to Major Arnold Willis. He knows everything about every case. He won't steer you wrong.

Keri gave me Willis' contact information. The major agreed to meet with me first thing Monday morning after I told him I was a friend of Keri's and might have some new information for him about the case. If he knew I was the one who discovered the body, he didn't mention it. I assumed that my name was probably in the report, but maybe he didn't connect this in our brief phone call.

After a quick run, a shower, and a cup of coffee, I headed to the police department. As expected, Louise was still sleeping when I left. I peeked in on her and noticed that, at least this time, she had bothered to get under the covers. It was just before 8:00 in the morning, halfway through the day in my book, but I kept remembering that Louise was getting her first break in a very long time.

The Cape Mayson Police Department was in a low brick building about six blocks from the beach. The brick was painted white to try and give it a more modern look, but I still placed the building circa the 1970s. Two large palm trees framed the double glass doors that appeared to be the main entrance to the station. I parked in one of three visitor spots near concrete stairs with a blue painted handrail that led to the entrance.

"I'm here to see Major Willis," I said through a small hole in the plexiglass window to a young, tanned woman with long brunette hair and a large silver cross around her neck.

"And you are?" She replied, not looking up from her computer screen.

"Maddie, Maddie Arnette."

"One minute, please. You can have a seat," she said, finally looking up at me and gesturing to the two tired upholstered blue chairs with faded, threadbare fabric behind me.

I took a seat and absentmindedly began scrolling through messages on my phone. I tried to respond immediately to texts and flag emails that I would answer later. Everything was pretty run of the mill—a reminder that the deadline for registering for the second month of camp was coming up, a reminder that I needed to get my teeth cleaned, and a coupon for twenty percent off sandals at the local discount shoe warehouse. Most of my friends and colleagues knew I was on a sabbatical and were respectfully leaving me alone. That's when I noticed a text from Damien.

> Give me a call at this number, and I will tell you what I know.

"Mrs. Arnette, the major, will see you now," the receptionist behind the plexiglass yelled in my direction as if I might be talking to a crowded waiting room when it was just me sitting there by myself.

I shoved my phone into my pocket, making a mental note to call Damien as soon as I was done at the police department. The receptionist buzzed me through the door and then got out of her chair and beckoned for me to follow her down a long narrow colorless hallway. It was clear I had interrupted something she was doing that was much more important than walking me a few doors down to a meeting with Major Willis. So, I decided to stay quiet and forgo the small talk that might make her even more annoyed. She stopped in front of a doorway, stepped back, and gestured with a tired wave of her hand for me to go into the office.

"Good morning, Mrs. Arnette," Major Willis said, standing up from his large wooden desk to reach across it and shake my hand. "Please, have a seat," he said, pointing to a plush green armchair across from him.

"Please, call me Maddie."

Arnold Willis was a large man with sandy blond hair graying at the temples. He wore a dark suit and a red and white striped tie. On his desk was a picture of him with a petite dark-haired woman and two adult children, a boy, and a girl, who looked to be in their twenties or so. The daughter took after her mother, while the son was an identical younger version of his father.

"Okay, Maddie. What can I do for you?"

"Well, first, I just need to mention, for full disclosure, I am a television reporter in Oak City, but that's not why I'm here."

"I know. I already looked you up. I figured that if you knew Keri, you were probably in the same line of work."

"Right, and so I'm actually on sabbatical at the moment, not working on a news story, just to be clear."

"So, what is your interest in this case, Maddie?"

"Well, you may or may not know this, but *I* was the one who found the body."

"I do know that. Thought your name sounded familiar, so I went back and looked at the file."

"Well, as you can imagine, it's been weighing on me. I heard you are pretty close to ruling it an accident, and I just feel like that would be a mistake. I think the case deserves more investigation. I've been talking to a few people around town, and it seems like there's something off about the whole thing."

"Really. That's interesting. Because my guys have been talking to a lot of people, too, and we've come up empty. Seems like the party on the boat was a little wild and that he either fell in by accident or decided to take a swim. Either way, *no one saw it happen.* They didn't even know he was gone until they got back to the dock. The family didn't want an autopsy, but the medical examiner did a tox screen on him. Pretty sure we'll find something in his system that contributed to his lack of judgment."

I sat there for a moment studying this man. I couldn't think of any reason he would have to lie, so I assumed he really believed what he was telling me. I was surprised that the family had the right to decline an autopsy in a suspicious death.

"So, the family has the power to say no to an autopsy? Even when foul play could be a factor?"

"Foul play is *not* suspected."

"You've talked with all the people, the people from the party who were on the boat, you've spoken with all of them?"

"I really can't get into the specifics of an ongoing investigation, but yes, mostly by phone. A lot of them are no longer in the area. They came from Oak City for the party and have already left town, gone home."

"You don't find it strange that no one heard or saw him go in the water?"

"Pardon me, Mrs. Arnette, I mean Maddie—when alcohol and loud music are involved, it's pretty easy for me to imagine that happening. No, I do not find it strange. I actually have another meeting to attend, if you'll excuse me."

Major Willis stood, making it clear that our meeting was over. He handed me his business card and told me to feel free to contact him if I heard anything *specific* that would give me cause to believe some type of foul play was involved in Max Prince's death. I took the card and reluctantly turned and left his office. When I got to the door to the lobby, the receptionist hit a button from behind her desk and the door buzzed as it unlocked to let me pass through it.

I walked outside into the bright sunlight and looked back at the small brick building. I knew being a police officer at the beach was probably frustrating. I imagined most of their calls were related to annoying tourists—calls about swimmers who ventured too far out in the waves, calls from business owners who found illegally parked visitors on their property, calls about rowdy, drunk college kids who spilled out of bars in the wee hours of the morning and urinated on people's lawns.

They were not like the Oak City Police Department, that had a lot of experience dealing with suspicious death cases. I still didn't know what the case here was. But at the very least, I believed it involved negligence. How could an entire boat full of people stand by when a man was drowning and see nothing?

"Damien, this is Maddie Arnette, Janie's co-worker."

I was sitting on a bench in front of a fountain outside my building after making the short walk back from the police station. I decided to sit there and make my call to Damien so I wouldn't wake up Louise.

"Oh, wow, hi. Thanks for calling. My friend Jason is the guy who knows a lot about this situation. But I told him I would talk to you first because I knew you were cool; that's what Janie tells me. Jason works part-time for Perry Spotz, the captain of Ripple, and he was on the boat last weekend when everything went down. He got there just before it happened. He has another job pumping gas at one of the marinas. He closed up around nine, and then Perry picked him up at the dock so he could help with the charter."

"What does he do for Perry?"

"Odds and ends mostly keeps the boat clean during an event and makes sure the passengers are happy. So, by the time he got on the boat, between 9:30 and 10:00, everyone was pretty trashed. He knew a lot of the guests because the girl whose birthday it was,

Stella something, they went to high school together."

"So, what did he say happened?"

"He'll have to give you all the details, but he says there was a fight between the dude who drowned and another guy who was totally wasted. He says the drunk guy punched the dude, and he fell overboard. And then the next thing you know, the boat was hauling ass back to the dock."

"And no one tried to save him?"

"That's what Jason says. He says it all happened so quickly. He heard someone yell; we're *out of here.* Maybe Perry, the captain, maybe someone else. He's not sure."

"That's quite a story."

"I know, right?"

"Can I talk to Jason?"

"He's really scared. The police have already interviewed him twice. He didn't tell them the whole truth about what happened. He's afraid of this guy; Perry, says he's connected to a rough crowd."

"But maybe if he talked to me, I could get the information to investigators without using his name."

"I don't know if he'll go for that. I mean, he feels awful about the dude, that's for sure. He knew him a little bit. They went to the same high school a few years apart. It's kind of been wearing him down. He can't eat or sleep. He's even talking about leaving Cape Mayson, maybe moving to Oak City, which is so weird because he's a total water person. I don't think he could survive inland."

I thought about the burden this guy must be carrying around. Watching someone fall into the water and not jumping in to rescue the person is not against the law—but not calling 911 and leaving the scene *is* a crime. There had to be more to the story. There had to be a reason that others on the boat, including the captain, decided to leave and not report the fact that Max had been missing for several hours.

"Look, why don't you talk to Jason and let him know that I will keep his identity confidential. I do it with my sources all the time."

"Okay, I'll talk to him. Like I said, Janie talks about you a lot. I know you're cool and all, but I've got to watch out for my bro. He's in a really tight spot on this one. He wants to do the right thing, he really does, but he's freaking out. Thinks someone is coming after him if he narcs on them."

"I get it," I said. But I didn't really get it. Why come to me? What did Jason think I could do about the situation after he had already lied to the police? My instinct was always to believe what people told me unless they gave me a reason not to—*truth default*. So, if what Damien was telling me was the truth, potentially twenty people left a man to die.

I told Louise everything I had learned from my phone call with Damien and everything I didn't learn from my meeting with Major Willis.

"Sounds like a bunch of bullshit to me," Louise said as she blew into her hot mug of coffee to cool it off. "Sounds like the detective is either lying or in denial. Probably doesn't want to upset the rich guy who owns the boat. It's a liability thing. The dead guy's family is probably going to sue the pants off the boat owner whether this becomes a criminal case or not."

"True," I said, staring out into the water, imagining Max's body floating all the way from the backside of the island where he allegedly fell off the boat to the spot right in front of my condo where he had ended up. How many boats had floated by him in the water? How many times did the current threaten to push him onto a beach or beneath someone's dock? How had a boat propeller cutting through the waterway not sliced him into pieces? I shook my head, trying to erase the image from my mind, *those eyes* again looking up at me from beneath the surface of the water.

"And that Damien guy. Didn't you tell me he was kind of a loser, that you didn't care for him much?"

"Also, true, but that doesn't mean he isn't telling the truth. What reason would he have to reach out to me on behalf of his friend if he didn't want to get to the bottom of this, to do the right thing?"

"Good question, but I'm still skeptical."

We sat in silence on our lounge chairs for a moment, watching boats whiz by on the waterway in front of us, their wakes trailing in foamy white ribbons behind them. Because sound carries across water, I could hear their music playing and people on the boats talking and laughing. I couldn't make out what they were saying, but I could tell from their tones that they were having fun. If only they knew the crystal blue water they were gliding through was also a death knell for Max Prince.

7

THE LAST STRAW

IT WASN'T HARD TO FIND INFORMATION about Mark Maron online. He had established himself as a premier boutique hotel owner in North Carolina from the mountains to the coast. He went into resort towns, bought the biggest dumps, and then transformed them into something chic and magical.

I looked at a few photo galleries of his before and after projects where he revealed that a rundown old hotel could become modern and hip with a pricy renovation, a little bit of paint, and the right décor. One of his hotels in Cape Mayson was a historical property from the 1800s that he brought back to life with oversized animal print-covered wingback chairs surrounded by huge potted ferns in large ceramic blue pots. The walls in the lobby were pale blue and held framed black and white photos of the hotel's former glory days. The hotel was now called "Exit Zero" because the interstate highway from Oak City literally dead-ended into the beach community.

Maron and his family stayed in an exclusive little community at the tip of Cape Mayson called Harbor Light. Zillow estimated the value of his home at five million dollars. It was clear that his little luxury charter boat was one of his many investments, and it was more than likely that he had very little involvement with its daily operation. Other than not wanting to assume legal liability in court for a dead passenger, I figured he was pretty much hands-off when it came to Ripple.

So, I turned my attention to Captain Perry Spotz. After all, he was there, and presumably, he was the one who made the decision to leave the location immediately after Max Prince went into the water. I looked up his criminal record and discovered that he had a history of drunk driving, minor drug charges, and petty theft. Still, the convictions were all fifteen years or more old, which usually meant the person had gotten their act together.

Weirdly, Perry had very little social media presence, with the exception of a Facebook Fan Page dedicated to the charter boat. I scrolled through the photographs. Most of them were from events on the boat the previous summer. A few featured a group of young women holding up champagne glasses, all wearing matching t-shirts that said "Bridesmaids." In the middle was a woman dressed in a white bikini wearing a veil who was obviously the bride. Another group of photos showed an older couple arm and arm with a group of family members around them. In front of them was a cake that read "50th Anniversary."

It seemed a little odd to me that a man who lived in such a fancy house needed this little side-hustle to supplement his income. But on the other hand, what did I know about accumulating real wealth? Maybe this is how you did it, by cobbling together lots of investments, big and small.

As I scrolled further down, I discovered what appeared to be the only photo of Perry Spotz. He had wild, untamed red curly hair and was wearing a baseball hat that said "Captain." His name was embroidered in red on the right breast of his white polo shirt. He was standing on a dock in front of Ripple with his arm around another man whom I recognized as Mark Maron from his LinkedIn photo. Something seemed odd about these two men joining forces in this venture. How in the world would someone like Perry Spotz have connected with someone like Mark Maron? They hardly ran in the same circles.

I noticed Perry had something in his free hand in the photo, and I zoomed in on the picture to see if I could make it out. It was a bronze coin with a triangle on it and an "1" in the center. Quickly, I Googled "AA tokens," and there it was—the bronze coin signified one year of sobriety. I had a feeling that Mark was Perry's sponsor, and maybe the charter boat business was Mark's effort to help Perry get his life in order.

The caption beneath the photo read: "Ready to take the reins? From one Cappy to another."

My phone rang, jerking me away from my research. Zack's name flashed across the screen.

"Hello, Maddie, it's Zack."

"Hi, Zack. Are you here, in Cape Mayson?"

"Yes, got here last night, as a matter of fact. The website doesn't lie; Cape Mayson is really beautiful."

"1 know, it really is. We're lucky that it's so close to Oak City, just two hours."

"You are," Zack paused. He sounded awkward, like a teenage boy about to ask a girl on a date. "So, 1 know it's kind of last minute. But are you free for lunch today? 1 know you're working on your podcast, so if you can't fit it in today, maybe tomorrow?"

1 looked at my watch. Between meeting with Major Willis, talking to Damien, debriefing with Louise, and researching the Ripple, 1 had wasted away most of my morning. What difference would lunch make to my self-imposed work schedule? Something inside me was fluttering, tickling my stomach, making me feel a little jumpy and heady.

"Sure, why not," 1 said as casually as 1 could, lest my swirling stomach butterflies make their presence known in my jittery voice.

"Okay, since 1 don't know the area, do you want to pick the place?"

"How about The Last Straw Café? They have a nice little patio on the beach and a great lunch menu. I can ride my bike there, and it's not far from you, maybe a mile."

"Perfect. 1:00?"

"Great, I'll see you then," 1 hung up abruptly so as not to give my excitement away. 1 could hear that he was still talking when 1 ended the call. I had a bad habit of doing this because my brain was already on to the next thing once I made a plan. Hopefully, he would think the call had just dropped.

My decision to go to The Last Straw Café was not purely because of their delicious menu and excellent wine list. I had also done some research on Stella Avery and discovered that her mother, Dawn, owned the restaurant. I figured that Stella had already returned to Oak City to her job as a physician's assistant. So, talking to her mother was the next best thing. Right now, the way I saw it, all the roads were leading back to Stella on this one. It was Stella's party. She invited the guests. She presumably stood by like the others and watched Max Prince fall into the water.

When I told Louise I was having lunch with Zack, she jumped up and down like a little girl on Christmas morning and then pulled me in for a tight bear hug.

"Louise, *it's just lunch.* You're the one who told me it was no big deal."

"Well, I lied. It most certainly *is* a big deal. You're finally stepping out with a man. It's about time. He may not be *the* man, but at least you're breaking the seal."

"You are crazy; you know that?"

She let go of me and held me out to look at me like a proud parent about to send her daughter to the school dance.

"That's why you love me, darling. What are you going to wear?"

"Wear? I hadn't thought about it. I guess this?"

I looked past her to the mirror on the wall. I didn't have a lot of in-between clothes. I was either dressed to the nines for television or in workout clothes. My feeble attempts at smart casual were usually pretty lame. I was currently wearing an old red sundress of Miranda's. Even though she was only twelve, we were roughly the same size as she had gotten her height from Adam's mother. I had to admit the look was less than stellar. It hung limply from my bony, tan shoulders. Unraveling threads poked out from the bodice in the blue and yellow embroidery here and there. Once form-fitting, it had all but lost its shape.

Louise steered me into my walk-in closet and started to scroll through the options, pushing each hanger aside and dismissing my "beach dresses" one by one.

"Wow, okay, not a lot to work with here. We want you to look good without looking like you tried too hard. Lucky for you, none of these dresses will make you look like you're trying at all!"

I swatted Louise on the back, and she made a mock pain face. We finally settled on a blue and white halter dress that looked breezy and summery and most importantly, was short enough so I could ride my bike without it getting caught up in the wheels. I pulled my hair back in a tight ponytail, applied powder, mascara, and lip gloss, and decided this was about as good as it was going to get. I slipped on flip flops, which Louise promptly nixed with a roll of her eyes, so I substituted them for some flat, white strappy sandals that would still allow me to pedal my bike.

"Twirl for me."

"You have got to be kidding."

"No, I'm not."

"Do you think he's putting this much effort into what he's wearing?"

"You'd be surprised; some men do."

"Not the kind of men I like."

"How do you know what kind of men you like? You're practically a nun. Plus, Adam was a nice dresser."

"He was, but I didn't care for his fashion-forward focus. I like it when a guy is a little rumpled, you know, dressing out of the laundry basket."

"You are too much; you need to go, or you'll be late."

"True, I actually want to get there a little early. Remember the girl who had the party on the boat?"

"Of course, Stella, something or other?"

"Yes, Stella Avery. Well, apparently, her mother, Dawn Avery, owns The Last Straw Café, where I am meeting Zack for lunch."

"Mixing business and pleasure, that's my girl. Are you sure that's a good idea for a first date?"

"Nope, I'm not sure about anything. But I might as well show him the real me upfront. No sense in beating around the bush. I'm not interested in playing games."

"Good point."

The Last Straw had perfected shabby chic—rustic whitewashed picnic tables adorned with massive deep blue glass candle holders sat on a patio beneath a large white flowing piece of canvas tied to four posts with ropes. The drinks arrived in mason jars, and the cutlery came wrapped in light blue linen napkins tied with thick tan twine that looked like straw. The menu was online, easily accessible with a phone.

I got there early and was lucky enough to get a table at the front of the patio that looked directly over the white sand at the endless blue ocean disappearing into the horizon. I noticed that the water was extremely flat today, no doubt a disappointment for surfers like Zack. I didn't picture him as a surfer, but truth be told, I didn't know him at all. I tried to envision him in longboard shorts catching a wave and riding it all the way into the shore. I shook my head. I still couldn't see it—this landlocked boy, this cop, hanging ten with hipsters on the North Carolina coast. I recalled our first meeting in Pennsylvania—his slicked-back hair, bow tie, and suspenders. He was like a throwback to some bygone era. There was not a hint of surfer in him at that meeting.

"Would you like something to drink while you're waiting?"

The waitress was dressed in all white with a crisp, starched apron that matched the clean décor of the restaurant.

"Sure, I'll have an unsweetened iced tea."

"You can access our menu on your phone by hovering over this plastic card."

"Got it, thanks."

"I'll also bring you some pita bread and hummus while you're waiting. Just one person is joining you?"

"Yes, thanks."

When she turned to walk away, I thought that this was the perfect moment to ask whether Dawn was here. Chances were slim that the owner worked on a quiet weekday shift, but it couldn't hurt to ask.

"Quick question, is the owner, Dawn, here? I'd love to ask her some questions about the restaurant, like where she got the name."

"Well, I can answer that one. When she got divorced, she sold her husband's fancy boat out from under him as part of her settlement and bought this restaurant. And he told his lawyer, *This is the last damn straw. I never want to see that woman again.* Voila!"

I wasn't so sure Dawn wanted people to know this story, or maybe she did? If the wait staff here knew the answer and felt confident enough to share it, maybe Dawn encouraged it as part of her catharsis.

"Wow, that's a great story!"

"I know, right? Anyway, Dawn is here. She loves chatting with the customers. Let me check and see if she's available."

The white-clad waitress disappeared behind two wooden swinging doors into a small cottage-like building that probably used to be someone's private home.

"Welcome," a petite redhead in a white apron appeared. "Shelby said you would like to know more about the restaurant."

Dawn was tiny, tan, and muscular. She had the look of someone who worked hard and worked her body hard. She had the voice of a smoker, which I guessed based on her healthy appearance was simply the voice she was born with. Her whole face smiled, and her green eyes twinkled with an openness that was immediately engaging.

"Yes, hello, nice to meet you. My name is Maddie, Maddie Arnette."

"Oh, I know you—you're the TV lady! My daughter lives in Oak City. I always watch your news when I'm up there."

"Thanks for watching." I realized suddenly that this would make the next part of the conversation tricky. Now that she knew who I was, she would assume I had questions about Max's death because I was doing a story on it.

"So, what do you want to know about The Last Straw? I am an open book!"

"First of all, I love your style; it's really inviting. I've been here one other time, and your menu is amazing, really creative."

The white-clad waitress I now knew as Shelby moved silently in between us to put down my iced tea and a rustic straw basket full of pita bread cut into triangles along with a small bowl of spicy hummus.

"Thanks so much. I've always loved cooking, but I only thought of making my hobby my career a few years ago when my girlfriends told me how much they enjoyed my recipes. And here I am, living my dream," she said, gesturing to the patio and the ocean in the distance. "Couldn't have a better spot. Used to be a down and dirty fried seafood joint; the guy was retiring and itching to sell. I came in just at the right time. It was kind of a dump, but I did most of the renovation and decorating myself with the help of some friends and family."

"Well, you did a great job. Thanks for sharing that history with me. I love learning what's behind small businesses like yours. I know everyone has a story."

"That's for sure."

"Can I ask you one more question?"

"Sure, shoot, anything," she said with a chuckle, casually leaning one hand on the back of the chair across from me.

For a minute, I thought I might chicken out. This woman was one degree removed from Stella but many degrees removed from what happened on Ripple. I felt bad approaching her on the pretense of learning about The Last Straw. And now that she knew I was a reporter, my next line of questioning might rub her the wrong way. This was always one of the toughest things about being a reporter; one minute you were pleasantly chatting with someone, and the next moment you were asking them the hard questions that could easily turn a friendly chat into something very uncomfortable. I decided there was no other direction to go but forward.

"So, you're Stella Avery's mother, correct?"

Suddenly, Dawn's engaging face went from open to dark—her eyes tightened, her mouth pursed, and her casually laid hand now tightly gripped the chair.

"Yes, why do you ask?"

"Well, I was just wondering because I'm the paddleboarder who found Max Prince in the water."

One of Dawn's hands went to her mouth, the other hand gripped my shoulder. She looked like she was about to cry. That's when Zack cruised up to the table, oblivious to the fact that I was in the middle of a crucial conversation.

"Ladies," he said, nodding his head in our direction and pulling out the chair across from me. He unfurled his napkin and put it on his lap, completely unaware of the moment he had just walked into. He gazed absentmindedly out at the water. "Wow, what a beautiful spot."

8

BURYING THE LEAD

FOR A DETECTIVE, I WAS SURPRISED that Zack was so oblivious that he had walked into a serious conversation between myself and Dawn. But at the same time, I also realized that he was probably nervous about meeting me for what seemed like a first date. For this reason, I didn't want to hold this lack of awareness in this one single moment against him.

When Zack came to the table, Dawn abruptly excused herself and walked quickly back through the swinging wooden doors into the kitchen. He kind of rolled his eyes as if to say *what's her deal?* I sat with his reaction for a moment, trying to decide whether to tell him what had just happened, but I decided against it. It wasn't that I didn't trust him. I just didn't want him to think I was obsessed with this case. I would let him learn about my obsessions later when he really got to know me. No need to show my entire hand so early in what may or may not be a budding relationship.

"So, sorry I'm a few minutes late. I should have walked, but I drove, and it was hard to find parking."

"Yes, parking is crazy here. You should rent a bike while you're here. It's the best way to get around, and you never have a problem parking."

He flashed his smile with his perfect white teeth framed by his perfectly tanned face and topped by a cascade of dark unruly hair. Gone was the business suit and slicked-back hair from our first meeting in the spring. Now, in this laid-back attire, khaki shorts, and a hip short-sleeved button-down, he actually did look like a surfer. I still couldn't figure out where he got his deep tan from living in central Pennsylvania. But then I remembered that he told me he was a cyclist and spent a lot of weekends on his bike climbing hills around the rural farmlands.

"That's a great idea. I passed a bike rental place on the way here. I might just do that. Should have just thrown mine in the truck. So, how are you? How's the sabbatical going?"

"Good, weird, I don't really know."

"Weird?"

It was like everything I just told myself about, *not* telling him anything, had vanished the minute I looked into his eyes. They were honest eyes, credible eyes, the eyes of a helper. I could sure use a helper right now.

"I mean, television news has always been such a big part of my life; it's how I define myself. I'm not sure who I am without it," I told him the truth, but not the whole truth. "I'm trying to figure all that out."

"Well, I'm kind of in the same boat. I've got almost thirty years in as a police officer, minus all the vacation time I've built up. I'm thinking about my next chapter too. It's time to redefine myself. I know this sounds crazy, but I've always wanted to run a bed and breakfast, something in the country with farm-to-table food, great views, and places to hike and bike. A real retreat."

"That sounds amazing," I replied, thinking about how much this man was continuing to surprise me.

"Law enforcement has really changed. I honestly got into it to help people. And I think I did a lot of good along the way, but I think I also ignored a lot of bad behavior from my colleagues who didn't get into it for the right reasons. Frankly, I'm exhausted by it all. In reality, I'm an old hippie, which really doesn't fit with the law-and-order lifestyle I've chosen. I want to find my peace and help others do the same by spending time in nature and nurturing their bodies and souls."

"So, basically, you're looking to open a commune?"

We both laughed. His was a hearty laugh. I hadn't seen that coming either. A good laugher was at the top of my checklist when it came to liking people. Then he ran his fingers through his hair, brushing it out of his face. It was a self-conscious movement that made me like him even more.

We both ordered salads—mine with salmon, his with chicken. We devoured the pita points and hummus and then capped off the meal by sharing a homemade triple berry cobbler topped with a generous scoop of vanilla ice cream.

I was surprised that Roger had not yet appeared in our conversation, but I also knew it was inevitable. As Shelby cleared our lunch plates and refilled our waters, Zack raised the elephant.

"So, I don't want to tread into dangerous waters after such a nice meal, but I would be remiss if I didn't tell you that it looks like Roger *is* going to get another hearing soon. I thought it was going to be pushed off until October, but it looks like it could be as early as August or September now. There's a good chance he could be released."

I got quiet. I knew that if Roger was released, it was because I had discovered new information, information that showed that another man, a drug addict named Clifton, had killed my mother. I had given that information to Kojak, who in turn gave it to Zack. The information came in the form of a bag full of paperwork that Clifton's mother, Esther, had given me just before she died. Roger and Clifton had known each other casually, so I assumed that Roger had hired Clifton to kill my mother. But now, I was starting to doubt this assumption.

"Well, it was all in the files that you gave me, or I guess technically that Kojak gave me. Clifton's mother spelled everything out: how your father and Clifton were at a bar near your grandparents' house in Pennsylvania, and he told Clifton how your mother, Patty, had left him, that she was a real bitch, and that she was going to try and get full custody of you which he said would kill him. So, Roger says something off-the-cuff like 'everything would be so much easier if she was dead.'"

"That's it?"

"That's it. He didn't tell him to do it. He didn't hire him to do it. No money exchanged hands. He just suggested it. I mean, really, he just made a crazy statement that Clifton ran with. Clifton was a blackout drunk and a drug addict at the time. Your dad left the bar and went to some rundown roadside motel. The overnight desk clerk saw him check-in, and says his car never moved. He could see it from where he was sitting. He left the next morning early to go back to New Jersey.

There was DNA at the crime scene that we could never place. Esther included a sample of Clifton's hair in that bag. We had it tested—*the DNA is a match*. Clifton was in your grandparents' house the night your mother was killed. It all adds up."

When I had visited Roger, he admitted to knowing Clifton, but in a letter that he wrote to me after our visit, he said he was still responsible for her death. Roger obviously felt guilty about what he had said to Clifton at the bar and decided to spend his life in prison paying that penance. Clifton was dead now, killed by his father Pete, after breaking into his parents' house one night to steal things he could fence to pay for drugs. There was no one left to blame for my mother's death. Releasing Roger seemed a likely end to the story at this point.

"I don't understand why none of this came out at my father's trial."

"I don't either. The only thing I can think of is that your dad refused to rat out Clifton due to some misguided guilt over what happened. He is guilty of being an accessory after the fact to murder and obstruction of justice because he basically protected the killer by hiding this information from investigators. He protected Clifton from prosecution. But he's been locked up for nearly four decades; he's more than served his time for those crimes under Pennsylvania law."

As if my life needed more complications. Suddenly, the narrative that I had built my entire world around—that my father killed my mother and went to prison for the crime—was being undermined. It would have been so much easier for me to stick with the original script, but when I met Esther, and she told me what she knew, what she believed to be true, that her son had killed my mother, my conscience wouldn't allow me to ignore it. Esther made it pretty clear that knowing this information, keeping this secret, had destroyed her life. I was determined to do the right thing, even if it meant Roger would be set free. I needed to be a mother that Miranda and Blake could be proud of. I couldn't let the lie destroy my life the way it had destroyed Esther's.

Suddenly, my mind drifted to the kids at camp. I wondered what they were doing at this very minute while I was sitting in a restaurant learning the news that my father might be released from prison. I quietly sent positive energy to them in my mind as I pictured Miranda mastering kayaking, slicing gracefully through the water. I pictured sweet Blake playing piano, his tiny fingers dancing across the keys, in a bright room with an open window that let in the cool Maine summer breeze. And then I drifted back into the moment with Zack.

"I see."

"I'm sorry to have to tell you all of this. But giving me these files, asking me to look into the case was the right thing to do. Like I said, if I've learned one thing from police work, it's that you need to stay true to yourself no matter what someone else does. There's this famous quote by the first University of Pennsylvania provost, William Smith. He said, 'Laws without morals are useless.' So, what I'm trying to say is that you did the right thing. You should be proud of yourself. You could have just ignored it, thrown the files away, and gone on with your life. But you didn't. I admire you for what you did."

Zack's gaze was so intense, I was sure he was going to burn a hole right through my head to the other side. I almost turned around to see if there was someone else that he was looking at. Instead, I bucked up and returned his gaze. Maybe he could see me the way I wanted to be seen, as a strong woman who didn't take crap from anyone and made the necessary tough decisions even at my own expense. But if I was going to let him in, to truly let him see the real me, I had to be real with him about everything.

"So, not to change the subject, but there is one other weird thing that happened this week. I hadn't planned on talking to you about this, but Saturday morning, you know, the day I talked to you on the phone, I found a body, a dead body floating in the water."

"What do you mean by *a body floating in the water?*"

"Pretty much exactly the way it sounds. I was paddleboarding, and my oar caught on something hard, something big. I thought it might be driftwood or even a tire, so I turned around to see what it was, and *boom*, there was a dead guy floating on his back, his eyes wide open, staring up at me from the water."

"You must not be a very good reporter."

"What do you mean?" I quipped, annoyed by his dig.

"Because I've never seen anyone bury a lead like that one."

I told Zack pretty much everything, including the fact that I had chosen the restaurant because I wanted to speak with Dawn Avery about her daughter. Instead of being put off that I was trying to conduct business on a date, Zack put on his detective hat, and we talked through all the possible scenarios.

Most importantly, Zack agreed with me that this should not be an open and closed case, and he wondered out loud why the police seemed in such a rush to deem it an accident.

"Maybe Mark Maron has some influence. After all, any criminal charge against anyone on the boat will hurt him if Max Prince's family decides to file a civil lawsuit alleging negligence by the charter boat company and its crew," I hypothesized.

"Maybe," Zack said, stroking his chin. I noticed he had about two days of stubble. I assumed it was because he was in full vacation mode. "But a guy like Maron, who is hands-off his smaller investments, probably wouldn't blink at a lawsuit like that. He'd just settle out of court and pay the family off. Not sure it's worth it to him to coerce the police into shutting down a criminal investigation."

"So, someone else on that boat must have an in with the Cape Mayson Police," I mused.

"Could be. It sounds like there are a lot of layers to this. First, was what happened—Max going into the water—an accident or intentional? And then, was the aftermath—leaving him to die—a product of panic, or was *that* intentional?" Zack posed.

"Wow, good points. I hadn't thought of all that. I guess it helps to know someone who investigates crimes for a living," I replied playfully, trying to move away from the serious tone of our conversation.

Zack smiled at me, and our hands almost touched across the table, *almost.*

"So, you're divorced?" I asked, rapidly changing the subject. I felt like I was squandering our time on all the wrong things. I had learned nothing about this man during our meal as I was so self-absorbed with my own baggage.

"Yep, divorced. Moved to Pennsylvania with my wife. She's a professor. I was married to my work, and she wanted more than to be a cop's wife. She wanted to travel and see the world. She didn't want kids. That was a sticking point for me. I *did* want them. There wasn't any big drama; we just grew apart, *fell apart*, really. It was sad. So, now I'm a single uncle to three beautiful nieces, my sister's kids, and I'm pretty good at it."

"Ah, the picture I saw on your desk when I first met you, that was your sister and her girls."

"You're a bit of a junior detective, aren't you?"

"No, just very observant. Most people aren't very aware. In fact, they're oblivious, kind of sleepwalking through life. You miss so much when you're like that. I try not to miss *anything*."

"I'll say. And I hope you don't mind, but Kojak shared with me that you are a widow?"

"Yes, my husband died after being diagnosed with a brain tumor in 2016. I'm not going to sugarcoat it. It was very rough. And now I'm a single mom to a boy and a girl, twins, they're twelve."

"And where are they now?"

"Oh my God, I knew I forgot something at home!"

We both laughed again, and this time his hand brushed mine as he moved it to take a sip of his water. Electricity shot up my arm. What was going on here? Was I a teenage girl or a grown woman?

"I'm assuming they are somewhere else, like maybe summer camp?"

"Bingo. In Maine. They're having a ball, well, at least one of them is. Miranda, she's my tough one. Blake is having a little more difficulty adjusting, but he's coming around. It's the same camp my husband Adam went to, their father."

I felt strange saying Adam's name out loud in front of Zack for some reason like it was a betrayal of my marriage. Intellectually, I knew that it wasn't, but it still felt wrong. The words had tumbled out of my mouth in a jumble and landed on the table between us. Instead of looking like he wanted to run, Zack looked like he wanted to give me a hug. But he didn't. We just sat there in awkward silence for a moment.

Thankfully, Zack excused himself to make a call, saying he needed to check in with his office briefly, and asked if I wouldn't mind waiting a few minutes. It was a relief to be released from the uncomfortable moment. I took another sip of iced tea to calm my nerves and shooed him away with a cheerful wave of my hand, looking down at my phone to indicate that I, too, had important things to do.

He walked out onto the sidewalk to make his call where he wouldn't bother the other diners in the restaurant. I found this refreshing as I had overheard so many people through the years screaming into their phones in public with no sense that they were impacting others around them, not to mention sharing personal information. I thought of scolding people for their lack of phone etiquette on more than one occasion, but as a television reporter, I had to avoid public conflict at all costs lest someone video me on their phone and post it on social media. One unguarded moment like that, right or wrong, could tank someone's broadcasting career.

Just as I was falling deep into the black hole of scrolling through my endless list of unread emails, I felt a hand on my shoulder. I assumed Zack must have returned and snuck up behind me. I turned and looked up, smiling, but it wasn't Zack. It was Dawn Avery.

"Ms. Arnette, I just wanted to apologize for my reaction earlier. This tragedy has been so hard for our family. Max and Stella went all the way through school together. He was two grades behind her, I think, but they ran in the same circles, and they were friends. This whole thing has been so heartbreaking. And when you told me you found him in the water, I just lost it. But honestly, that was selfish of me because I know it must have been hard on you, too."

"I totally understand. And I'm sorry for springing it on you like that. I just couldn't think of a way to say it. Do you want to sit down for a minute?" I said, gesturing to Zack's empty seat. She sat down, and we continued our conversation.

"Well, you can probably imagine Stella is a wreck. Not only was he a friend, but it happened at *her* party. I mean, it's not her fault or anything; I've told her this a million times. But she's a physician's assistant. She took an oath to help people, and she didn't get the chance to help him. It's tearing her up.

"And I'm going to tell you this in confidence, the family was so distraught, they couldn't bear to identify the body. They asked her to do it. She didn't hesitate. She left work, jumped in the car, and drove all the way down here from Oak City. She went right to the coroner's office. She said it was awful, just awful. But she felt like it was something she *had* to do. I tried to call her afterward, and she wouldn't return my calls for a whole day. Max's parents were so torn up, Stella told me this later, that they begged the investigators not to put Max's body through an autopsy; they just couldn't imagine him being picked apart like that. They were so broken, and for some reason, this was really important to them. So, there was no autopsy, just a toxicology report that hasn't come back yet."

I recalled the conversation I had with the patrol officer at the scene, the one who told me a "friend of the family" had been asked to identify the body. Dawn's story was matching this detail. It made what she was telling me more credible.

"Stella had to go back to Oak City to work right after the party, but she's not doing well. I told her to take a leave of absence and come home and stay with me for a little while, but she insists she *needs* to work, to get her mind off it. Of course, she'll be here for the funeral. At least, I guess she will if she's up to it."

"If you don't mind me asking, does she know what happened? Did she see anything?"

"No, nothing. Everyone just assumes he either fell in and hit his head, or he had some crazy idea to go swimming at 10:00 at night, and jumped in, and then got into trouble in the water because he was drinking. I mean, *they were all drinking*. It was a party, you know. No one was supposed to be in the water at night. It's just such a tragedy."

"That's so weird that no one saw anything."

"I agree. And I'm pretty sure the police have talked to everyone by now, I think. Stella gave them the guest list and contact information for the guests. They all say they didn't know he was missing until they returned to the dock at the end of the night."

I had no reason to doubt that this woman was telling me the truth as she knew it. Her tone was sincere. And clearly, she had no reason to doubt her daughter. Stella could be telling the truth, or she could be protecting someone. The only way for me to truly figure out what Stella knew or didn't know was to talk to her myself. But I wasn't sure how I was going to get Dawn to agree to connect me with Stella, given her daughter's current fragile state.

"Dawn, please call me Maddie. And I want to be clear; I'm not talking to you as a reporter right now. This has been pretty traumatic for me, too, and I'm just trying to process it."

"I completely understand," she said, putting her hand over mine and clasping it.

"Do you think Stella might talk to me?"

Dawn looked at me wide-eyed. She pulled her hand away, obviously unsure of my motives.

"I don't know. I'm not sure that's a good idea. But she's a grown woman. It's her choice. I will give her your contact information and let her decide."

I slipped a business card out of the small purse I had slung over my shoulder that was just big enough for my keys, phone, and glasses. I was glad I had thought to stick a few business cards in the pocket of the bag.

"Thank you. I just think it might be cathartic for both of us to talk about it," I said sincerely. I still couldn't let go of the image of the man I now knew as Max floating in the water next to me, pleading with his eyes for me to help him. I was too late to save him, but maybe I wasn't too late to find out what happened to him. *Laws without morality are useless.*

Dawn relaxed a little when I used the word "cathartic," her face softening, her eyes returning to an empathetic gaze across the table in my direction. As she stood up to leave, she quietly slipped my card into the pocket of her apron. She squeezed my shoulder again and walked away silently.

When Shelby returned to clear the rest of the table, I asked for the check.

"It's taken care of," she said with a polite smile. *A gentleman,* I thought of Zack.

"Okay, great. I didn't realize he had paid the bill already."

"No, sorry, it wasn't your lunch guest who paid the bill; it was Dawn. She told me to tell you it was on the house today."

I nodded and smiled self-consciously. I then left Shelby a fifteen-dollar tip on a thirty-dollar meal. I headed to the sidewalk to find Zack and tell him what kind of progress his junior detective had made while he was gone.

9

UNSTEADY AS YOU GO

As I rode my bike back to the condo, so many things were swirling around in my head, cluttering my brain. First, there was the fact that my father, Roger, might not be guilty of killing my mother and might be getting out of prison thanks to new information that I had uncovered. The worst part about this was that I wasn't sure I wanted Roger out of prison. I had *no* intention of having a relationship with him. There was no way we could just pick up where we left off when I was twelve, the last time I visited him as a child. Yet, I knew he would surely want to have a relationship with me.

Then there was Stella Avery, the young woman who hosted a party where a man died—not just any man, but her friend. And now, she was falling apart either because she was grieving and felt guilty for what happened, or because she was complicit in some foul play or negligence that had contributed to his death.

And then, to cap it all off, there was Zack. Smart, kind, funny, attractive Zack. There was no doubt I felt something when he casually brushed my hand at lunch, but I didn't trust my instincts when it came to men. It had been so long since I dated; what did I know about men? I knew about Adam; that's all I knew. Now, I was starting from square one again, trying to decipher who this man really was and whether he was showing me his true self or some dating version of himself.

All of it was *exhausting*. By the time I locked the bike in the rack and jumped on the elevator, I was wiped out. I decided the best thing I could do was throw myself into my work on the podcast.

Kai had texted me several times in the past few days, saying things like *Just checking in* and *How's it going?* I was so consumed with the Max Prince case that I really hadn't even thought about the podcast once since I found the body. But I knew it was time to get down to work. It would be a welcome distraction from everything else that was going on in my life.

When I got into the apartment, Louise was sitting on the couch waiting for me, clearly hoping for a play-by-play of my lunch with Zack.

"So?"

"So, what?"

"Come on! You know what I'm talking about. *Zack?* How was your date?"

She enunciated the word "date" like she was repeating it in a spelling bee. I almost thought she might spell it out. *Date, d-a-t-e, date.*

"It was good, I mean fine. It was fine and good. I don't know. I have no idea what I'm doing here."

"Sure, you do, it's like—"

"Please don't say *swimming*," I grinned and settled into a wicker chair with overstuffed pillows facing her.

"That's not what I was going to say at all. I was going to say that it's like being in high school again, like starting all over. You get a second chance, but with life experience as your guide instead of just hormones. Do you know how many people would kill for a second chance, a do-over in the romance department?"

I could sense that she was talking about herself. She and Scott lived frenetic lives between their intense careers and their sons' busy sports schedules. I imagined this didn't leave too much time for them as a couple. Truth be told before Adam got sick, we had been in a bit of a rut ourselves. The twins had been a handful, testing limits daily, pushing our buttons and each other's. Miranda was always poking the bear when it came to Blake's sensitivities—telling him he was "a baby," that he whined like a little girl. And my job as a crime reporter was like being on a treadmill without a kill switch. The only way for me to slow down was to jump off in mid-stride and hope I didn't break a leg. So, I knew exactly what Louise was referring to.

"I hear you, and I appreciate what you're saying. But *this*, whatever *this* is, it is still really new, and I haven't defined it yet. Nor do I know how I feel about it," I said as I clutched a throw pillow to my chest as if it might protect me from Louise's prying questions.

"But do you like him? That's all I'm asking you," she said gently this time, in a way that would be impossible for me to ignore.

"I do," I said immediately. I even surprised myself hearing the words out loud. "I like Zack Brumson."

The Jones brothers stole large farm equipment, equipment that cost tens of thousands of dollars, from farmers in Pennsylvania. They would back up a tractor-trailer in the middle of the night, load it up, and by dawn, they would be on their way to the Midwest to sell a stolen tractor to some unsuspecting farmer in middle America.

Eventually, as the men's teenage sons got involved in the family business, they brought in a new side hustle—*drugs*. This, of course, featured a seedy element that threatened to bring down the whole house of cards. So, it was decided by the brothers that the younger members of the organization had to be eliminated—*all of them*. This included the ringleaders' own son and his friends, and that's when the murders started.

With the help of Kai, I had found the original investigator on the case, and he agreed to do an interview with me. It was a two-hour interview, and I needed to listen to it, log the pertinent pieces of sound that I wanted to use, and then begin writing the first episode with his interview as the framework. It was a tedious but ultimately fulfilling process. When I started to see the shape of an attack coming together—that arc that made it into a story people would be compelled to listen to, my heart skipped a beat.

Louise and I sat side-by-side on the chaise lounges on the porch, both of us balancing computers on our laps. She had her AirPods in and was on a conference call while I had my headphones on, listening back to my taped interview with Detective Pat Zaminski. He was eighty-two now, but his voice and train of thought were clear and direct. I had never met him in person as we did the interview on my computer, but Kai had sent me a few old pictures of him. In one photograph, he had one of the brothers by the crook of the arm with his wrists handcuffed behind his back. Both men had long hair and Elvis sideburns. Detective Zaminski was wearing tight plaid polyester pants, a thick white vinyl belt with a large shiny silver buckle next to his gun holster, and a white sports coat. My favorite part was that he had a lit cigarette dangling from his pursed lips. This moment in time said more to me about this man than just about any written biographical information Kai could have sent me.

"They were mean; I mean the dark-heart sort of evil that you hope as an investigator you don't ever come across in your career," Zaminski's booming voice said, filling my headphones as I watched boats whiz by on the waterway below the balcony. "When you are confronted with that kind of evil, a man who is willing to have his son assassinated to save his own skin, you have to watch your back. No one had house alarms back then; they didn't exist. But I had a big dog who would attack on demand, and I kept my gun in a holster hanging over my bedpost, ready for anything."

I closed my eyes and pictured the man with the long sideburns from the photograph asleep with his gun dangling just a few inches above his head. There was probably a wife sleeping soundly next to him, maybe a few children in their own bedrooms nearby, and they all depended on this one man to keep them safe. It was these vignettes that interested me maybe even more than the facts of the case, the real-life moments that painted a vivid picture of a person's character. I silently wondered if Zack was like this. Was he the sort of man who would protect a family at all costs?

"Paddleboarding?" Louise said it like maybe she had said it a few times already, trying to get my attention, but I hadn't heard her.

"What?"

"We deserve a break. We've been working for *hours*," she said, stressing the word "hours" like we were digging ditches in the rain instead of working on our laptops on a sunny balcony overlooking the water on a beautiful day.

By "hours," Louise meant two hours, which hardly registered in my book as a solid work session. But I could use a break, some exercise, and some peace on the water. I hadn't gone paddleboarding since the day I found Max's body. It was time to get back in the saddle.

"What do you say?" Louise said, her laptop now closed and perched at the edge of the chaise lounge. She had turned to face me; her legs now swung over the edge of the chair.

"Okay. I guess, but I need to do some more work when we get back. I feel like I've gotten so far behind this week. I've been so consumed by this whole Max Prince thing."

"I agree; you're under a lot of stress. That's exactly why you need to get out on the water and take a break. Clear your head."

I wasn't sure this was the thing that would clear my head, but I decided it was worth a try. And at least if I had a panic attack, Louise would be with me. What could go wrong?

I had brought my paddleboard with me—a small board called a "Little Teddy" that was basically for women and children as it was only rated up to 150 pounds. It was just nine and a half feet long with a rounded front end that gave me a lot of stability, but it didn't cut through the water nearly as fast as the newer, more modern boards with sleeker designs.

The yacht club at the condo had several used boards anyone could borrow for a couple of hours. The dockmaster fit Louise with a board similar to mine but longer and more stable after telling him she was just a beginner.

Right away, I thought maybe I had made a mistake as I watched

Louise spin in circles, not able to get control of the direction of the board between the current that was slowly picking up and the significant breeze that made us feel like loose sails flapping in the wind.

"Louise, sit down and paddle like you're in a kayak until we get around the corner where the breeze will let up."

She looked at me bewildered as she repeatedly tried to get away from the dock and the boats that zigzagged around her, trying to avoid hitting her. I paddled closer to her and sat down on my board with my legs crisscrossed as I moved the paddle from one side of the board to the other to model the proper form. She nodded at me and unsteadily lowered herself to a sitting position. Slowly, she followed me out of the high traffic area until we turned the corner into a quieter canal bordered by single-family homes with small docks. The water was almost still here, and the breeze had all but subsided. I got to my knees and then stood up, one foot at a time, holding my paddle horizontally at my waist for balance. Louise paddled over next to me, still sitting.

"So, you can stand up now," I said gently, not wanting to undermine her confidence in what I was asking her to do. "It's easy. Just take your time. First, get to your knees, then come up to a standing position one leg at a time."

She nodded at me, but her expression was fearful like she might be about to cry. It was strange to see Louise this way. She was so strong and capable in every aspect of her life, but then I realized I had taken her out of her comfort zone.

"Okay," she said, her voice wavering as she began the unsteady process of trying to come up to a standing position. At first, I thought she had it, but then I saw her falter as she tried to push up on her right leg. The board rocked, and she tried to use her left leg to steady herself, but it was too late. I heard a splash as I watched her tumble into the water backwards. Her paddle floated in one direction while her board floated in the other direction. Luckily, she had the board attached to her leg with a Velcro cuff connected to a rubber leash that was tied to the board so that it couldn't go too far.

"I'll get the paddle; just pull yourself back up on the board," I said, stifling a laugh as she surfaced, wiping saltwater out of her eyes and squinting into the bright sunlight.

"Whose idea was this anyway?" Louise said sarcastically as she clumsily pulled herself back up onto the board like a shipwreck survivor crawling onto land. The water was only about four feet deep, so I was pretty sure she was going to be okay. I paddled over to her oar and pulled it close to my board with my paddle until I could reach down and grab it. I laid it on my board and paddled back over to her to return it.

"I think you're really getting the hang of this," I smirked, handing her the paddle, no longer trying to hide my amusement.

"I think I've found my new passion and lost my sunglasses in the process," she replied with more annoyance than humor this time.

Louise adjusted her wet baseball hat, which she miraculously did not lose in her fall from the board. She stood up, this time with some actual grace, took the oar from my outstretched hand, and started to paddle forward. I moved quietly in time next to her; the only immediate sound was our paddles cutting through the water as we glided swiftly down the canal. Small motorboats and fishing boats cruised up the waterway near the horizon, bouncing on the surface of the deep blue water, their fluffy white wakes snaking behind them, a distant rumbling of their outboard engines hitting our ears a few seconds after they had already passed.

"Look at you," I said with sincerity, glancing over at Louise as she concentrated on her form, staring straight ahead beneath the brim of her dripping wet hat.

"I just had a little bit of a rough start. I will conquer this."

"I know you will."

Louise was nothing if not persistent. She was the type of person who would fall and get up a hundred times until she mastered something. It was one of the things that I loved most about her. She wasn't too proud to *try* new things or *fail* at new things. I believed it was this quality that kept her young because she was always willing to learn something new. It was one of the admirable traits about her that I was always trying to incorporate into my own life.

As we rounded the next corner, I realized that we were entering the exact area where Max had fallen off the boat. Even though it was hot and humid, a shiver went down my back. It was one thing to look at it from land. It was another thing altogether to be on the water in the actual spot where he slid beneath the surface and took his last breath. I wasn't sure if Louise recognized the location since she wasn't that familiar with the area and had only seen it briefly from land. So, I decided not to mention it, not wanting to break her focus on trying to stay upright on the board.

"Holy crap," Louise said suddenly, pulling her paddle out of the water and letting the board slow to a crawl, moved only by the tiniest of currents. I paddled backwards to turn my board around and meet her where she had stopped. "This is it. This is the place we took pictures the other day, where that guy drowned."

"Yes, it is," I said, trying to act surprised as if her declaration had just jogged my memory.

"How deep do you think it is?"

"I don't know, maybe a few feet."

"Why don't we jump in and see?"

"Hold on, newbie. You stay right where you are. *I* will jump in."

I handed her my paddle and slid off the board into the dark, still water. I hit the bottom almost right away, jarring my back a little bit. I was surprised at how shallow it was.

"Three feet, I'd say."

The surface of the warm water hit me just above the waist.

"How do you drown in three feet of water?" Louise said a little too loudly, loud enough for recreational boaters who were anchored at the little sandbar nearby to hear us.

"Well, first, who knows what the depth of the water was that night? It depends on whether it was low or high tide. I can check the tide charts for that day. I think it was probably high tide. Even so, it would only have been about six feet deep. And secondly, anyone can die in any depth of water if they are intoxicated or hit their head."

I could see the wheels turning in Louise's head as she took in everything I was saying. She scanned the area with her eyes, squinting again to avoid the bright sunlight. People sat casually on the edges of boats, country music blaring from their stereos. Kids splashed in the water nearby.

"I still don't get it. Something is not adding up here," Louise said, shaking her head as I watched a man overthrow a frisbee to his dog. The dog paddled out to retrieve it a few feet from my board.

The truth was, I didn't get it either. And I wasn't sure I wanted to get it.

10

TRUTHSAYER

When we returned from paddleboarding, I saw that I had a missed call from an unknown number. I wrapped up in a towel and went back to my chaise lounge on the balcony while Louise took a shower.

The mystery caller had left a message: It was Jason, Damien's friend who was on Ripple the night Max died. According to Damien, Jason was the only sober person on the boat. He had come straight from his other job pumping gas at a local marina. Captain Perry Spotz had picked Jason up at a nearby dock because he had agreed to help him with the party that night.

I called the number and got Jason's voicemail. I decided against leaving a message. But he must have seen a missed call from me because he called me back thirty seconds later.

"Hi, this is Jason. I think I missed a call from you. I'm Damien's friend."

"Thanks for calling me back," I said a little too enthusiastically.

"No problem, but this all has to be confidential, *for real*. This guy I work for part-time, Perry, Perry Spotz, he's a tough dude. I can't afford to get on his bad side. That's why I didn't tell the police everything I know. I can't risk having this guy pissed at me."

"I get it. I will keep your name out of it. I'm just trying to figure out what is going on here."

"Me, too," Jason said after a long pause. "So, basically, I had only been on the boat for about twenty minutes. I have a captain's license, so I help Perry drive and dock it sometimes. But he didn't really need me for that kind of help that night, so he gave me a trash bag and just asked me to walk around and clean up what I could. You know, it was a typical party; there were plastic cups, napkins, plates, bottles, and basically stuff all over the place. The partiers were dancing, singing along with the music. They weren't wasted but definitely buzzed. I don't love cleaning up after people, but Perry pays me well, so it's worth it. I was just doing my job, trying to stay out of everyone's way. Of course, I was still checking out the ladies. There were some cute girls there, dressed pretty provocatively and dancing like there was a stripper pole in front of them. I mean, I'm a guy; it was hard not to notice them. I wasn't being creepy or anything."

I sat there on the chair, wrapped snugly in the towel, silently willing Jason to get to the point. I was sincerely hoping he had a point to get to.

"Anyway, out of nowhere, I hear two guys yelling, calling each other names, shouting all kinds of curse words at each other. I mean, stuff like this happens from time to time; people get into fights when they party. But this was like way over the top. It got my attention. I had already put the trash bag down because I was taking video of the crowd dancing with my phone. It was something Perry had asked me to do because sometimes he liked to post it on our Facebook fan page to encourage other people to charter the boat. You know, advertising how much fun people were having. But when the yelling started, I walked in their direction, thinking I might be able to calm them down. And just as I get close to them, one dude punches the other one, and he falls into the water. I'm like ten feet away at this point. Everything kind of like stopped at that moment, like that game you play as a kid where someone yells *freeze*. It was like that. Everyone just froze in place, stopped talking, and stopped singing. The music kept playing, though. For some reason, I totally remember it; it was that song "Old Town Road" by Little Nas X with that old country guy, Billy Ray something."

While I appreciated Jason's attention to detail, I was itching for him to tell me what happened next.

"So, then what?"

"Well, I was about to dive in and help the dude. No one else seemed like they were going to do anything, and I was clearly the only sober person besides Perry on the boat. And then, without warning, Perry yelled *we're out of here.* We had been cruising slowly, and suddenly he gunned it. It was crazy. I honestly didn't know what to do. It was pitch dark, and once he started moving, I lost sight of the spot where the guy went into the water."

"What did you think? Did you think Perry knew what was happening?"

"For sure; Perry is always in control in every situation. He was trying to get out of there as fast as possible."

"Did you know the guys who were fighting?"

"I didn't recognize them at the moment. Later I found out that it was Max Prince who went overboard. He went to the same high school that I did, but he was a couple of years behind me. I didn't know him well. He was good friends with the girl whose party it was—Stella Avery. She graduated with me, same class. The guy who punched Max kind of just blended back into the party crowd, and I couldn't tell who he was."

"How did everyone else react?"

"Like I said, they froze; they got real quiet. On the way back to the dock, no one said much. Just talked in whispers to each other. It was like everyone knew something bad had happened, something they were all now a part of. It was like they all had a secret now, a secret they had to keep *or else.* They were bonded by it. Once we got back to the dock, they couldn't wait to leave. They grabbed their stuff and got off quickly, practically running to their cars and Ubers."

"And then what happened?"

"Perry called 911 and said he did a headcount when he returned to the dock, and someone was missing. He told the 911 operator that the guy was drunk and must have fallen into the water when no one was looking."

"How did that make you feel, to hear him tell it like that? I mean, he just lied about a man drowning."

"*Sick.* I felt sick to my stomach. And when Perry hung up the phone, he looked right at me and said, and I'll never forget this, he said: *That's the story, that's the one we're going with. Do you understand?* And I did understand. I understood completely. It was Perry's world, and I was living in it."

"So, you lied to the police about what happened," I said, trying to keep the judgment out of my voice.

"I did. I didn't feel like I had a choice. I still don't feel like I have a choice, but I'm sick about it. I can't sleep; I can't eat. I just keep picturing Max struggling in the water, calling for help, and seeing the wake of the boat just screaming away from him. It's like a nightmare that keeps replaying over and over in my head. That's why I wanted to talk to you. I'm hoping you can get this to the right people without throwing me under the bus. I didn't know the dude well, but no one deserves to go like that."

"Agreed, and as far as you being the tipster, I mean, there were like twenty people there that night, right? No one would know for sure it was you."

"True, but I think they may all be protecting this guy that hit him for some strange reason. They're all friends."

"I get that. But why would Perry cover it up?"

"That's the weird thing. Maybe he's worried about his boss getting sued?"

"Sure, but there's still potential liability for losing a passenger whether he knew it at the time or not, and leaving makes it a criminal act."

"I know; it's insane to even say it out loud. The only thing I can think of is that Perry panicked. He thought in the dark there was no way we would find the guy, so he decided it was better to get back to the dock as soon as possible and pretend no one saw it happen."

"That's pretty risky with all of those witnesses."

"Sure, but they're drunk, and not one of them even made the slightest move to help."

"Doesn't sound like they had time."

"True, but someone should have yelled at Perry to turn the frigging boat around, to at least *try* to find the guy. Not one person did that. I didn't do it either. I should have done it. The blood is on my hands as much if not more than it is on theirs because I was sober."

I could hear Jason's anguish over the phone. On one hand, I was stunned that neither he nor anyone else on that boat tried to help Max, but more curiously, I couldn't figure out the motive for Perry Spotz to cover it up. There had to be something more going on here. I felt like Jason had told me everything he knew. He had unburdened himself as much as he could, given the circumstances. He had no reason to hold back any details at this point. *I believed him.*

When we hung up, I sat and stared at the phone in my hand for a long time. I looked out at the water and pictured someone slipping beneath the surface. I tried to imagine what that must be like, a helpless feeling as the air begins to leave your lungs, then desperation to claw your way to the surface, and panic in the dark when you can't tell which way is up. As much as I loved the water, I also had a deep respect for its power—not so much a fear but an understanding that, like driving a car, it came with inherent risks. On the road, the danger came from other drivers, but on the water, the danger was part of nature. For me, it made being on the water at once exciting and daunting.

I just couldn't believe that none of the people on the boat had told the police the truth. I would have thought some of them would have confessed to save their own skins, unsure of what others were saying. All they had to say was that they were drunk, that they didn't realize what was going on until it was too late. And then, they got scared, and that's why they didn't call 911 right away. As far as I could discern the liability was squarely on the shoulders of the man who assaulted Max and on Captain Perry Spotz, who made the choice to leave the scene. But the others, whether they knew at the moment what was going on, they certainly knew by now what had happened. How could they live with themselves? Maybe, like Jason, they were not doing very well; the death of a man would weigh heavily on their shoulders. It had to change a person, knowing they may have contributed to someone's death.

Suddenly, as I watched a boat whiz by on the waterway below, its white foamy wake snaking behind it, I felt completely and utterly alone. I was sitting on something so big, so important, yet I had no idea who I should tell. I needed to tell the right person, a person who would understand the importance of the situation and help me navigate my next steps. Without hesitation, I dialed his number.

If I didn't have Kojak in my life, I was pretty sure I would be dead by now. We had been in a lot of tight spots together. There was the literal protection he offered me as a detective, but then there was the emotional protection he gave me as a father figure. He knew about my mother, he knew about Adam, he knew how vulnerable I could be at my core, and most importantly, how obstinate I could be when I fell backed into a corner.

"So, let me get this straight. All of these dumbasses saw this crap go down and did nothing?"

"Pretty much."

"That's some crazy frigging evil."

"Yes, it is. So, what should I do? Should I go back to that Cape Mayson cop, the one I talked to the other day? Major Willis?"

"Let me think about that for a minute. I'm not so sure that's a good idea. You told me in your text that he seemed pretty dismissive. Said it was an accident, *case closed*."

"Yep, that's how it went down."

"Well then, he's not your guy. He's either a lazy bum who doesn't want to do the extra work required to get to the bottom of this thing, or he's hiding something. Small towns are funny; everyone knows everyone, and it's not unusual for people to look the other way. Especially in a swanky little beach town like that. When people got money, you can make all kinds of things go away, *even a dead body."*

As Kojak said these words, I suddenly felt a chill even though I was sitting on the porch on a beautiful, balmy summer day. I wasn't naïve. I knew that he was right, but I just couldn't picture any cop ignoring a case where twenty people had let a man drown.

"So, what do you suggest? I mean, I can't exactly ignore what I know now. I'm in too deep."

"As usual."

"What's that supposed to mean?"

"It just means that you can't seem to pull yourself away from the darkness, kiddo. You were supposed to be at the beach relaxing and working on that casting thing."

"Podcasting."

"Yeah, whatever. Never listened to one of those things in my life. How do I get it, anyway—on my radio?"

"Nope, only on your Sony Walkman; it comes on a cassette," I said with laughter in my voice.

"Really?"

At this point, I knew the cheerful banter was meant to take my mind off the terrible predicament I was in, but it wasn't working. I simply couldn't ignore the fact that, for some strange reason, Max had floated up to *my* paddleboard. It was like he knew even in death that I would try to find the answers as to how this horrible thing had happened to him. It was in the moment, as Kojak continued his playful side of the conversation, that I knew what my next step needed to be.

"It's not like I asked for a dead body to float up to my paddleboard."

This statement quickly halted Kojak's standup comedy routine. For just a second, I thought he had hung up—the silence between us was heavy, waiting for someone to punch through it.

"I know, kid. I really do. Listen to me, just sit tight. Don't go back to that detective. I got a bad feeling about the guy. Probably just a lazy dude resting on his laurels, doesn't want to get his hands dirty; maybe he's close to retirement, but I don't want to take a chance if it's something else. I got a buddy at the Attorney General's Office; maybe I can get him to take a look at it."

And then, suddenly, I felt guilty for making Kojak feel bad. I knew that he was only trying to help. And I really needed his help. I had a habit of pushing people away who were trying to help me. It was as if I couldn't risk showing weakness. After Adam died, I vowed to myself that I would be strong, that I could take care of myself and the twins, that I didn't need anyone's help. Lately, I realized that I *did* need help. I needed Kojak's help, Louise's help, and maybe even Zack's help.

"Okay, that sounds like a plan."

"And hey, how's my boy Zack? Heard he's vacationing down there, that you guys might get together."

"Who told you that?" I quipped, letting the playfulness creep back into my voice to signal a truce.

"You know me. I got people everywhere. That's what makes me such a top-notch detective."

11

IDENTITY THIEF

As a television reporter, I had been to more wakes and funerals for people I *didn't* know than for people I *did* know. For the most part, I stayed away from funerals, as a general rule because I always found them to be so depressing. But it was a necessary part of the job, and it was one place where I always knew I could find people who might be willing to talk about the victim.

When I looked up Max Prince's obituary online, it was very brief.

> Our beloved son Max Prince departed this world on Friday, June 7, as the result of a boating accident. He leaves behind a family that loved him very much and an army of dedicated friends. He was passionate about introducing children to the world of health and fitness in his role as an elementary physical education teacher. He was just as passionate about his role as a lifeguard in Cape Mayson, where he spent his summers keeping the beaches safe for swimmers. A celebration of life will be held Thursday at the Little Chapel on the Beach. The family will receive visitors at the Windstream Funeral Home Wednesday afternoon.

In lieu of flowers, please make donations to the Cape Mayson Turtle Hospital in Max's honor. There will be a private burial and reception for immediate family only following Thursday's service.

I looked up the turtle hospital whose motto was *Rescue, Rehab, Release.* Their mission was to rescue injured sea turtles and nurse them back to good health so they could be released into their natural habitat—the ocean.

I felt like I was in familiar territory again. It reminded me of a place where I might do a story for "Amazing Animal Tales." Sometimes, it was a bit hokey, but it filled my need to continue reporting without the day-in-day-out feeling that I was drinking from a fire hose. Crime reporting was dark and demanding, and now, as a single mother, I had two children who demanded my attention much more than the mean streets.

Even with the job change, I hadn't been able to completely extricate myself from crime reporting. I could still feel the pull of it tugging at me, begging me to solve the mysteries that kept falling into my lap, including the puzzle of my mother's death, which I had remarkably not thought about since my lunch with Zack. I was still having a hard time unpacking the fact that Roger might be innocent. But I had put this aside for now, preferring to focus on the fire right in front of me.

I decided I would attend Max's wake and see if I might be able to get a minute with someone from his family. I wondered if they too had suspicions about how their son had died. I also wondered who might show up at the wake. Would the people from the party be there? Would they dare show their faces after what Jason said they had collectively done?

I knew I had one powerful ace in the hole in terms of getting to speak to the family—*I found the body.* My guess was that they would want to speak with me, that this discovery would bond them to me in some strange way, and that they would not be able to turn away from me.

I would be ready for their questions, ready to lie. I would not tell them about his eyes being wide open and staring up at me from the water. I would tell them he appeared peaceful, floating there, suspended near the surface like an angel with the early morning light surrounding him like a halo. There was no reason to tell them the truth, the truth about the fact that I couldn't get his dark, piercing eyes out of my mind. I wouldn't tell them that when I closed my eyes and laid my head down on the pillow every single night, I saw him staring back at me.

I looked up the turtle hospital and realized I would have to pass it on the way to the funeral home, so I decided I would swing by there first. When I told Louise about my plan, she insisted on tagging along. At first, I told her no, but then I realized I could use the company. Since I was turning over a new leaf of learning how to accept help in my life, I decided this might be a good first step.

"I'm in," Louise said, twirling in a black hippie-looking sundress that she happened to bring with her. "Who knew we'd be going to a pop-up funeral?"

"It's a wake, not a funeral."

"It's all the same. There's a dead body. Everyone stands in line and whispers while they're waiting to have an awkward moment with the dead person's family. The only difference is that you don't sing at a wake."

"True. But I do need to make a stop on the way; you might be a little overdressed for it."

"What's that?"

"A turtle hospital."

The turtle hospital was a single-story, light blue cinder block building. On the front, someone had painted a mural of two bright green sea turtles swimming underwater. The turtles were more cartoonish than realistic. They looked carefree and had big smiles on their animated faces. I could see the comedy of the mural immediately reflected in Louise's snickering face.

"I think those two turtles in particular need to be saved," she said, pointing at the painting as we parked in front of the building. "They need to be saved from that terrible piece of artwork."

We paid the admission fee, which was labeled as a "donation" to the hospital. Then we followed the bright red arrows as they led us through the facility by different tanks with individual turtles of varying sizes in each one. Each tank had a sign on the front indicating the sex and age of the turtle and where it was found. The signs also included the turtle's injuries and prognosis. My favorite part of the exhibit was that the staff had apparently named each turtle.

Romeo: male, three years old, located at Lea Island by swimmers, injured by a boat propeller, expected to make a full recovery in 3-4 months and be released back into the sea.

At the edge of each tank was a "turtle ambassador," as indicated by the title on their bright yellow t-shirts. Most of them appeared to be teenagers or college students, probably volunteers, who shared their wealth of turtle knowledge with anyone who was interested in listening.

"If you find an injured loggerhead sea turtle, you need to call the local Wildlife Alert Number—we have cards at the front with that number on them. Feel free to grab one on your way out. These turtles are endangered species; they are being threatened with extinction, and that's why they are covered under the federal government's Endangered Species Act. The biggest threats to these magnificent animals include fishing lines, nets, and boat propellers. We are also very concerned about people disrupting their habitats, their nests on the beach. That's why sometimes you may see rope around a particular area asking you to stay out because turtles are nesting there."

As I listened to the young woman named Jessie with a mass of blond curls and a swath of freckles across her round face wax poetically about turtles, I silently wondered if Max had been a turtle ambassador. Was that why his parents chose this particular charity for donations in his honor? Or was it simply a choice made because his family happened to be animal lovers?

I decided to wait for the young woman to finish speaking so that I could pull her aside, but the words were tumbling out of her mouth so fast, without breaths in between, I wasn't sure when there would be an opening.

As I waited, I thought about all the animal stories I had covered for "Amazing Animal Tales." I honestly thought it was a joke at first, that it wouldn't stick. But it turned out that with all the bad things going on in the world, people would rather watch an animal story than just about anything else on the news. Animal stories did especially well online and on social media. They often trended as the top news stories of the day even when there was something else much more important going on. I thought about how much our viewers would love a story about budding scientists nursing injured loggerhead sea turtles back to health. I made a mental note to tell Janie about this place so that we could do a story here when my sabbatical was over.

"Any questions?" Jessie asked the group of five people lingering at the edge of her tank. Romeo, who had multiple barnacles adorning his shell, was turning around and around in the water like a kayaker practicing a roll.

"What happens to their shells if they don't make it? What do you do with them?" A woman asked.

"That's a very interesting question. We actually cremate their bodies and take their ashes out to spread at sea to honor where they came from. But the shells, they're quite valuable. Some people use them as artwork. They're so valuable that there are even poachers who illegally capture and kill turtles just for their shells. There's a nonprofit turtle rescue and museum in Florida; they display them at their facility, and once a year, they hold an event where they auction some of them off to raise money. The proceeds go back to the turtle rescue that donated the shells. So, we ship them there, to Florida."

The wheels in my head were turning faster than Romeo in the water. What a great story this would be to follow the journey of one of these turtle shells. But as soon as the crowd shuffled away to the next tank, I saw my opening to speak with Jessie about Max.

"Jessie," I said, referencing with my hand to her name, which was embossed on a white and red plastic tag pinned to her shirt. "I have a slightly unrelated question. Do you have a second?"

"Sure," she said, motioning me to the far side of the tank, a place too narrow for a group of visitors to walk through. She obviously sensed my desire for privacy. "Shoot."

"It's about Max Prince."

Her reaction was immediate. She hung her head and gripped the side of the tank, staring down into the water as if Max might just magically appear there, swimming happily with Romeo.

"He was a volunteer here, and he was also my friend."

At this point, Louise had wandered off with the group. I could see her out of the corner of my eye taking selfies with the turtles behind her in the tanks.

"I'm so sorry," I said, and lightly put a hand on the young woman's shoulder.

"He was involved in a lot of the rescues, you know, where they go out to the location where a turtle is found and try to transport them here safely. He worked here on his days off from lifeguarding in the summer, not as much in the winter because he was a teacher and couldn't fit it in. But he was a great guy. He loved the turtles so much. When one passed away, he was so sad. I saw him cry more than once. We're all in shock about what happened to him, sick about it, honestly."

With that, she gripped the side of the tank even harder and seemed like she was trying to steady herself. I could now see small tears running down her cheeks.

"The wake is today; funeral is tomorrow."

"That's what I heard," I said, trying to sound casual.

"He won an award for a really difficult rescue like two years ago. The turtle was tangled in a fishing line and up on some rocks at Masonboro Island. He paddleboarded to it, cut the line with a knife, and somehow managed to get the turtle onto the board and then safely onto the boat. Luckily, it was a baby. I mean, adults can be three hundred to a thousand pounds."

Jessie wiped her eyes with the back of her hand. I looked across the facility and saw Louise taking photos of a family in front of one of the tanks. I could hear the pinging of raindrops on the tin roof above us that provided shelter for the turtles from the sun. Jessie silently motioned for me to follow her with the wave of her hand, which I did. She led me out of the shelter into a low concrete building, down a long hallway into what appeared to be the main office. She pointed to a framed picture on the wall of Max, surrounded by a group of turtle ambassadors, holding up a plaque in front of a stage. The picture was grainy, overexposed with backlight coming in from a nearby window, probably taken on someone's phone and then blown up to fit the frame. I looked closely at it. It was definitely the same man I had seen in Max's obituary online and possibly the same man who was in the photo on Facebook with Stella. But something bothered me about this picture on the wall—*it was his eyes.* Even in the bad lighting, I could see that they weren't dark at all; they appeared to be green or maybe blue. I closed my eyes and tried to imagine the body in the water, slightly bloated, the skin a purplish tinge, with brown wavy hair. The basics matched up, but the dead man's eyes had been *so dark*, staring back at me from just beneath the water's surface. I could never forget that. Yet, the man in this photo, his eyes were bright. Was my mind playing tricks on me? Or maybe death, specifically death in salt water, had the power to change the color of a person's eyes, to make them dark and foreboding? I was starting to second guess everything I thought I remembered.

Suddenly, the small concrete office felt like it was closing in on me, like the walls might collapse in on themselves, suffocating Jessie and me beneath their weight. I quickly thanked her and ran back down the hallway, through the door, and outside into the parking lot, where I found Louise scrolling through her pictures on her phone.

"What's up? You look like you just saw a ghost."

"It's a long story. I can't really explain it right now," I said breathlessly, not knowing how to tell my best friend about how my mind was playing weird tricks on me, making me doubt things that I knew to be true. I didn't want to worry her any more than she already was about me.

"Try."

"It's nothing; I was just talking to a friend of Max's. He volunteered here. It sounds like he was a really good guy. She got very upset while she was talking to me. I just felt bad about bringing it up."

"Got it. Well, let's continue the joy-fest. We've got a wake to go to."

Just like Louise had predicted, there was a long line of people waiting to pay their respects to Max and his family. Everyone was appropriately dressed in black or other dark, muted colors. You could hear their whispered murmurs as they exchanged pleasantries while they patiently stood in line.

Even though it was a wake, it was a *beach* wake. So, the dress was less formal—sundresses, shorts, even some flip-flops. There were people of all ages—some clearly his contemporaries, twenty-somethings in little clusters. There were young women with big sunglasses obscuring half of their faces, sporting long sun-kissed locks and short skirts. There were young men looking awkward and uncomfortable in polo shirts and wrinkled khaki pants probably grabbed right out of the hamper; their floppy surfer hair wet down into some semblance of submission.

There were also small groups of adolescents with their parents; I assumed they were some of Max's students. They were dressed more formally, holding their parents' hands tentatively, looking sad and somber as the line shuffled slowly forward.

I turned around, and I spotted Jessie and the turtle ambassador crew, all cleaned up in their Sunday best, coming in the door and stepping to the back of the line. She had told me they were ending the tours early today so that everyone could attend the wake. They stood in a tight circle, their heads close together, speaking in low voices, occasionally laughing; I guessed they were sharing funny stories about their friend.

I was trying to be unassuming like I had a right and a reason to be there. In my heart, I felt like finding Max's body was a very good reason to want to pay my respects to him and his family. But in my head, I was also aware that I was there more as a journalist than as a witness to his death. It was this cognitive dissonance that I was struggling with when Louise, fresh off editing her turtle pictures for social media, grabbed my arm.

"Check out that girl; she looks horrible. Maybe anorexic, *poor thing.*"

I didn't want to be too obvious, so I glanced down the line behind me at the person Louise was talking about. She did indeed look thin—gaunt. She was an attractive woman with big brown eyes, but they were sunken into her face and rimmed by dark circles. Her brown hair hung limply around her shoulders like she hadn't washed it in days. A dark romper hung from her thin frame like it had been draped over the wrong mannequin in the store—one far too small for all the fabric it contained. She looked familiar to me, but I couldn't place her until she tilted her head back a little, and I got a glimpse of the woman behind her. Dawn Avery had her palm on the woman's back. The painfully thin young woman had to be Stella Avery, but she looked so different from the happy, healthy-looking photographs I had seen on her Facebook account.

"Oh my God," I said too loudly for my surroundings. Louise slipped her phone into her pocket as a signal that I now had her full attention.

"What?" She whispered, also too loudly. The people in front of us turned around with a *shush* in their eyes.

"That's the girl from the boat. The one who had the party. That's Stella Avery. She's the one who identified Max's body for the police. She looks *awful.*"

"Uh, pretty sure 'awful' is an understatement."

"Frankly, I'm surprised she's here. Her mom told me she wasn't doing well."

"Clearly, she's not."

"No, but I guess anyone in a situation like this would be sick about it."

"Yep, especially if you might have been able to prevent it."

"We don't know that," I said, bringing my finger to my lips to quiet her. "Not the place."

"Got it," she said, looking straight ahead, obviously a little miffed at me for scolding her. But I knew she would be over it before we left the building. Louise didn't hold onto things.

As the line moved forward, I could begin to see Max's parents, a small couple, looking weary but appreciative as they hugged their visitors and held onto their hands tightly. Max's father was a handsome, graying brunette with an athletic build and a youthful look despite the small wrinkles around his eyes and mouth. Max's mother was blonde and plain but also had a pleasant round face that exuded sincere warmth. She looked each person in the eyes as she spoke with them, holding their gaze stoically for as long as they stood in front of her. She acted unhurried like she had all day to spend with each visitor.

At this moment, I thought about my own children and the unbearable grief this couple must be experiencing. I always wondered in these situations how parents were able to go on, to cope, to get out of bed every day, and function.

I recalled when Adam first died and everything seemed so hard, even the simplest things—like brushing my teeth, washing my hair, putting away groceries. It all felt pointless. And even when I managed to go through the motions, my limbs felt heavy, like it required so much extra effort for me just to walk to the mailbox or put gas in the car. Eventually, I snapped out of it. I started running again, getting more sleep, and I began focusing on my raison d'être—my children. But if they were taken away from me, I knew I couldn't function.

I paused for a moment and thought about the kids. Whatever they were doing at camp, it had to be more fun than attending a wake. I would send them some postcards later to let them know I was thinking about them and missed them terribly.

Suddenly, I realized the line was moving, and it would be our turn to greet the family soon. I hadn't decided what I was going to say to the Princes. It felt inappropriate and bizarre to just blurt out *I'm the one who found your dead son.* But on the other hand, they would surely ask me how I knew him. I would have to lie. I was too old to be in his circle of friends. I would have to say I knew him from the school where he worked or the turtle hospital. I figured I could easily be the mother of one of his students, but lying in this situation just didn't feel right. The problem was that the truth didn't feel right either.

I wanted so badly to workshop this with Louise, who was still brooding next to me, staring straight ahead. Our shoulders brushed one another like strangers as we stepped forward every few seconds. But I knew that we were too close and that there was no way to have a private conversation with her at this point, even if I could penetrate her bristle. I wished I had brought it up in the car on the way over, but like so many moments, I just figured I would ad-lib it, and see what felt right at the moment. And that moment was *now.*

Just beyond the Princes, I could see the corner of the open casket. A beige, puffy satin material peeked above the edge, but thankfully, I couldn't see the body yet. Strangely enough, even though I had been a crime reporter for many years, I still always felt a little squeamish about seeing dead bodies. I knew that it would be rude not to at least stop momentarily at the casket after greeting the family to pay my respects. I reminded myself that I had already seen this man dead, and this would be a much gentler view: a body that was cleaned, embalmed, dressed, and surely touched up with some makeup. *I can do this,* I said quietly to myself.

"Mr. and Mrs. Prince, I am so sorry for your loss," I said with the utmost sincerity reaching out to first shake her hand and then his. They both clasped my right hand with two hands for a few seconds before letting go.

"And you are?" Mrs. Prince said with tears in her eyes and a receptive expression on her face. She was not trying to pry but to learn one more thing about her son from this stranger standing in front of her.

"Maddie, Maddie Arnette. And this is my friend Louise Chance."

We exchanged pleasantries as I circled around the truth of how I knew their son. Louise was giving me an evil glance that I could see out of the corner of my eye that said, *don't do it.* But somehow, as I stood there trying to work it all out in my head, I couldn't come up with a better path than telling this devastated couple the harsh truth. These two grieving parents standing in front of me with their eyes red and puffy from hours of crying and faces painted in pain deserved the truth.

"I was the one who found your son," I said abruptly in mid-sentence as they were thanking us for coming. It was like someone took control of my brain and forced the words right out of my mouth. As soon as they escaped, Max's mother threw her arms around me in a dramatic gesture and held onto me tightly, squeezing harder and harder as tears began to flow down her face onto my bare shoulder.

"Thank you, thank you, thank you," she said in between sobs.

Max's father touched his wife's shoulder and gently pried her off me.

"What she means," he said, pulling his wife into his chest so that she could continue sobbing, "is that without you, we might never have known what happened, that Max had died. We may have gone through life, always wondering if he was out there somewhere. It may not seem like it right now, I know it sounds a little crazy, but you gave us a gift— *you gave us our son back.*"

It was the reaction I hadn't expected, but inside I was silently congratulating myself for following my gut and telling them the truth. I nodded at the couple, unsure of how to respond. After a few seconds of awkward silence punctuated by Max's mother's cries, I realized that they didn't expect a response from me. Instinctively, I reached out and touched her back lightly, and started to move in the direction of the casket. I sensed Louise's awkward presence looming in lockstep behind me.

"Miss Arnette, thank you for coming," Max's father said to my back as I was making my getaway. "How can I reach you in case we have questions and want to talk later?"

I reached into the outside pocket of my small purse, where I always kept a handful of business cards. It didn't seem like the right time or place to whip out my phone and ask him for his contact information. I turned and slipped the card into his extended hand. He nodded gratefully, his eyes full of fresh tears.

"What just happened?" Louise leaned in and whispered as if she had stepped out of the room for a minute and missed the whole thing.

"I think they just thanked me for finding their dead son."

All I could think about was getting up to the casket, counting to five in my head, which seemed like a respectful amount of time to stand there, and then getting the heck out. As the line shuffled closer to the body, I took a deep breath and thought about what I was about to see. I knew that Max would be presentable, not a bloated face with dark eyes staring at me from beneath the surface of the murky water. *I could handle this.*

When it was our turn, Louise and I stepped up to the edge of the casket and stood solemnly side-by-side. We both folded our hands in front of us reverently and looked at the young man lying there in the dark suit, white shirt, and red tie. His face was tan, *too tan*, covered in too much makeup, and his brown hair was combed back neatly behind his ears. Padded cream-colored silk bubbled up around his head and shoulders. It took me a minute to really focus on what was in front of me. I had to resist the urge to grab Louise's hand and run out of the room.

My heart started to pound. There was a ringing in my ears that blocked all the hushed conversations happening in the background behind me. I closed my eyes for a second and reopened them. Nothing had changed. How was this even possible? Nothing was making any sense. I was at Max Prince's wake. I had just met Max Prince's family. But I was very sure of one thing: This dead man in front of me was *not* the man I found floating in the water.

12

BODY DOUBLE

"Okay, so let me get this straight," Louise said for the fifth time as we sat on my balcony overlooking the water, trying to figure out what in the world was going on. "You're telling me that the guy in the casket, the dead guy, is *not* the same dead guy that you saw floating in the waterway?"

"That's exactly what I'm telling you."

"But how is that possible? Somebody had to identify the body. And there had to be some sort of medical exam, if not an autopsy. What happened to the dead guy you found? Did he just disappear on the way from the waterway to the coroner's office?"

"I don't have any idea. But I know that *it isn't him.* And I don't think there was an autopsy done, at least that's what Stella's mother, Dawn told me. The family didn't want one. They just asked for a toxicology report that isn't complete yet."

"How can the family say no to an autopsy in a criminal investigation?"

"That's the thing. It's *not* a criminal investigation. It's believed to be an accident, so if the family doesn't want the body decimated by an autopsy, I guess they have some say in it."

"How can you be so completely sure it's not him? I mean, they clean them up pretty well. You only saw the dude for a split second, and he was underwater, not exactly a clear view."

"Louise, it may have only been a few seconds, but I know exactly what I saw. His face is etched in my mind forever. I can close my eyes right now and picture him like he's right in front of me."

"Okay, so what is it about that memory that has you so convinced it's not the same guy."

"They look similar; there's no doubt. But the guy in the water had a mole on his right cheek. It was obvious, something that stuck with me."

"Okay, so playing devil's advocate, maybe they covered it up with makeup in the casket. He sure had a lot of makeup on."

"True, but the mole was raised. I don't think any amount of makeup would make it disappear. I searched for it on the man in the casket—looked for it hard. *No mole.*"

"So, let's just say you're right. This means that someone switched the bodies between the drowning and the funeral. What in the world? Why would someone do that? How could someone do that?"

"And the thing that is so crazy is that Stella identified the body. She obviously knew it wasn't Max. I told you her mother, Dawn, told me that. She just mentioned it in passing; I really didn't think too much about it at the time. She told me the family was too distraught, so they asked Stella to do it for them."

"The skeletal chick?"

"Yes, which may explain why she looks so horrible. It's not grief—it's *guilt.*"

"Okay, I'll play along. But I still don't see a motive for switching the bodies of two dead guys. And so, *who* is your dead guy, and where is he now?"

"Great questions. I wish I had the answers to them. I don't. But I intend to find out."

This definitely wasn't turning out to be the relaxing getaway at the beach that I thought it would be. Louise was so distressed by the day's events that she told me she needed some retail therapy and decided to head to the mall on the mainland. I begged out and stayed behind, feigning fatigue. I wanted to start searching missing person cases online to see if I could find a John Doe with a mole who just happened to disappear around the same time that Max Prince died.

Because it was a tourist town, the dead man could be from anywhere. If no one reported him missing, there would be no record of his disappearance. When my phone rang, I was scrolling through the NAMUS website, the National Missing and Unidentified Persons System—the clearinghouse for data about missing people in the United States. It was a caller from Pennsylvania. I almost let it go to voicemail, but curiosity encouraged me to answer.

"I'm trying to reach Maddie Arnette."

"That's me, can I ask who is calling?"

"Sure, this is Belinda Parsons. I'm a real estate attorney calling from Dilltown, Pennsylvania."

"What's this in reference to?"

"Well, it's a little bit complicated. I'm sorry to interrupt you in the middle of the day. Is this a good time to talk? Do you have a few minutes?"

"Go on." I was starting to regret picking up the phone. I had an urge to hang up, but my polite gene stopped me.

"Well, you are the granddaughter of Glen and Rachel Hartsell, correct?"

"I am. What's this about? I'd rather not answer any more questions until I know more about your reason for calling."

"I know this is coming out of the blue. And I'm really sorry about that—so I'll just cut right to the chase. Apparently, you own their farm and their farmhouse."

My mind immediately flashed back to the dilapidated farmhouse I had visited when I went to see my father in prison in Pennsylvania earlier that year. It was dilapidated, overgrown with weeds, an eyesore, in complete disrepair. The property, once a working farm, was now nothing but fields of brush gone wild. I had gone there to pay respects to my mother, to the place where she was born and the place where she was murdered. When I watched the house disappear in the rearview mirror of my rental car, I put it behind me forever. Now, this woman, this stranger, was telling me I owned this dark piece of my family's past?

"You must be mistaken; they had two sons; it surely would have gone to them before me. I know they've also passed away, but I'm sure they had wives, children, next of kin."

"True, that's where the confusion lies. Their sons had lifetime rights to the property, but upon their deaths, your grandparents' will says the property and the house should be divided equally between the grandchildren. And you're it. Your uncles had no children. You're the only grandchild."

"So, why am I just finding out about this now, thirty-some years after my grandparents' death?"

"Excellent question. Apparently, a clerk at the old courthouse misfiled the paperwork, so when your uncles died, the state took control of the property since there was no next of kin and no one who could locate the will. The state didn't really want it. It pretty much just sat there neglected for years. But we recently built a new courthouse—it's amazing, you should see it. Looks like a shopping mall with shiny marble floors and very tall escalators. Anyway, as the clerk's office was preparing for the move, they decided to take all the old estate files and put them in a digital format because they didn't have space to store them in the new building. During that process, they found your grandparents' misfiled will and realized the mistake. So, you own the house, what's left of it, and the property, 127 acres."

As if my life couldn't get more complicated. I stared out at the water and caught the snippet of a pop song emanating from a boat below. Three young girls in bikinis were dancing on the bow of the boat while a shaggy white dog slept in a large marine beanbag at their feet. The bright sun glistened off their sunglasses as the thin white trails of wake snaked behind the boat. What in the world was I going to do with an old farm in Pennsylvania?

"So, you are an attorney? Who do you represent? How are you connected to this?"

"Well, I'm actually a real estate attorney. I handle large residential and commercial developments, mostly mixed-use projects. I got wind of this situation because one of my clients is interested in purchasing the property. He was researching it and discovered the discrepancy about the same time as the clerk's office did. You'll be getting a letter from them, by the way, from the clerk of court's office explaining everything. But in the meantime, my client is prepared to make you an offer on the land. He wants to put up a mixed-use development—condos, apartments, single-family homes, maybe some retail, even office space. He's eager to get started. So, I thought I would call you, break the news, and get the ball rolling as I assume you have no use for the land given that you live and work in North Carolina."

Here I was, talking to a stranger, finding out that I owned something that could be precious to me, and now she was asking me to part with it before I'd even had time to think about what it meant. I had no concept of how valuable the land was. After all, it seemed like it was in the middle of nowhere to me, but this woman's urgency made me realize I needed to get some more information before I said anything.

"Miss, what did you say your name was?"

"Belinda, Belinda Parsons."

"Miss Parsons..."

"Just call me Belinda."

"Okay, Belinda, I really need some time to process this. I've only known about owning the property for two minutes; I can't exactly turn around and sell it without thinking it over."

"Of course not; I don't mean to rush you. I know it's a lot to take in. I'll give you my contact information, and then just take the time you need to think about it and get back to me when you're ready. We're prepared to make you a very generous offer."

As soon as I hung up the phone, I sat back down on the chaise lounge and closed my eyes. Again, I pictured the old farmhouse winking at me with its sagging eaves and broken windows, sunlight streaming through the roof's patchy shingles. I felt a closeness to my mother there—not because she was murdered in that house, but because she was raised in that house. She ran through those green rolling fields, her red hair streaming behind her, her parents watching at a distance from their rocking chairs on the front porch. It had once been a special place before someone took it all away by tainting it with her blood.

Could it be a special place again? Was this my destiny—to pick up my family and move hundreds of miles north to a rural town where we knew no one and start over? Maybe the universe was trying to send me a message.

Suddenly, I realized I did know one person there. I picked up my phone and hit the contact number for Zack.

13

WARNING

WHEN I TOLD ZACK ABOUT THE CALL concerning my grandparents' property being left to me, he was very quiet on the other end of the line. At first, I wondered if one of us had a bad signal, but then he spoke, just one word—*fantastic.*

I felt like it was a strange response to learning I had just inherited the property where my mother was murdered, but then I tried to see it from his perspective. It was his adopted hometown. He loved the rolling farmlands that defined Dilltown, and he probably saw some bizarre potential in the property that I did not. Then I let myself go one step further. Maybe he saw potential in us? Maybe that was the genesis of his response? I shook my head vigorously to try and get the thought out of my mind. *What was wrong with me?* Was I a 14-year-old girl with a crush on a boy, or was I a 40-something widow with two kids to raise?

Miranda and Blake's sweet faces popped into my head. What was I thinking? I hardly knew this man, and he was acting far too excited about my news like he had some underlying agenda. Whatever it was, my priority had to be my family, not a new crush or an old farmhouse with too much land to take care of.

After our brief conversation that ended as awkwardly as it began, my phone rang, and I thought it might be Zack again calling back to expound on his "fantastic" declaration. I looked down at the name and realized it was not Zack but Damien.

"Maddie Arnette," I said in my business tone, not wanting to give Damien the satisfaction of knowing that he was already programmed into my phone.

"Maddie, it's Damien, Janie's Damien."

It irked me the way he said, "Janie's Damien," as if I might possibly know another Damien. But I let my annoyance pass. I was curious about everything that had transpired at the wake to find out what he had to tell me. I would not share with him that the body I saw in the casket was not the man I saw floating in the water. I planned to hold that information close to the vest until I could figure out what was really going on.

"Hey, Damien, what's up?" I said with as much casualness as I could muster.

"So, I hear you've been asking around, asking a lot of questions about Max."

I was sitting on a chair at a small table on the patio, my computer in front of me. Max's obituary photo was pulled up on my screen. I had checked it again as soon as I got home from the wake. And I was right. *No mole.* Max was definitely the person I saw in the casket based on the photo I was looking at, but he was definitely not the man I found floating in the water. No way.

"What do you mean, Damien? I'm just doing my job. Beating the bushes a little. Nothing unusual for a reporter."

"Gotcha, but that's the thing—you're dealing with some pretty heavy stuff here. These guys don't play. I really regret bringing you into this. Janie would kill me if something bad happened to you. I think you should just drop it. Forget everything I said, forget whatever Jason told you, just leave it alone. It's too dangerous."

"Leave it alone? Damien, at first, I thought we were talking about a tragic accident where people panicked and did the wrong thing. But now I'm starting to get the feeling there's a lot more to this story. Was there a plan to kill Max? If that's the case, then we're not talking about an accident; we're talking about *premeditated murder.*"

"Look, I don't know what happened. I wasn't there. But I do know this crew that Jason hangs with, works with, and if they think for one minute someone is going to sell them out, they won't hesitate to do something crazy."

"Damien, has someone threatened you?"

Damien was silent on the other end of the line. I was now staring at the photo of Stella and Max on my computer. Max's face filled the screen. His smile was wide; his eyes stared right into the camera lens. His hair was blowing in the wind behind him. He did not have a mole on his cheek in this picture either. It was also clear to me that his eyes were not brown—they were much lighter, maybe green or hazel. It was like he was looking right at me, begging me to solve the mystery surrounding his death. And then I thought of the dead man I found in the water staring at me with his dark eyes, and I suddenly realized I had two people reaching out to me from beyond the grave looking for answers,

"They didn't have to threaten me. I already know what they're capable of."

Zack stirred his coffee nervously as I entered the coffee shop. I wasn't sure why he was so nervous. Did I make him nervous? I had so much I wanted to tell him. I wanted to tell him about the body I found not being Max Prince. I wanted to tell him about Damien's call, his warning to be careful and watch my step. But it was clear that Zack had something else on his mind today, something that had nothing to do with my agenda.

"Hey, you," Zack said as I sat down across from him. It was an almost too familiar greeting that made me shiver a bit for some reason. He sat at a picnic table outside the coffee shop that was just a short walk from my apartment.

"Hey, how are you? Sorry I haven't touched base since our lunch the other day. Things have been a little crazy. I know you sent me a few texts. I wasn't ignoring you, just a little overwhelmed."

"No worries. I get it. I'm just glad you're here now. Sit down. Got you a skinny honey and cinnamon latte, no whip. Correct?"

"Correct," I said, trying not to sound too excited that he remembered my high-maintenance coffee order as I straddled the picnic bench. Wait, when did I tell him that? *Did* I tell him that? *Breathe.* I suddenly realized I was making everything more complicated than it had to be. Clearly, I had mentioned the coffee order before, and he had remembered it. That was a good thing, not a bad thing. He was a detective, after all. It was his job to pay attention to details.

"So, you go first. What's going on with the case, with the dead guy in the water case? I assume that's the *crazy* you're referring to."

"Yes and no. I mean, yes, for the most part. I don't even know how to explain it all. There's a lot going on with it. But the biggest issue—and *it's a pretty big one*—is that I went to the wake, and something really strange happened. I don't know what to make of it. I'm actually afraid to say it out loud because you're going to think I'm nuts, certifiable, gone off the deep end for sure."

"Nope, nothing freaks me out. For real. I'm a detective, remember? I've seen just about everything you can imagine. You would be hard-pressed to blow my mind. But feel free to try."

He squinted to see me as the sun was directly in his eyes. I got up, walked around the table, and sat down next to him. As soon as I did this, I realized he thought I was trying to get closer to him when I was honestly just trying to make it easier for us to talk without the sun burning holes in his retinas.

"Sun," I said, pointing to his eyes as I dramatically slid away from him on the bench to demonstrate that I was not making a move. He turned to meet my gaze. The sun was now blocked by the side of his head.

"So, tell me, what happened?"

"Well, you know, I went there to pay my respects. It felt like the right thing to do, considering that I had found the body. I'm not going to lie; I also wanted to know more about Max to see if I could learn anything that might give me insight into the case. I brought my best friend Louise with me. I think I told you she's staying with me for a few days. Anyway, right away, the whole thing felt super awkward, and I decided I had made a terrible mistake. But it was too late. I was already in line to greet his parents. I was committed. I had no idea what I was going to say, so I just kind of blurted out that I was the one who found the body."

"How did that go?" Zack said with a genuine mix of curiosity and sympathy.

"Emotional. The mother, Max's mother, clung to me and started sobbing. The husband, Max's dad, was very kind. Tried to gloss over the moment, tried to make me feel okay for the abrupt way that I told them. They said finding Max was a gift to them because they might never have known he was dead otherwise."

"That's one way to look at it. I'm sure it was a blessing in a bizarre way."

"But here's the thing: *I didn't find Max.*"

"What are you talking about? Of course, you did."

"No, I didn't. When I got up to the casket and saw the body, saw Max, I realized something was terribly wrong. It wasn't him."

"How is that possible? That it wasn't Max?"

"So, this is where it gets really complicated. It *was* Max Prince, but it *wasn't* the man I found in the water. I know this for sure."

"How is that even possible? Why are you so sure about this?"

"Because I will never forget that man. His face is etched in my mind forever. For one thing, the man in the water had a pronounced mole on his right cheek."

"So, maybe the funeral home covered it up with makeup for the wake."

"I thought about that, so I went back and looked at Max's pictures on social media. *No mole.* And you know what else—he didn't have dark eyes like the man I saw in the water. In every picture of Max, it is very clear that he had light-colored eyes, green or hazel maybe, but definitely not brown."

"Okay, so back up. You found a body. Police reported that the body was identified as Max. Who identified him?"

"Stella. The girl who had the party."

"What motive would she have to lie?"

"No idea, but it's the only thing that makes sense."

"So, she lies, and then sometime in between that identification and the wake, the real Max appears and ends up in the casket. So, where is the other guy? *Who* is the other guy, and where was Max's body hiding?"

"I told you that you would think I'd come unhinged."

"I don't think that. But I'm trying to make sense of it all. Because if what you're telling me is true, there are more people in on it than just Stella. Someone with some pull had to switch those bodies and deep-six the other one. And why would anyone do that? That's a lot of work. What would the purpose be?"

"Good question. I have no idea. And then the guy I told you about, Damien, the guy who dates my colleague—he calls a little while ago and tells me to back off. He's had this sudden change of heart, doesn't want me to pursue it anymore, wants me to leave it alone. Which, of course, only makes me want to pursue it even more."

"I'm sure it does."

With that simple declaration, Zack reached in my direction and put his right hand over my left hand. It was less of a holding hands thing than it was a comforting gesture. But it felt odd—the weight of his hand on mine. I wanted to immediately pull away, but I thought it might offend him. I also did not want to give him the wrong idea. So, I counted to three and then casually pulled it away, acting like I had an itch on the tip of my nose.

Zack agreed that I needed to take Damien's warning seriously and said that he also wanted me to step back a little. He said he would subtly check into the Windstream Funeral Home and see if he could find out anything about them. He said that there was no way a body could be switched without some collusion from the funeral home. He then told me he had something very important that he wanted to talk about. He said he understood if I wasn't up for it, for another heavy conversation after what I had just told him, but I urged him to go on. I suddenly felt selfish for having monopolized the conversation with my personal drama.

"Please, what is it? I'm sorry; I've been talking about my stuff ad nauseum."

"Well, it's about what you told me on the phone earlier today."

"Oh, you mean about my grandparents' property?" It hadn't occurred to me until just now that *this* was what he wanted to talk about all along, not Max Prince. I started to get a funny feeling in my stomach. This was a red flag that a man I had just met was suddenly interested in my real estate.

"Right, well, remember how I told you I was retiring soon, thirty years in minus all my unused vacation time? Anyway, I got to thinking about what I want to do next, and I think I know for sure now."

"That's great. What is it? Don't keep me in suspense."

"Remember at lunch I mentioned that I had always wanted to open a bed and breakfast? I know where I want to do it now, in Dilltown. I know it sounds crazy, but it's the perfect place, the perfect fit. I'm pretty good with my hands, with renovating. I love taking something old and making it brand new again, but at the same time maintaining the historical integrity of the property."

I appreciated his passion, but I couldn't figure out why Zack was telling me all this, and why now, with everything else that was going on? And then it dawned on me. He didn't want to just do this in Dilltown; he wanted to do it on my property. I decided I would play dumb and see how long it would take him to bring it up.

"That's awesome, Zack. What a great dream to have, and I know you will make it happen." This time it was I who put my left hand over his right hand and gave it a little squeeze. "Let me know if there's anything I can do to help. I'm not really very handy myself, but I do have some pretty great design ideas."

"Well, there actually is something you can do," he said, looking at me coyly, picking my hand up now and holding it in between his. "If you would consider selling me your grandparents' property, I think it would be the perfect place for a bed and breakfast. And I promise I would return it to its former beauty, bring it back to the way you remember it as a little girl. You could help me. We could do it together. I know we haven't known each other for long, but I just have this feeling we could be a great team."

He squeezed my hand and looked at me like a little boy on Christmas morning, seeing his presents for the first time. My brain was confused by his brazen request, but my heart felt like it was swelling with each smile and each squeeze. I was sure of only one thing: that I was not sure of anything in this moment.

14

LEFT ALONE

ZACK HAD SURPRISED ME with his bold request and his enthusiasm. I had only just learned the property was mine, and now he was asking me to part with it, just like Belinda Parsons. On the other hand, if I did sell it to him instead of the developer, I would know that it was in good hands, that someone wasn't just bulldozing my family's legacy to make way for fancy condos and restaurants.

Still, when he told me he had to go back to Pennsylvania, to go back to work, and that I should think about it and call him, I wasn't sure if I was sadder about possibly letting the property go or the fact that he was leaving. It was a funny thought, the thought of missing someone I hardly knew. I hadn't truly missed anyone since Adam, and I wasn't sure exactly what it meant.

To make things even more complicated, Louise also had to get back to her busy life in Oak City. So, once again, I was left alone with my thoughts and a death investigation that I couldn't seem to let go of.

My phone vibrated, and I looked over at it on the old wooden desk that I had placed in front of the glass sliding doors to give me a premium water view. It was a text from Zack.

Hey there, sorry to leave so quickly today. Things are piling up at the office. I will keep you posted on

Roger's case and let you know if I find anything out about Windstream. Think about what I asked you earlier. I had another idea after I left. We could be partners, but you wouldn't have to do anything. I would do all the work and then run the place. You would be a silent partner—just something else to ponder. And I hope this isn't too much, but I think I miss you already. I know it sounds strange because we hardly know each other. Come to Pennsylvania and visit me soon. Please...

It was a whole lot to think about. I barely knew this man, and now he was asking me to come visit him in Pennsylvania and possibly be his business partner? It all felt too fast and too intimate, like his hand on mine. But there was something about the way he used the word "ponder" that hooked me. Who used that word, let alone in a text? There was an old-world charm about Zack Brumson that intrigued me. It also scared me a little bit.

But I hardly had time to *ponder* his intentions before my phone rang. I could see the number had a Maine area code. It had to be the twins calling from camp. I had mailed their postcards on my way home from meeting Zack the previous day, so they had obviously not gotten them yet, which meant they were calling just because they missed me, and that touched my heart almost more than receiving their letters.

"Mom," Blake said excitedly. "I got a bullseye in the bow-and-arrow competition. I went on a zip line. It was *so high*. You would have totally freaked out. Some kids closed their eyes, but I didn't! And, oh, one more thing. There's a girl, a girl named Kelly, and I'm pretty sure she likes me, at least that's what everyone says."

Blake was talking so fast that I could barely understand him. I couldn't get a word in. I could hear Miranda in the background trying to wrestle the phone away from him. Finally, her loud voice came on the line.

"Mom, we want to stay for the whole eight weeks. That's what *we've* decided."

As usual, Miranda's voice was strong and unwavering.

"Are you sure, honey? That's what Blake wants, too?"

I could hear him in the background say "yes" with conviction.

"Yes, Mom. It's so fun here. The kids are cool, and so are the counselors. It just makes sense. There's nothing to do at home. It's so boring. Plus, I know you're working a lot, as usual. This must be a nice break for you, to not have us to take care of every day."

I suddenly felt guilty, like my kids thought they were in the way, which was absurd. I pictured us all snuggly sharing the condo in Cape Mayson together, walking on the beach, swimming in the ocean, and sharing dinners at sunset on the balcony. It made me sad to think of losing them for the entire summer. Maybe they should be right here with me? Maybe our break from each other had been long enough?

"Miranda, why don't you guys think about it a little more before you make your final decision. I think I have a week before I need to pay the tuition for the balance of the summer."

"Mom, we have thought about it, and this is what we want to do. Okay?"

"Okay."

I wanted them to be independent. We had always wanted that. Adam and I worked toward that goal together. And now that they were exercising that independence, it felt lonely. The thing I thought I wanted the most, *to be left alone,* was turning out to be the thing I now wanted the least. Here I was—no kids, no Zack, no Louise—and I didn't like it one bit. But I gritted my teeth and did what any good mother would do.

"Okay, if that's your decision, I think it's great. I know you two will have an awesome adventure there this summer."

Quietly, I realized that my summer was also shaping up to be quite an adventure.

I knew I should be working on the podcast, but my brain just couldn't focus on it at the moment. I promised myself I would just do this one thing, and then I would concentrate on work for the next few days.

I had to go to Oak City to pick up my mail, pay a few bills, get my hair highlighted, and have lunch with Kojak. So, I decided while I was there that I might as well pay Stella Avery a quick visit.

It wasn't hard to get an appointment with her. I told them my doctor had retired and I was shopping for a new provider. It wasn't a complete lie. My doctor did retire, and I was in between providers temporarily. I just went to the local urgent care when I had a medical need, which was, thankfully, very rare.

I thought about being upfront—just calling Stella Avery, telling her whom I was, and asking her to meet with me—but I had a strong hunch she would turn me down. I decided this approach, pretending to be a new patient, while it was a little bit of an ambush, would make her a captive audience in a professional setting where she couldn't blow up at me.

When she walked into the room, she looked even thinner than she had at the funeral, which was less than forty-eight hours prior. It wasn't just that she was so thin. Plenty of people wore thin well. It was that she looked physically ill like something was eating her from the inside out. It was clear right away that she didn't recognize me and was trying to put on her bravest face.

"Hello, Ms. Arnette; I'm Stella Avery. I understand you are in the market for a new medical provider."

And then I saw it; the look come over her face, the look of recognition that told me I had less time than I thought to plead my case and get her to talk to me.

"Actually, I came here for another reason today. I am—"

"Yes, I know who you are," Stella said, backing away from the chair where I sat as if I might be radioactive. But she didn't turn towards the door to leave. At least this was something.

"I'm sorry. I didn't think you would see me."

"You were right. I have nothing to say to a reporter."

"You and Max were friends, old friends, good friends."

"That's right," she replied, fiddling with a stethoscope that hung loosely around her neck. It was obvious that she was trying to figure out my game in the same way that I was trying to figure out her game.

"So, I understand that you're grieving."

"Very perceptive. How can you tell that?" She said in a mocking tone.

"I just mean it must be very sad for you to lose a friend that way."

"What's it to you? Get to the point," Stella quipped, crossing her arms now and widening her feet in a power stance like a superhero getting ready to unleash her secret powers on me.

"The one thing I can't figure out is that if you were such good friends, how could you tell the police the body *I* found was Max when it really wasn't?"

Stella's eyes widened in the middle of her gaunt face, making them look almost cartoonish. Of all the things she had expected me to say, this was clearly not one of them. Instinctively, her hands went to her hips to continue the ruse of confidence when I could see that it was draining exponentially out of her body with every word I spoke.

"Why did you do it, Stella? Why did you misidentify the body? Who made you do it? Why?" Despite the boldness of my statements, I kept my tone neutral and calm.

With these words, Stella started to back towards the door. She kept her eyes on me the entire time and reached behind her to grab the handle.

"You have no idea what you're dealing with here, lady. If I were you, I would make a U-turn. You don't want to go down this road."

With that and a click of the door, Stella was gone, leaving me alone in the exam room with my thoughts. I had obviously touched a nerve. But now she knew that I knew she had misidentified the body. I was exposed. Whoever made her do this would now know I was onto them. It was an unsettling feeling, but it was one I had felt many times before. I knew that my only option was to keep going until I had the answers I was looking for.

As I was walking out of Stella's office, my phone rang. I looked at the number and realized it was Zack. I hadn't expected him to call so soon, but I was pleasantly surprised.

"Guess where I am?" he said with no introduction.

"I have no idea."

"I'm standing right in front of your grandparents' house. Excuse me, *your* house."

I pictured Zack there all spiffed up in his dress pants and suspenders; his unruly hair slicked back, a red bow tie at his neck, "beach Zack" put away on a shelf until his next vacation. I also pictured the sad house with its sagging eves, buckling boards, and a jungle of weeds threatening to swallow it. What did he see in that house? For the life of me, I couldn't figure it out. It was clearly a teardown, but that's not what he saw. He saw *potential.*

"Very interesting..."

"Yes, yes, she is."

It jarred me for a moment, his speaking about the house as 'she.' I wasn't sure why it annoyed me so much, but maybe it was because I wanted to be the one to see the diamond in the rough that could be transformed. I wanted it to be my vision, not his.

"By the way, got some intel on that funeral home of yours."

"Windstream?"

I was suddenly a captive audience; my concerns about his obsession with the house took a backseat to my obsession with Max Prince's case.

"Yes, Windstream. I didn't realize it at first, but I know an old college buddy who works there. I found him on Facebook, and he was more than happy to speak with me on the down-low. It seems that Miss Stella Avery did identify the body you found as Max Prince shortly after the cops fished him out of the water. They didn't have any reason to question her identification. Body went to the medical examiner for an autopsy, but before he could be examined, the parents quashed it and said they didn't want his body to be compromised. They agreed to allow a toxicology blood screen; that was it. He was sent directly to Windstream at the parents' request. But no one from the family ever came to look at the body. So, they went ahead and embalmed him and got him ready for the funeral.

"Around the same time, they had a gunshot victim, self-inflicted apparently, found at the edge of the marsh, a guy who was on vacation from another state. A man claiming to be the dead man's brother identified him to the police and handed them a suicide note. Open and shut case. So, my buddy gets this guy ready for his funeral. It turns out that my buddy likes to look up pictures of people he embalms on social media so he can see what they looked like when they were alive, so he can make them look realistic. He doesn't want to make them look too freaky with too much makeup or anything. He can't find the name of the gunshot victim—it's like he doesn't exist, like he's a ghost. But he finds Max Prince's obituary, and guess what he learns?"

"I have absolutely no idea."

"He realizes that the dude the cops pulled from the water is *not* Max Prince. The other guy—the one with the hole in the back of the head—he's *the real* Max Prince."

"Okay, so this isn't making any sense. I saw the body in the casket. No gunshot wound."

"Back of the head, like I said. It's amazing what people who work in funeral homes can do to fix bodies for open casket funerals."

"Back up. What did your guy do? Did he tell the cops they had the identifications mixed up?"

"He wanted to be sure, so he asked Max's parents to come take a look at the guy he believed was Max in the casket before the wake. They were very reluctant, but Max's father agreed to come. My buddy showed him the gunshot victim—of course, all cleaned up, with the wound concealed, and the father thanked him for making sure he still looked like 'their Max.' So, it was confirmed."

"Oh my God, my head is spinning. So, what about the other guy, the one I found in the water? What happened to him?"

"That's the really weird thing. When my buddy got back from Max's wake, he was going to call the police and explain the situation, but the other body had already been cremated by one of his co-workers. The guy told him the family called and changed their minds, that since it was a suicide, they decided not to have a service after all and just wanted the body cremated, said that they would pick up the ashes later. My friend didn't know what the heck was going on. But he didn't want to get mixed up in it. I told him I wouldn't use his name, and I wouldn't tell the local cops anything. He doesn't want to get in trouble for not reporting what he discovered about the bodies as soon as he figured it out. He's glad he got Max reunited with his family, but he feels awful about the other guy. He really is a good guy; I don't want to throw him under the bus."

I thought silently for a moment about Zack's loyalty to his old friend, a loyalty that was so strong that he wouldn't give him up even though what he did probably bordered on criminal obstruction of justice. Surprisingly, instead of it making me think less of him, it made me admire him more.

"Why would someone go to all the trouble to do this? It's such an elaborate plan."

"Someone who wanted everyone to think Max Prince drowned when he was really shot to death."

"What happened to the alleged brother of the gunshot victim?"

"Disappeared, gave Windstream false contact information. He obviously snowed the police as well, convinced them it was a suicide."

"Those Cape Mayson police sure don't dig too deep, do they? So, the real Max Prince was shot, and we have no idea who the other guy is, and because he was cremated, we may never know."

"That's it in a nutshell."

"Wow, I didn't see that one coming."

"Me neither. You couldn't make this one up if you tried."

15

BATMAN

LONG BEFORE POLICE RECORDS were computerized, I was reading them in big three-ring binders in the lobby of the police department every morning. Eventually, all the records became digital, but there was something lost in the transition. It wasn't the same as holding a piece of paper in your hand and being able to examine it from top to bottom.

I decided to pay the Cape Mayson Police Department another visit, and this time ask them if I could see the list of calls they had received around the time Max disappeared. I didn't want to raise any red flags with the investigators on the case, so I just went to the records department and told them I was a journalist doing a story on a series of robberies on the island, and I was trying to track down a few specific cases. The records clerk printed out a list of calls for the dates I requested and handed them to me beneath her plexiglass window. She motioned to a small, scratched wooden table in the corner of the lobby and told me I could look at them there, and that if I needed her to print any specific reports, she could do that for twenty-five cents per page.

As I glanced at the list, I realized that most of the crimes in Cape Mayson were pretty minor—someone's bike getting stolen, trash cans getting knocked over, someone taking beer from an unlocked garage. Max's case was listed as a "possible drowning call." At first, as I scrolled down the list, I didn't see anything else that jumped out at me. I went through it a second time, and that's when I saw it, "drunk man possibly needing medical attention."

I casually asked the bored clerk if she could print this specific report. I had completely forgotten my ruse about the robbery trend, but apparently, so had she. She printed the two-page report, and I handed her fifty cents that I dug out from the bottom of my purse. I so rarely carried cash anymore that I was always surprised to find some hidden in a pocket or in the deep recesses of my bag.

The report was brief, but it told me exactly what I needed to know. A man and woman walking their dog that night had seen two men walking along the sidewalk next to the marsh. One of them was very drunk. According to the report, he kept stumbling and was having a hard time getting up. The other man, who was young and muscular, kept yelling at the drunk man to get up, saying, "Come on, Marine, get your butt up." The couple was worried that the drunk man needed medical attention. But when the Cape Mayson police arrived and stopped the young, muscular man, he said his buddy was fine, that he had gone back to the hotel where they were staying. They took him at his word and left.

The woman who called 911 had described the drunk man as wearing a white shirt, red shorts, and a gray and black baseball hat with a Batman emblem on it. I couldn't help but flashback to the body I had found in the water, the billowing white shirt, and the bright red shorts.

The police never did find the drunk man the 911 caller reported seeing, but the next day she called back to see if investigators had learned anything. They told her that they believed the man was okay, that he had gone back to his hotel. That's when she told them she had found a Batman baseball hat on the sidewalk the next morning when she walked her dog near the spot where she had seen the men the night before.

Was the drunk Marine the person I found in the water? Did he fall into the marsh in the middle of the dark night and drown? The marsh was just a few feet from the sidewalk, a few stumbles away.

And, as the crow flies, it was much closer to my condo than the location where Max went into the water. If this were the case, it was pretty convenient for Max Prince's killers that they had a body they could use to prove he had drowned instead of being shot.

And who was this mystery man who was now a pile of ashes? There were no missing persons reports in the log from that night or the next day. But someone had to be missing him, especially if he was a Marine. He would have had to report back to where he was stationed, which was likely Camp Lejeune, about an hour and fifteen minutes from the island. I made a mental note to call over there later and ask the public information officer if they had any missing Marines.

I thanked the clerk, who was now totally ignoring me, so involved in staring at her phone that she didn't even look up when I spoke to her. I folded the report and put it into my back pocket. As I walked to my car, all I could think about was the name and phone number of the dog walker burning a hole in my jeans.

I was almost to my car, rehearsing exactly what I would say to the dog walker, Gina Finkel, when I just about bumped right into Major Arnold Willis.

"Major, so sorry," I said, realizing how distracted I must have been to not see his imposing frame in a dark suit coming at me across the parking lot.

"No worries, Miss Arnette, I'm glad we're running into each other, pardon the pun. I just wanted to let you know where the case you inquired about stands."

"Oh, thank you. I appreciate your following up," I said, trying to hide my skepticism at what appeared to be his sudden gentle tone. Gone was the chill that he dismissed me with at our last meeting.

We were both standing awkwardly in the middle of the parking lot between the rows of mostly patrol cars. Neither of us seemed to know what to do with our hands. I fidgeted with my phone while he shoved his hands in his pockets.

"You're welcome. The truth is that we've talked to everyone we could. I think I already told you that a lot of the people who were on the boat that night, they left town immediately. They don't want to have anything to do with this, understandably. It was a tragedy. And so, the chief, he's shutting it down for good. Not putting any more resources into this one. We're officially going to rule it accidental. We just don't have anything else to go on. At this point, it does seem like an accident. Sure, could some of those people could have done more to help? *Absolutely.* But does that mean there was a crime committed? No. No, it does not."

I stood there assessing this man and his credibility. In my gut, I believed that he was covering up for someone. But who? And why would he risk his career to protect someone, or maybe even multiple people?

"Well, that's too bad that there won't be more investigation. But I get it; I do. You can't throw a lot of resources into a case when it appears to be an accident," I said, trying to sound sincere but failing. The wheels were spinning so fast in my head that I was pretty sure he could smell the rubber burning.

"That's right. I hope you understand. It's not for lack of caring or trying; it's just the way these things shake out sometimes. We're a small department. We do what we can. But we don't have the manpower like departments in big cities have."

Obviously not, I thought to myself as I considered the fake suicide story they had accepted without any further investigation from the so-called "brother" of the possible dead Marine.

"Understood. Well, thanks for at least looking into it. I appreciate it."

We shook hands, and I watched as Major Willis swaggered into the police station confidently, like a man who had just crossed something off his to-do list.

Gina Finkel was happy to take my call when I told her what I was interested in talking about. She said she couldn't stop thinking about the young man who kept stumbling and trying to get up off the ground every time the other man yelled something at him about being a Marine. She told me it was like watching another person being tortured, and while she and her husband didn't want to get too close for fear of what the other man might do to them, she felt compelled to call 911.

She told me the man who was yelling was wearing all black, and the thing she remembered the most was the fact that the drunk man had on a Batman hat.

"I don't know; it seemed like some weird military hazing incident gone wrong. I just felt so bad for the guy and thought he was in trouble. We were afraid to get too close because the other guy was mean-looking, big, muscular, you know, and I assumed he was a Marine too, and maybe drunk. I thought it was too dangerous to confront him."

Could this vanished, drunk Marine be the man I saw floating in the water? I was trying to imagine a scenario in which he went missing. Maybe everyone thought he had just run away, quit, skipped town, gone AWOL.

"But then I didn't hear anything that night or the next day. I was worried, stayed up tossing and turning half the night. The next morning when I walked my dog, I found a hat, *the* Batman hat. All I could think about was that maybe he had crawled away from the sidewalk to get away from that jerk and fell into the marsh and drowned. It's only about ten feet from the sidewalk, and if you're drunk, disoriented, and you don't know the area, it could easily happen."

"Well, you did the right thing by calling 911, even if they didn't find him. At least you tried." *It was more than the police had done*, I thought.

"I just kept thinking if he had drowned, surely he would have washed up by now, surely someone would be missing him, don't you think?"

"Usually, that's the case. You're right. But you'd be surprised how many people go missing and they don't find them. Or they do find remains, and they're never connected to a specific missing person case. There's a lack of resources dedicated to these cold cases. I'm sorry; I don't mean to make you even more concerned. I'm sure he'll turn up. Like I said, no matter what happens, *you* did the right thing by calling the police. Not everyone would do that."

"Thank you. That means a lot to me. I've been worried sick about this since it happened. I hope they find him."

When I hung up with Gina and looked out the window across the choppy water, in my heart, I knew that I had found her Batman.

16

RED SKY

I DECIDED THE BEST WAY TO CLEAR MY HEAD was to go for a paddleboard excursion. The oppressive North Carolina humidity that felt like a wet blanket during the day gave way some in the early evenings. The sun would be setting soon, so I knew I had at best thirty minutes.

It was risky to start out so late because paddleboarding after dark was not an option—there was no way the boats could see you, plus sharks liked to feed at night. Both these factors were very good reasons to stay on dry land. But I ignored the red flags.

As I paddled hard through the small swells that formed tiny whitecaps, I marveled at the red sky tinged with orange stripes above me. I had never seen sunsets like this before I came to Cape Mayson. They looked more like paintings of sunsets than natural ones, with their rich hues slathered across a canvas, morphing into one another and changing shape every few seconds. I quietly thanked nature for giving me such a fantastic show, one that was momentarily distracting me from Max Prince and the dead Marine.

Nothing was making sense. If everything that Zack found out was true, it was now clear that Max didn't drown. He was shot. It was also clear that whoever killed him wanted to make it look like an accidental drowning. Was it possible that coincidentally around the same time, there was a drowning and that the killer was able to initially pass off the dead Marine as Max until the bodies were switched by Zack's well-intentioned college friend?

I wished Louise was still here so that I could say everything out loud to her, and she would organize it for me. Then, she would ask the relevant questions so that we could begin the process of figuring out what made sense and what didn't make sense. I decided I would call her when I got back and workshop this with her over the phone.

Then Zack crept back into my mind—funny, handsome, kind, helpful Zack. What was going on here? Was I falling for him? It didn't seem possible. Adam had died less than three years ago, and I wasn't ready for another relationship. It felt like I was disrespecting my marriage to even be thinking about Zack. But at the same time, Adam was gone. He wasn't coming back. Was I supposed to go through life alone? Sure, I had the twins, but they had their own lives, and in a few years, they would grow up and leave home, and then I would really be alone.

I looked up from my reverie and noticed I was losing the light. The orange sun was now dipping beneath the horizon, washing the sky with pink lines. As much as I wanted to keep going towards the rich palette, I knew darkness was not far behind, so I pulled my paddle backward and turned the board around to head back to the marina.

I noticed a few small boats were coming into the Intracoastal Waterway from the direction of the ocean, most likely recreational fishermen or people just enjoying a beautiful summer day on the water, eking out every last minute. By law, each boat had to have a red and green light on the bow and a white light on the stern as soon as the sun started to dip. They chugged along quietly past me in the No Wake Zone, heading for their homes or boat slips, their lights twinkling in the descending darkness.

Suddenly, I noticed a boat coming fast in my direction. It was still light enough for them to see me, but the boat kept charging like the driver wasn't about to change course despite my being directly in his path. I started to paddle fast to the right to get out of the way, but then he turned slightly and continued to head right for me.

The general rule of thumb was that the vehicle that had the best ability to move over quickly did so. Clearly, a motorboat had more flexibility than a sailboat, for example, or a paddleboard. But the captain of this boat didn't seem to know or care about this rule; *he kept on coming.*

I decided I would paddle left and try to head towards the docks lining the shore. But then he also changed course slightly and continued to head straight for me. I wasn't wearing a lifejacket, but I had one attached to the front of my board as required by law. There was no time to unfasten it. This had always been a quandary to me— why they would allow you to just carry the life jacket on the board when in a real emergency, you would never be able to access it. I would have to jump and take my chances. I didn't want to believe that this was really happening, that someone was deliberately trying to hit me. Yet, there was no other scenario that made sense.

I realized that I would have to wait until the boat was close to me to jump off. Otherwise, he might just try to run over me in the water. I had to let the driver think he was about to hit me. As the boat screamed in my direction, my heart pounded out of my chest. I had to time it just right to get off the board and away from the boat so that I could quickly swim to a nearby dock to safety.

I counted to ten as the light on the bow blinded me, and I leaned left and dove into the dark water in an arc, like a dolphin putting on a show. *One, two, three, four, five strokes.* I was out of the path of the boat and gliding toward a nearby dock. Then I heard the awful sound, the sound of the boat hitting and shattering my paddleboard. I turned around just in time to see the two halves of the split board flying through the air and then falling straight down into the boat's wake as it passed. The boat was a ghost now, skimming the surface of the water in the distance, getting smaller and smaller. I couldn't make out much about it. There were two words in blue on the side. There was a "T" and maybe a "Y." Not much to go on.

I was breathing hard and shaking as I climbed the metal ladder onto a white floating dock lit up by small round lights lining the edge of it. I could see an impressive white beach house with floor-to-ceiling glass windows in the distance at the end of a long wooden walkway. I pulled myself up and collapsed on the dock, reaching down to make sure my dry bag with my phone was still around my waist. Then, I heard the sound of feet pounding down the wooden walkway and short breaths trailing the heavy footsteps.

"Are you okay?" said a breathless man who was reaching his hand down to help me up. I looked at him through fuzzy eyes. "I heard it. He must not have seen you. That was crazy. You're *very lucky.*"

I let the man help me up and ease me into a nearby wooden Adirondack chair, handing me a beach towel. I wondered if the beach towel was already there on the dock or if he had brought it with him from the house, which seemed like a strange thing to do in an emergency.

"Yes, that was a close call," I said, surprised by the sound of my own voice, surprised that I could form words with so little air left in my lungs.

"Are you hurt? Do you think you need to go to a hospital?" He was looking at me intently now, a middle-aged, white-haired man dressed in a pressed golf shirt and madras shorts. He was wearing flip-flops and the concerned look of a father as he stared at me intently. "Are you staying near here? The least I can do is get you home."

I stared at the man, my eyes now adjusting to the bright lights as I cried saltwater tears. He looked like someone who was safe, someone I could trust. And at this moment, I didn't really have another choice.

"That would be great," I heard myself say.

"Come on in for a second. My wife is in the house. We can get you some water and some dry clothes."

He helped me out of the chair by my elbow and steered me down the walkway in the direction of the house, which was so bright it looked like a spaceship about to launch. I put one foot in front of the other, but I was so shaky it was like I was walking on a high wire. The man patiently walked with me, holding my elbow firmly, guiding me down the path. Silent alarm bells were going off in my head as I let this stranger lead me into his home, hoping his mention of a "wife" was credible and not just something meant to put me at ease, not something to trick me into going with him.

"What's your name, young lady?"

"Maddie, my name is Maddie."

"Nice to meet you, Maddie. My name is Mark, Mark Maron. I'm very sorry this happened to you. But I'm very glad you're okay. We'll get you fixed up and get you home in no time."

I sat with the name for a second, scrolling through my brain's massive Rolodex for a reference. Just as we stepped off the wooden path onto the concrete patio in front of the home, I remembered where I saw that name before. *Ripple.* Mark Maron owned the boat that Stella Avery chartered, the boat where Max Prince began his journey to death. This was turning out to be a very odd coincidence.

Mark took me into a sparkling white kitchen with marble countertops, stainless steel appliances, and delicate silver pendant lights with white frosted globes dangling from the high-pitched ceiling. He motioned for me to slide into one of the high-backed white leather bar stools. I pulled the towel tightly around me to keep from getting the stool wet and to stay warm in the air conditioning that made it feel like I had just walked into a freezer.

"Randi," he yelled to someone I hoped was his wife. "Can you get me some dry clothes? This woman has just had an accident on the water."

My eyes were clear enough now to observe this man who had brought me into his home. He was tall and thin, gray-haired, with the beginnings of a summer tan, and he wore glasses with tortoiseshell frames. He wasn't exactly handsome, but he was well-maintained. He wore expensive clothes and looked like he probably took care of himself.

"What kind of an accident?" Randi asked.

The woman who glided into the kitchen was dressed simply in black leggings and a long taupe, loosely fitting t-shirt. Her short blonde hair was perfectly coiffed, and a single diamond pendant hung from her neck. She was statuesque—at least 5'10", and wore little makeup, but she was stunningly beautiful.

"It was nuts. She was on a paddleboard, and a boat came right at her. Tore the board in two. You didn't hear it?"

"No, I was running the bath. It must have drowned out the sound. Are you okay?"

Randi put her hand with flawlessly manicured nails on my shoulder and looked at me with pity in her eyes.

"Yes, I think so. Just shaken."

"That's unbelievable. I guess they didn't see you," Randi said, shaking her head.

"Maybe," I said, regretting my hesitancy as soon as the word came out of my mouth. I realized there was no need to share my suspicions with these people, especially given Mark's potential connection to Max's situation.

"Maybe?" Mark asked, making my reply sound much more sinister than I had intended.

"I don't know. It kind of seemed like they were coming for me, like every time I moved, tried to get out of the way, they would turn more in my direction."

"That's awful," Randi said. "Let me get you some dry clothes."

She left the room and left me sitting in the bright light of the kitchen across from Mark. He studied me as he pulled a glass from a cabinet behind him and filled it with water from the refrigerator door, and then handed it to me silently. I had to unwrap the towel partially to release my shivering hand so that I could grab it. He saw me shaking from the cold and misinterpreted it as fear.

"Wow, you're really shaken up by this. Who in the world would want to do this? Who would want to hurt you? Do you have any idea?"

Once again, alarm bells were going off in my head. I knew it wasn't safe to share my concerns with anyone right now, *especially* not this man who owned the boat connected to Max's demise, but I wasn't sure what to say. I so wanted to pull my phone out of my dry bag and call Zack, but I knew that wasn't an option.

"Probably just some drunk people messing around. They probably thought it was funny," I said, not believing my own words as the lie came out of my mouth.

"That seems like a pretty cruel joke even for a bunch of drunks. Maybe we should report it to the police?"

"No," I said a little too emphatically. "I mean, no use. I didn't get a good look at the boat. It would be impossible to figure it out. There's really no point."

Mark shook his head in what appeared to be disbelief. If he knew anything about what had happened to me, he was an excellent actor because he seemed genuinely concerned. At that moment, Randi returned with an armful of dry clothes and another towel.

"Here you go. This will be more comfortable, and then we can take you home. Unless you're hurt. Do you think you need to see a doctor?" Randi said as she handed me the stack and pointed in the direction of what I assumed was the powder room.

I took the pile gratefully and gingerly edged down from the stool.

"Nope. I'm not hurt, like I said, just shaken. Thanks for this. You are very kind."

I peeled off my bathing suit, t-shirt, and shorts and put them into a plastic bag that Randi had given me as I examined my face beneath the harsh bathroom light. I was pale and drawn. My eyes were red, and my hair a wild matted mess that was slowly drying and would be impossible to comb through if I let that happen. I wet my hands, smoothed it down, and slicked it back into a tight ponytail with a hairband that I always kept around my wrist.

I used the dry towel to wipe away any lingering moisture from my skin and pulled the cozy sweatshirt over my head. It gave me the immediate rush of warmth that I was craving. Randi had also given me some exercise shorts and a pair of flip-flops.

As I finished pulling myself together, I noticed a framed photo of a boat on the wall next to the sink. It was a photograph of Mark Maron and the man that I now knew from social media was Perry Spotz. Perry had his arm draped casually over Mark's shoulder. They were smiling and standing on a dock in front of a large white boat. Mark was gesturing to his side, pointing at the name of the boat. In large blue cursive letters, it read: "Ripple." I remembered this photo from Facebook with the caption: "From one Cappy to another."

Next to it was another framed photo. This one was of Mark and a younger version of Mark. I decided it must be his son. The father and son looked playful and happy, standing on the dock in front of the house with the sun setting behind them as they leaned casually against the railing. They were both wearing matching blue baseball hats with the word "Captain" on the front in yellow stitching. They could be the same person, just twenty-five years apart in age. They looked like they had just shared a private joke with one another right before the photo was snapped.

Randi offered to drive me home, and I gladly accepted. My body felt like it had been run over by a truck, flattened on the pavement. Between the fear I had experienced when I saw the boat careening towards me and the emotional trauma of trying to figure out who would do this to me, I was completely drained.

Randi tried to make small talk as she slowly maneuvered her large SUV through the quiet, dark streets from her house in the exclusive gated community of Harbor Light. Harbor Light was technically a separate little island just off the tip of Cape Mayson, connected by a small draw bridge. You could get there by boat, but not by car unless you were a guest of someone who lived there. Once she pulled past the guardhouse and onto the main road, we were just a few blocks away from my apartment.

"So, you're just here for the summer?"

"Yes. I am on a sabbatical from work. Working on another project, a true-crime podcast."

"Oh, I love true crime," Randi said with a tiny bit of shame in her voice. "I love those true crime documentaries on TV. I watch them all the time. So, what are you on a sabbatical from?"

"I'm a TV reporter in Oak City. Just taking a little break. My kids are at camp this summer. I have twins, a boy and a girl. So, it just worked out," I felt embarrassed for telling this stranger too much too quickly. I was just trying to fill the silence and be polite. I hadn't meant to reveal this much about my personal life to Mark Maron's wife.

"And your husband?" Randi asked as she pulled into the parking lot of the condo.

"He's dead. Cancer, a brain tumor, a couple of years ago." Again, I was stunned by my lack of filter and my bluntness. I definitely needed to get out of this woman's car as fast as possible.

"Oh, I'm so sorry," Randi said as I was opening the door to get out. I could see sincere concern on her face beneath the harsh dome light. She was not the problem. It was me. I was unraveling, and I needed to unravel privately. I was thinking about the twins and how the last thing they needed was to lose another parent.

"Thank you. Thank you for everything. You guys were great. I don't know what I would have done if you hadn't been there."

Randi gave me a little wave and then pulled out of the parking lot. I kept hearing Damien's words in my head, telling me to be careful, to back off, telling me I had no idea what I was up against. Were these the people I was supposed to be afraid of? This kind man who had picked me up from his dock after I was nearly killed and took me inside? This kind woman who gave me dry clothing and drove me home? If they were the people Damien was warning me about, then my radar for danger was not operating properly. Nothing about them sent up red flags.

Leave it alone, Damien had said. *Janie would kill me if something happened to you.* He talked about the people being involved as *powerful.* Could he be talking about Mark Maron? I honestly didn't know. But what I did know was that there was a hot shower waiting for me, and everything else would have to take a backseat.

17

DAY IN COURT

AFTER THE SHOWER, I put on a big, fuzzy terrycloth robe and lay down on the bed. I had a soft throw blanket at my feet that I eventually pulled across my legs, but I never made it under the covers. I also never closed the blinds. I woke up with the sunrise, bright light streaming into the room directly into my eyes. I squinted and looked at my phone on the bed next to me. I couldn't believe that I had fallen asleep right after the shower and slept through the night. I must have been wiped out. I also couldn't believe that it had been one week since I found a body floating next to my paddleboard. So much had happened in the past week that it felt like weeks or months had passed instead of just a few days.

And then, as the fog of early morning suddenly evaporated, I instantly remembered what had happened the night before, that someone had tried to kill me by running me over with their boat. I shivered against the image of my paddleboard in pieces flying through the air, and I pulled the plush blanket even tighter around my legs to ward off the cool draft descending from the ceiling fan above.

I knew that I needed to tell someone about what happened—if nothing else, to let someone know that I was in danger in case something else happened to me. I could call Major Willis, but it didn't feel like this was the right choice. I still wasn't sure that I could trust him. Plus, I had no real information to share. I couldn't identify the boat that sped at me as dusk was blanketing the waterway. I couldn't see who was driving. There was no point.

Maybe I should tell Kojak? But then I shook the thought out of my head. This would only make him worry about me more. He would tell me to pack my bags and come home. So, like many other moments in the past week, it seemed like my best choice for a confidant was Zack. After all, he was the one who discovered what had happened at the funeral home.

Yet, I was conflicted. I hadn't yet made a decision about my grandparents' property, and I was afraid he was going to rush me. I wasn't sure if we could have a conversation without his bringing this up. It was like the elephant in the middle of our relationship, whatever that meant—*relationship*. I couldn't even say the word in my head without feeling guilty again like I was somehow being disloyal to Adam. I knew this was not a sane way to think, that it was truly time to move on. Louise had made this very clear to me, and she was right. But was this the right person to move on with? I still didn't have an answer to that question. Then, my phone rang.

I looked at the screen and saw a smiling picture of Zack sitting at The Last Straw Café from the other day. I had taken it as a selfie with me in the foreground and then cut myself out. I had taken it for Louise because she wanted to see what he looked like, but I was trying to be sly about it in front of Zack. She had approved when I came back to the apartment and showed her "casual Zack," not the one from work in suspenders and a bow tie behind a big desk, but the one in a t-shirt and cargo shorts on vacation at the beach.

"Hey there, I was just thinking about you," I said, wishing the words hadn't come so quickly from my brain to my lips.

"Excellent. Must have been that dark web tracking us and reading our minds again."

"For sure."

"So, I've got some *big* news," Zack said.

I propped myself up on one elbow and pressed the speakerphone button, so I could lay the phone down on the bed and listen without pressing it to my ear.

"Go on."

"It's happening. He is getting his day in court. He's going to have a chance to tell his story."

For just a minute, I was confused. Suddenly all the possible "he's" started going through my mind—the person who hit Max Prince and knocked him off the boat, the people who watched and did nothing, Perry Spotz, who sped away from the scene, Mark Maron, who owned the boat, and the still undetermined mystery person who had put a bullet in Max's head. But then I pulled myself out of the dark spiral and realized he was talking about my father, Roger. Roger was finally going to have his day in court.

I didn't know how Roger had spent nearly forty years in prison for a crime he may not have committed. He tried to tell me he was innocent so many times. He tried to tell me in the letters I never read. When I visited him in prison in Pennsylvania this past spring, he tried to tell me again, but I wouldn't listen.

Roger wrote me one last letter after my recent visit where he told me that he didn't kill my mother, but he felt responsible. I now knew he felt this way because he had suggested to Clifton that he wanted my mother out of the way. That's what Zack had told me. Roger never meant for it to actually happen. He couldn't live with himself for what his words had led to, so he decided to pay the price. Once the police came for him, he shut his mouth and took the punishment that he felt he deserved—life in prison.

I finally did go through some of Roger's unread letters that had been collecting dust in a box in the back of my closet for decades. It was after I got out of the hospital fresh off the near-death experience of having a gun pointed at my head. I had some forced downtime while I was supposed to be recovering. So, I spread the letters out in the spare bedroom and started reading parts of them, not every single word, but significant chunks. After all, there were hundreds. He had revealed things to me slowly over the years, in little bits and pieces. What I gleaned from them was that Clifton was a follower, a drifter with no friends who had a difficult relationship with his family. He desperately wanted to be accepted by someone. That, someone, turned out to be my father.

Clifton's mother, Esther, died of cancer shortly after we met, and Clifton was also dead—tragically shot and killed by his father, who mistook him for an intruder. All I had now were the files that Esther left behind along with Roger's letters and now Zack's insistence that Roger *deserved* his day in court.

I hadn't spoken with Roger since the new information had opened the door for his possible freedom, but he knew through his attorney that *I* was the one who brought the new evidence to light.

I wasn't exactly sure how I felt about the whole thing. I had gone from spending my life enraged that Roger had killed my mother to now being angry at him for taking the rap for someone else and thus abandoning me. I knew I wasn't ready to speak with him yet, that I needed time to process all these new feelings. I was pretty sure I could never love Roger like a father, but maybe there was something else in between, a relationship where there was mutual affection, something less than love but more than casual acquaintances.

"Wow, it's finally happening. That's amazing."

"It is amazing, and it's all you. You made this happen. If he gets out, you will be responsible for giving this man his life back. It was the right thing to do."

"Right. But what about my life? Who can give me my life back?"

Zack was quiet on the other end of the line. I realized right away that it was unfair for me to put him on the spot like this. He had been nothing but honest, kind, and supportive of me throughout this whole ordeal of revisiting the Pandora's Box of my mother's murder. It was not right for me to cast my unresolved bitterness at him, but I couldn't help it. He was the one on the other end of the line, and I needed somewhere to put the dark feelings.

"Maddie, I can't imagine what you're going through. It's unconscionable, really, to think your dad is a murderer for almost your entire life and then to learn otherwise. But you've got to take this for what it is. He made a choice to go down for this, and now that you've brought the truth to light, he has a second chance at life. Sure, he's lost a lot. He lost *you,* for one thing. But because of you, there's a possibility he could walk out of prison a free man now. You need to give yourself credit for that."

Now, it was my turn to be silent on the other end of the line. I knew that everything he was saying was true, but for some reason, I couldn't bring myself to tell him he was right. It was like my mouth couldn't form the words. So, I just sat quietly, mired in the conflicted feelings that had stolen my voice.

"Maybe you should come here to Pennsylvania for the hearing. That might go a long way towards healing, to see it play out in real-time in a court of law."

Again, I was silent, but I was breathing loudly enough for him to know I was still on the other end of the line. *Could I do this? Could I face Roger in court?* I didn't know if I were capable of turning off the loathing that I had nurtured for so many years. It wasn't like flipping a light switch. It would take time to erase it.

"It would also give us a chance to go to the farm, to talk about my idea."

There it was in black and white, the thing I knew he really wanted all along. He wanted my grandparents' house and my land, not me. I could see red flags waving all around me where there had been affection just a few seconds ago. How could I have been so stupid, so gullible, so vulnerable? Clearly, now that I was back on the market, I had a lot to learn about men.

"I'll think about it," I said with an edge in my tone. "About coming to Roger's hearing."

I wanted to clarify that I was talking about the hearing and not about the sale of the property. How he thought it was appropriate to talk about the land right now was beyond me. He had finally shown me his true colors, and I was glad that I now understood the truth about him. To think I had almost gotten into a romantic relationship with him so soon after Adam's death. What a mistake that would have been. "I have to go," I said abruptly.

"Why, Maddie, what did I do? Did I say something wrong?"

The sadness in his voice almost made me feel sorry for him. But I realized it was all part of his nice-guy act. I hung up without saying goodbye.

"So, the guy came right at you, no question about it?" Kojak asked for about the sixth time as I relayed my story from the night before about the unfortunate encounter between the boat and my paddleboard.

"No question. Like I said, I tried to get out of his way, but he just kept turning the boat and coming at me."

"That's no coincidence; that's deliberate."

"That's what I think, too. I think someone was trying to send me a message to back off from the Max Prince investigation."

"Without a doubt, but *who* is the million-dollar question. I mean, it's pretty bizarre that you ended up on the ritzy dock of the guy who just happens to own the charter boat that the kid fell off of or whatever happened to him."

"That's what I think, too. But they couldn't have been nicer."

"Kid, sociopaths can be real nice when they need to be. They're smart cookies. They know how to make people think anything they want them to think. They're *chameleons*."

"Got it, loud and clear, but I didn't get a weird vibe from them. And I'm pretty good at that sort of thing. Catching vibes."

"Okay, so now we're judging people by 'vibes?' Maybe I should take out my Ouija board from the attic and dust it off. We could solve all sorts of crimes."

Kojak was always making jokes at the most inappropriate times, but he did know how to make me laugh, and if there was one thing I needed right now, it was to laugh. He knew how to put things in perspective. He also knew when it was time to get serious.

"Kid, here's the thing. There's someone who really wants you off this case; I mean, they want you off *bad*. So, the way I see it, you're in grave danger. You've got to get off that island while you can. It's not worth it. Let me take it from here. I got my buddy at the Attorney General's office looking into it hard. They're not going to let a Podunk police department turn their cheek on a possible murder investigation just because they don't have the kahunas to do something about it. I promise you that it won't be dropped. And I'll fill them in on everything you told me about the funeral home, the other body, the Marine, and so on. I could also bring Zack in since he's the one with the intel on Windstream."

"No, leave him out of this."

"Oh, do I detect a chilly breeze in paradise?"

"There is no paradise."

"Oh, sorry, I just assumed..."

"Well. You assumed wrong. He's got ulterior motives. I should have seen it from the very beginning."

"Whoa, whoa, whoa there, partner. It's fine if there's no love connection with my boy, but don't be dissing his character. He's a good man, as good as they come. What's this about an 'ulterior motives?'"

"He wants my grandparents' house and their land. That's why he's been talking to me, why he's been so nice."

"Wait a minute—I thought you just found out that you owned the property like two days ago? So, how could he have been scheming all this time? How could he have an angle before there was an angle to have?"

"I don't have an answer for that. He must have known all along."

"So, he somehow magically knew before you did?"

Even as Kojak said it out loud, I knew I must be wrong. Sure, Zack was excited about the possibility of buying the property, but I had known Zack for months. It didn't make any sense that he knew all this time that I owned the land that he wanted and said nothing about it. I suddenly realized it was possible for him to want me and to want the property at the same time.

"Okay, maybe you're right."

"Oh, wow, can you say that again a little bit louder so I can record it on my phone?" Kojak said with a chuckle.

"Very funny. Look, I've got to go. I need to do some work on this podcast."

"What you need to do is get your butt back to Oak City. It's not safe for you there anymore."

"I hear you. But if I just lay off the Max Prince case, whoever I've pissed off should leave me alone."

"So, you're really going to let it go. You're going to let me handle it."

"Yes, I've already let it go. I don't have the energy to deal with it. I created a Word document with everything I've learned about the case. I just sent it to you while we were talking. You can share it with the AG's office. Just keep my name out of it."

I felt bad about lying to Kojak regarding my intentions, but at the same time, I knew he would never let me stay if I told him the truth. I wasn't going to stop. I couldn't stop. I strongly believed that Max Prince was murdered—knocked off a boat and then shot to death. Someone had to pay for the crime. I owed it to his sweet, grieving parents to try and figure this out. I could still see their red puffy eyes and the way the skin drooped on their sad faces like wax melting on a candlestick. I had to find the truth for their sakes and for Max's sake.

18

THREESOME

When Janie told me that she and Damien wanted to meet me for lunch, I was immediately suspicious. Why in the world would they drive two hours from Oak City for the day just to have lunch with me? But they made it seem so casual, so I pretended it was casual as well.

I stood on the balcony, watching their car pull into the parking lot. I recognized Janie's old VW bug right away. It was gun-metal matte gray and in mint condition. As they got out of the car, I waved to Janie and Damien. I had only met him a few times when he joined her at company events, but I knew right away it was him from the green mohawk he insisted on sporting. I tried not to judge people by silly things like their hair, but because he was old enough to know better, I decided I was allowed to judge Damien for this poor choice that no doubt kept him unemployable in many circles.

Just as I turned to go back inside to prepare to greet them at the door, I saw another man out of the corner of my eye getting out of the car with them. He walked sheepishly behind the couple with his head down and his hands shoved deep in his pockets.

Had I really invited this couple I knew to my apartment, and they decided to bring a *random guy?* Even though I considered Janie to be a good work friend, this situation spelled out the differences between us. I would never invite a stranger to a friend's apartment without asking her first. But Janie lived in a world with very different rules. I just didn't know how different they were until today.

I opened the door when the bell rang to see Janie and Damien side-by-side in the hallway with their third wheel cowering slightly behind them. As soon as Janie saw me, she threw her arms around me, her wild blond curls bouncing in every direction. She held onto me like I was back from the dead and refused to let go until I practically pried her arms off me.

"Oh my God. I've missed you so much. When are you coming back to work?"

"End of the summer, most likely," I said, distracted by the young man whom I could barely see peeking behind Damien's stout mohawk.

"Cool. So, you know Damien," Janie said, ushering him into the apartment through the doorway in front of her. "And this, this is Jason Hubble, the guy you spoke with on the phone."

Janie waved Jason in, and he reluctantly crossed the threshold, brushing my shoulder and giving me a small nod. Compared to Damien, Jason looked like he was coming from church choir practice. He had short blond hair neatly combed to one side and a healthy, tanned glow from head to toe. He was wearing a yellow button-down short-sleeved dress shirt, khaki pants, and boat shoes. I put out my hand to shake his. I hadn't ever expected to meet Jason in person after our conversation about what happened on the boat the night Max died, and was curious as to why he was suddenly at my door.

"Jason, it's a pleasure to meet you."

He took my hand and shook it firmly, looking at me directly with his bright blue eyes.

"Would anybody like a drink?" I said to break the ice as we all stood awkwardly in the den avoiding eye contact.

"Hell yeah," Damien said. "What you got?"

Suddenly, I realized he thought I meant an alcoholic drink when I was just talking about seltzer water, lemonade, or tea. But then I decided alcohol might make this meeting less uncomfortable.

"Beer, wine, sparkling water, soda, tea, lemonade," I said, fully aware that the non-alcoholic drinks were not on their agenda.

"Beer, please," Damien barked, jumping in front of his girlfriend's request.

"I'll do a little white wine if you have some," Janie said bashfully.

I didn't like this version of Janie—demure, quiet, playing second fiddle to a man with a mohawk. Belle, my grandmother who raised me, always said *you must like who you are when you are with a man.* It was a piece of valuable wisdom that I carried with me throughout my life. I never had time for boys who made me feel that I wasn't worthy of their attention. One of the things that Adam had done for me was always make me feel important, important to him and to our family. I had started to sense the beginnings of that same feeling with Zack until he disappointed me with his true intentions. I was so glad I had spotted him for what he was before I truly fell for him. Clearly, I had avoided a potential train wreck by pulling back when I did.

"Me too," Jason said, following Janie's request. It surprised me a little that this seemingly polished young man would want to drink wine in the middle of the day when meeting a stranger for the very first time. But then I reasoned that he was nervous meeting me given our previous phone conversation and needed something to calm him down.

I went to the kitchen and grabbed three glasses, a bottle of chilled white wine, and a beer for Damien. When I returned, they were all still standing around awkwardly talking in hushed tones. I invited everyone out to the porch. Janie and Damien sat on a wicker loveseat next to each other. Jason and I each pulled up a chair from around the small table and made a semicircle with the loveseat.

"Cheers," Janie said with mock enthusiasm.

Everyone else followed suit with an equal amount of feigned enthusiasm. I waited for someone to speak, to tell me why we were having this strange meeting. I waited for them to tell me why they had invited me to lunch and then invited this stranger along who might somehow be mixed up in Max Prince's death. But nobody spoke, so I decided I would have to jumpstart the conversation.

"So, what brings you guys here? What's this all about? I'm pretty sure you didn't drive two hours just to have lunch with me."

"Right," Janie hesitated. "We just thought it was important for you to meet Jason and hear what he has to say in person. Like, see how credible he is. I know Damien told you to back off, but we're trying to do the right thing here. To figure out how to get this information to the right people."

Damien rolled his eyes when Janie mentioned his warning to me like he had just been messing around, that he hadn't really meant it when he said it.

"Okay, well, why don't you let Jason speak for himself?"

I regretted immediately how curt I was being to Janie. I didn't want to add to the undermining of her self-esteem that was already going on with Damien. She was my co-worker. She was my friend. She didn't deserve my tone, but I was fed up. I wanted these sketchy men out of my house. Despite Jason's clean-cut appearance, I didn't trust him.

"So, I didn't tell you everything about what happened that night," Jason jumped in.

"Go on."

"First of all, the guy who punched Max, the guy that made him fall into the water, it was Brett Willis, Major Willis' son."

"What?" I said, picturing Arnold Willis in the parking lot of the police station the other day telling me there was nothing to the rumors that Max's death involved any foul play. He had been covering up for his son. Now, his reluctance to pursue the investigation was making a lot more sense to me. "That's a pretty big deal, a pretty important piece of information you've been holding onto."

"Right, so this made it pretty improbable that the police were going to pursue this as anything other than an accidental drowning. Willis is not going to rat out his own son."

"That makes complete sense."

"But this is just the tip of the iceberg, really," Jason said, looking over at Damien. Damien nodded for him to go on. "It's just that Max didn't drown. I think it was all a setup to make it look like a drowning. As soon as he fell into the water, another boat came behind us and picked him up. Nobody else was paying attention. They were drunk and freaked out. But I saw this small boat whip around, and someone threw him a life preserver. They were pulling him in as we were speeding away. So, something must have happened to him later. I have no idea how he ended up dead, floating in the waterway."

I didn't correct him when he mentioned Max floating in the waterway. I wasn't going to reveal what I knew about the two bodies being switched, about the fact that Max was likely never floating in the waterway. The fact that Jason didn't know this detail meant it was unlikely he was involved in any way. This allowed me to breathe a little easier, considering he was sitting about two feet from me on a balcony six stories high.

"So, why didn't you tell me this when you called me? When we first talked?" I tried to keep the judgment out of my voice, but I could feel it creeping in.

"I don't know. I was scared. I thought maybe my mind was playing tricks on me. But *I know* what I saw. I saw him getting pulled out of the water in the distance. Like I said, no one else realized what was going on. They all believed he drowned at that moment."

"So, they're still all horrible human beings not to have said or done anything to help."

"Freaked out, scared, drunk; it was a lot of things all at one time. I'm not making excuses for them. I'm one of the bad people, too. I froze. I didn't help either."

"Okay, so why is this a 'dangerous situation'?"

Again, Jason glanced at Damien, who nodded for him to continue. Janie had one hand on Damien's leg and the other on the stem of her wine glass, that was now empty.

"Well, I got a text message from a blocked number telling me to tell no one what I saw *or else.* I really have no idea what's going on, but I do know that the captain, Perry Spotz, runs with a pretty rough crowd and that the man he works for, Mark Maron, is rich and very connected."

I pictured kind Mark pulling me up off his dock, handing me a towel, taking me into his home, getting me water and dry clothes. I couldn't imagine him being mixed up in anything violent.

"Clearly, someone knows you saw Max being pulled out of the water, and they want you to keep it quiet."

I wondered again if Jason knew that Max had been shot. It really didn't sound like he did. But again, I didn't want to reveal too much. I still didn't know what it all meant, and I also didn't know if I could trust Jason. I didn't want to risk letting him in on what I knew and having the whole investigation blow up in my face.

"Right," Jason said. "Because obviously someone did something to him after he fell off the boat; otherwise, he wouldn't have ended up dead. I probably shouldn't be telling you all this, but Janie said I could trust you with my life. That you wouldn't expose me, your source, no matter what."

"Janie is correct. Your name will remain confidential."

This time it was Janie, not Damien, who nodded fervently. Damien slammed his empty beer bottle down on the small glass table between us.

"Why don't we get some lunch, people? I'm starving."

It seemed very odd to go to lunch with this trio—my friend who was not acting like my friend, her boyfriend I couldn't stand, and now, this stranger who had just dropped a bomb in my lap.

We sat outside at a waterfront restaurant on the dock overlooking a marina full of bobbing boats. Damien, Janie, and Jason continued drinking while I decided to switch to lemonade. At this point, the conversation had completely changed from what happened to Max to what new schemes Damien was coming up with to make money. Janie listened wide-eyed, hanging on every word as if he might be a great inventor who just got a patent for a flying car.

"Like, the way I see it, people want their lawn seeded, but it takes a lot of time. So, you could just drop the seed from a drone, and it would take half the time," Damien bragged to his captive and increasingly inebriated audience.

Jason went on to tell me that he had been in the military for a few years but was honorably discharged after he lost part of his foot when the Humvee he was riding in tripped an IED in the Middle East. The other two soldiers were killed, but he was thrown from the vehicle and survived thanks to some quick medical attention from several troops riding in a Humvee behind them. Since then, he said, he had been here trying to figure out his next move, working at a marina pumping gas and working on the boat for Perry Spotz. It was clear to me that he felt like the accident had erased his purpose, and now he was in this unhappy limbo that he was struggling to fight his way through.

When I asked Jason how he and Damien knew each other, the conversation became awkward again. They danced around it while giving each other uncomfortable looks, cues with a nod of a chin or rapidly blinking eyes. But Damien wasn't picking up on what Jason was trying to tell him with his non-verbal language.

"Work, I mean way back. When was it? Long time ago. Can't really recall," Damien said, punctuating his sentence with a stilted laugh.

"It was after I got out of the service. Was looking for work. Damien hooked me up with a garage where I did some auto repair stuff. I was depressed and still in a lot of pain from all the surgeries on my foot. It was a rough time."

Damien nodded as if the story was just coming back to him while Jason was telling it. I'd been around long enough to know when someone was telling me a lie. Frankly, I was a tough audience; most journalists are because we're used to people trying to convince us of things that are often not true. I decided at this moment that I would not call their bluff, but I would file it for future reference.

The rest of the conversation was pretty mundane, strained at times, as we all tried to be polite without acknowledging why we were really together, a motley crew of unlikely lunch companions. As we finished our meal, Janie suddenly stood up and told Damien they had to get back to Oak City because she had to work early the next morning. Jason had just ordered another beer and looked up at them quizzically.

"Sorry, Maddie, I am filling in for Veronica. She's got a stomach bug, so I agreed to do the early morning shift in her place, which you know I absolutely *hate.* I know I'll never get to sleep tonight just thinking about how early I need to get up, but I am at least going to attempt to get to bed at a reasonable time, so I can function tomorrow."

As I listened to Janie's nervous rambling, I realized that she was trying to convince herself of her reason for leaving as much as she was trying to convince me. She knew I could easily find out if Veronica was sick and if she was truly filling in for her, so I didn't think she was lying, but I had also never known Janie to cut any social life short for a work obligation.

I looked over at Jason as the waitress put another beer in front of him and realized he wasn't leaving anytime soon. I was *stuck* with him.

"Jason came with us, so maybe you could take him back to his car?"

"Back to his car?" I asked, confused.

"He left it at the bar where we met last night after he got off work."

I started piecing everything together they had told me during the awkward lunch. Jason must have been with them all night long. They obviously didn't drive down just for the day. They must have all stayed somewhere together the night before. I could tell by the pained look on Janie's face that she realized her gaffe immediately—the lie about coming down for the day.

"I thought you guys came down this morning," I said, knowing my sobriety was a powerful weapon at this moment.

"Well, we were planning on that. But Damien wanted to hang out with Jason, so we came down last night and stayed at the Hampton Inn over the bridge. We met at Beerman's, and then he came back with us to the hotel because we didn't think he should be driving."

I pictured this in my mind. These were not college students. They were not kids out for a night of debauchery. They were three unrelated adults sharing a hotel room. It all sounded very odd to me. I couldn't imagine Adam having been comfortable with another man sleeping in our hotel room. Didn't they have Uber accounts? Also, I was pretty sure Jason didn't live that far away. Couldn't they have dropped him at his house? Something wasn't adding up. But against my better judgment, I agreed to take Jason to his car after he finished his beer.

About ten minutes later, as Jason and I were making small talk, Janie came back into the restaurant and handed Jason a shirt and a pack of cigarettes. She squeezed his shoulder, said a quick goodbye, and was off again.

"Bad habit," I said, pointing to the cigarettes.

"I don't really smoke. I use this," he said as he pulled out a pack of Nicorette gum and held it up for me to see. I wondered what his game was. He had just outed himself as a nonsmoker, yet Janie had deposited the cigarettes in front of him ceremoniously like there was no way he could live without them. "This shirt, the one I have on, I borrowed it from Damien, so he was just giving me mine back."

I hadn't asked for an explanation about the shirt, but it was clear he felt obligated to give me one after his cigarette faux pas. Then, without warning, Janie was behind him again, hand on his shoulder.

"Jason, I really need one for the road. I forgot mine," Janie said nervously. I had never known her to smoke. "Do you have a light?"

"I don't," he replied, obviously disinterested in her current crisis. "But I'm sure one of the wait staff might have one."

"Come with me," she beckoned, practically pulling him out of the chair.

They left, and he returned to the table alone, pack of cigarettes in hand.

"I'm ready if you are."

I drove Jason just five minutes down the road to where his car was parked in the far corner of the shopping center that housed Beerman's. As we drove in silence, I realized that I should have never let this strange man into my car. I knew nothing about him, and after the odd encounter with him, Janie, and Damien, I realized there were probably important things I was missing about the entire situation.

"Thanks so much!" He said, leaning in the passenger side window as he walked to his car. "Appreciate you hearing me out, and I appreciate you keeping my name confidential in this whole thing. It's a real nightmare. Let me know if you ever need anything, *anything at all."*

As I drove away, I kept replaying in my mind the creepy way in which he said "anything" as if we had some private joke between us, and he was asking me to read between the lines. I was convinced there was nothing more I needed from this man. I glanced in my rearview mirror and saw him pulling out of the parking lot. Then, I glanced in the backseat. The pack of cigarettes was still there, staring at me.

19

SHELL GAMES

I CALLED THE PUBLIC INFORMATION OFFICER at Camp Lejeune to ask if they had a missing Marine. Predictably, he told me that the names of servicemen and women who were AWOL were not public information. Before he could hang up, I gave him something that grabbed his attention.

"Officer Jackson, the reason I'm asking is that there is a chance a missing Marine drowned here in Cape Mayson. I don't know for sure, but I'm working on putting the pieces together. If you would work with me, we might be able to get to the bottom of it."

There was silence on the other end of the line.

"Miss Arnette, I will get back to you."

The line went dead. He was gone, but I was pretty sure I would be hearing from Officer Jackson again.

Zack had texted me multiple times since our last conversation. I wasn't sure if he had detected the ice in my tone as I stewed about what seemed like his singular focus on buying my grandparents' property or if he was like most men and had no idea why I was mad.

Hey, call me. Worried about you, he wrote in a text. *Sorry if I upset you when we were talking about Roger,* he added, completely missing the cues as to what upset me. *Really want to talk. Call me.*

I had learned the term "ghosting" from Miranda, and I supposed that's what I was doing to Zack. But at the moment, it just didn't seem like the most important battle I needed to be fighting. So, I shot him a text back with a thumbs-up implying that I *would* call him at some point. I had no intention of calling him, but I hoped this would keep him at bay and give me some space to think about everything that had happened.

Kai, my podcast producer, had also been texting me, telling me he needed me to finish the episode we were working on soon so that he could begin the tedious sound editing process. I decided I should take a break from the Max Prince saga; I would work on the podcast project to distract myself.

In this particular episode, I was writing about the arrest of the ringleader of the band of brothers, Bruce. The old photographs Kai had sent of the arrest were so compelling that I wanted to describe the moment in visual detail for the listener. Bruce, with his hands cuffed in front of him and his 1970's sideburns and Magnum P.I. mustache, dominated the black and white photo. Then there was Detective Tommy Zaminski in all his glory with his prominent squared-off sideburns, hippie-long hair, and tight plaid polyester pants juxtaposed by the gun in a holster on his left hip. He was gripping Bruce's arm, leading him through a maze of reporters with TV cameras, still cameras, and massive old-fashioned microphones shoved in his direction. But I kept returning to my favorite part of the historical photo—the lit cigarette hanging from Zaminski's mouth. It amazed me how smoking had been such a huge part of our culture less than fifty years ago, and now it was something taboo.

And then it hit me: smokers *had* to smoke. They couldn't go hours without having a cigarette. It didn't work that way, yet no one left our table during the two-hour lunch with Janie, Damien, and Jason to smoke. I was also pretty sure Janie didn't smoke. Jason told me he didn't smoke. That's when I realized something had to be in that cigarette pack other than cigarettes.

I pushed open the door and ran down the steps, taking them two at a time, my car keys jangling in my hand. I was breathless when I finally got to the car. Through the back seat driver's side window, I could see that the red and white pack of cigarettes was still lying on the seat where Jason had left it. It looked so foreign there. Not only had I never smoked, but no one had ever smoked in my car. For a moment, I considered that there might be a bug planted in the pack or even a small camera. Then my brain jumped even further to the next dramatic conclusion—maybe there was an explosive device inside. I pictured the booby-trapped box blasting my fingers and head off as I gingerly opened it, the twins orphaned as a direct result of my careless disregard for safety.

I took a deep breath and unlocked the car with my key fob. Intellectually, I knew that none of my hypotheses made any sense. *They came to me for help. They warned me. Why would they want to hurt me or spy on me?*

As I reached for the pack, I winced a little, my hands shaking. It was light. I didn't really know what a pack of cigarettes should feel like because I had never held one. Or at least not that I could recall. I leaned in. At first, the tips of my fingers just grazed it; then I grabbed it. I immediately opened it and looked inside. I expected to see drugs, or money, some furtive exchange between Jason, Janie, and Damien that had created such secrecy. Instead, I found a half-empty pack of cigarettes. I was disappointed that there was nothing inside the pack to confirm my wild theories, and I was disappointed in myself for hoping to find something in the pack to confirm my wild theories. Janie was my friend. I knew Janie. While Damien wasn't the most upstanding citizen, I didn't think she would get involved in something dirty.

I chuckled to myself and shook my head as I walked with the cigarette pack to the nearest trashcan. I held the pack hidden in the palm of my hand lest I run into someone and they might think I was a smoker. For some reason, that seemed like the worst thing that could happen at the moment. As my hand hovered over the trashcan, I turned the pack upside down to spill out the contents instead of just throwing the entire thing into the can at once. As I did so, a small piece of yellow lined paper fell out and fluttered into the bin. It was folded in half. It had to have been hidden beneath the cigarettes; that's why I hadn't noticed it before. Against my better judgment, I reached into the trashcan and quickly fished it out, trying not to make physical contact with the rest of the rubbish.

A short note in red felt tip pen was written on the tiny scrap of paper that looked like it was torn from the corner of a yellow legal pad. It read: "Beware of SHELL games." I stared at it for a few seconds trying to figure out what it meant and who was trying to tell me something. I was drawing a complete blank. I could ask Janie, but what if Jason or Damien wrote the note and didn't intend for her to see it?

I shoved the strange note into my pocket and headed back upstairs to wash my hands. As I climbed the stairs two at a time again, I thought of all the possible meanings of the word "SHELL." Written in all capitals, it was obvious the writer meant for me to focus on this specific word. But why? I thought of the literal meaning of "shell games"—deceit, illusion, thievery. I pictured a carnival worker taking someone's money while asking them which cup the coin was under as they performed a sleight of hand.

Then I thought of the literal meaning of the word "shell," something you found on the beach, something animals live inside. I couldn't understand why the person who wrote the note, whether it was Janie, Jason, or Damien, would make me guess what they were talking about. Why wouldn't they just come right out and say whatever was on their minds directly? I pondered this for only a moment as I lay my head back on the chaise lounge and closed my eyes. The one drink I did have earlier was long metabolized from my system, but it had made me sleepy. I listened to the soothing sounds of the boats passing below on the waterway, their motors creeping along as quietly as possible through the No Wake Zone. And then all the noise faded away as I slipped into a deep sleep.

I didn't know exactly how long I had been asleep when I woke up suddenly to the sound of a loudly churning motor below, someone who was clearly not abiding by the "No Wake Zone" signs posted on either side of the waterway in plain view. I was disoriented as I looked up and saw the sun dipping beneath the horizon. *Had I been asleep for that long?* I sat up with a start thinking about the cigarette pack and the note.

I stood up to clear my head and leaned over the edge of the balcony holding onto the railing as I deeply inhaled the salty sea air. I looked down just in time to see the loud boat pulling away, turning in the direction of the ocean. I picked up the binoculars from the glass table next to me that I had been using to bird-watch earlier and turned them in the direction of the boat. I couldn't make out any of the people on the boat, just a couple of men in baseball hats and sunglasses, but I could clearly see the side of the boat and the name written in large blue swirly letters. It said: "Knot Guilty." Clever, I thought, but he was still a rule-breaker, and I didn't like rule-breakers. There was something familiar about the phrase; maybe I had seen it in the marina next to the condominium. I made a mental note to approach the captain and chastise him about his speed in the No Wake Zone if I ever saw the boat again.

I sat back down on the chaise lounge and pulled my computer from the table onto my lap. I fully intended to finish the podcast script for Kai, but my curiosity about the note was driving me crazy. I knew that I would not be able to concentrate for one minute on the script while I was thinking about the little yellow piece of paper.

I Googled Jason and found several articles from his adopted hometown newspaper in Maryland. His parents had moved there after he graduated from high school. Even though they had only lived there for a short time, they wrote about his military accident and subsequent honorable discharge. He was considered a local hero, coming home to a small downtown parade where the mayor of the town gave him the symbolic key to city hall. Family and friends were quoted as saying things like *Jason would give you the shirt off his back. He goes out of his way to help people.* I read the glowing tributes twice, thinking about how they didn't mesh with the man who did nothing to protect Max Prince.

I then looked up Damien's criminal record again to confirm what

I already knew about him. It was all petty stuff, but it did include an older minor drug possession charge for marijuana and a more recent charge involving schedule two controlled substances, a class of drugs that included commonly abused narcotics like prescription painkillers. This alone didn't mean that Damien was involved in some bigger criminal enterprise, but it did raise a red flag to me about his character. I wished Janie would get away from him. Based on the weird bond between them that I had witnessed today, I was pretty sure this was not going to happen.

Then, on a lark, I decided to Google their names together, Jason Hubble and Damien Cooper. I got nothing in the search except for articles that included people named Jason and Damien, but not the correct Jasons and Damiens. Then I refreshed the search and only looked for images. This time I was rewarded with several group shots. I clicked on one of them and saw a group of young men standing behind the open tailgate of a box truck. They were loading something into the back of the truck. The caption beneath the photo had several names, including Jason Hubble, Damien Cooper, and *Max Prince*. I took my fingers and swiped the screen to zoom in closer on the photo. I could easily see the sign behind them on the building next to the truck: CAPE MAYSON TURTLE HOSPITAL. I zoomed back out a little to try and see what the young men were loading into the truck. The closer I got, the blurrier the object became. Finally, after adjusting the shot several times, I got it to the point where I could make it out. They were loading sea turtle shells into the back of the truck. I remembered the turtle ambassador, Jessie, who showed me around the day of Max's wake, telling me that they donated the shells of the turtles who died to a museum in Florida for an auction.

I sat back on the chair, confused, wondering what this all meant. I knew that Max had been a do-gooder, rescuing people as a lifeguard, rescuing sea turtles in his free time, and teaching and coaching children at school, but neither Damien nor Jason struck me as philanthropists. Yet here they were at a turtle rescue hospital helping to load these shells into the back of a truck. I also didn't recall either of them saying they knew Max very well. Jason had mentioned they had gone to the same high school a couple of years apart but weren't friends. And Damien had never said anything about knowing Max at all.

Something very strange was going on, and I knew that I had to get to the bottom of it, but before I could start to think it through, my phone rang. I saw Zack's name pop up on the screen. I hesitated, trying to figure out if I was ready to confront Zack about my concerns over how he seemed to be relentless in his pursuit of my grandparents' property. But I also knew that I needed him on multiple levels. I needed his expertise as an investigator to figure out what in the heck was going on with this situation, and as much as I didn't want to admit it, I needed his friendship or whatever it was that we were developing.

"Maddie Arnette," I said, pretending I did not have him programmed into my phone, which I'm sure he knew was just for dramatic effect, to make him feel like he wasn't important enough to have attained this status.

"Hey there, you. Where have you been? I've been worried about you. Especially with all that crazy stuff going on in Cape Mayson. I'm hoping you've decided to stay out of it to let the local guys figure it out."

I stayed quiet, uncharacteristically disarmed by his charm and his ease, like we had known each other for years instead of just a few months. Something about his protective tone made me immediately think of Adam.

"No; in fact, it just keeps getting crazier."

"I want to hear everything, but first, I want to apologize for how excited I got over your grandparents' property. It was very insensitive of me. It's yours to do with what you want when you want. I know I sounded pushy, and I regret how I handled it. Can we just forget about it and move on?"

The part of me that saw red flags around every single corner with Zack wanted to hang up the phone. The part of me that needed someone to help me navigate all the red flags in my own life pulled the phone away from my mouth temporarily so that I could inhale and exhale deeply before responding. For some reason, I could feel tears welling up in my eyes. I wiped them away with the back of my hand and put the phone back to my ear.

"Yes, we can move on."

As soon as the words came out of my mouth, large tears began to roll down my face. I was glad Zack couldn't see me. But I had a feeling he could sense my relief and my own surprise at being able to forgive, something that wasn't a regular part of my skillset.

"That's great, great news. I'm so relieved. I was so worried that I messed things up with you. I'm grateful that you're giving me another chance. Now, tell me everything that's been going on."

20

KNOT GUILTY

IT FELT RIGHT TO BE BACK ON GOOD TERMS with Zack. I attributed my momentary meltdown to the fact that this was all new territory to me, this relationship thing. After Adam died, I would watch our wedding video on my computer over and over. Each time I watched it, I would have the same horrible realization when I saw him dancing at the reception or shoving a piece of cake into my mouth—*he's dead, but he can't be dead; there he is, making a toast, there he is leading the conga line.* Yet I kept watching it over and over, like a kind of twisted self-punishment.

Then, to make myself feel better, I started noticing the other people in the video who were also dead. Natalie, my mother's friend from college, was dead—cancer. Adam's Uncle Joe was dead—heart attack. Annabelle, my roommate from D.C., was dead—car accident. As it turned out, noticing the other dead people in the crowd didn't help me miss Adam any less.

For some reason, knowing Zack did help. He helped me to see beyond the video, beyond the world I had so carefully constructed for myself that had come crashing down like a Jenga tower. For the first time in a long time, Zack made me feel calm. Not even Adam could do that on a regular basis.

Zack wasn't pleased that I was still involved with the Max Prince case. I told him everything I had learned since we last spoke about it—about Damien and Jason's warnings and subsequent weird behavior, about Gina Finkel spotting the Marine who drowned, about the near-death assault on my paddleboard and the unlikely rescue by Mark Maron.

"I can't believe you didn't tell me about all this earlier. You're really freaking me out. This sounds like you're in danger. I'm not good with this, not at all," he said with a mix of concern and clear hurt that I hadn't called him right away.

"It's all been happening so fast. I'm just not sure of anything right now, what anything means."

"It doesn't sound like a coincidence to me, the thing with the boat almost hitting you. It sounds *deliberate*."

I tried to change the subject by telling him about the detective's son, Brett Willis, hitting Max and sending him overboard. I told him about Jason seeing another boat pull Max out of the water. I told him about the strange note in the cigarette package and the photo of Damien, Jason, and Max at the turtle hospital.

"Shell, turtle shell," Zack said out of nowhere.

"What are you getting at?"

"The note, 'shell game.' Whoever wrote the note must have been talking about the turtle shells, the ones you saw them loading into the truck meant for the museum in Florida. There must be something funny going on with the turtle shells."

"Okay, Mr. bigshot detective, I guess you cracked the case," I said with a smirk he couldn't see but could no doubt hear. I just wanted to deflect his attention away from my safety as much as possible. It had crossed my mind the second I saw the photo of them loading the turtle shells into the truck that there was a connection to the note I found in the cigarette pack. "And all along, I thought it was Colonel Mustard in the library with the candlestick."

"I'm just saying; it makes sense. Either the word is meant to be considered as part of the phrase, or it is meant literally. I think there's a good chance it was meant to be taken at face value."

"Then why go to the trouble of making a riddle out of it and putting it in the bottom of a cigarette pack where I may or may not find it?"

"Excellent question—one I don't have an answer for. Maybe they've been streaming too many thrillers online. Or maybe they're genuinely frightened. They know something, and they want you to figure it out on your own because they don't want to be the ones to come right out and tell you for fear it might get back to the person who is behind this whole mess. The bottom line is that this is dangerous stuff. I'm really worried about you."

I hung up the phone, promising Zack, as I had Kojak, that I would pull back, that I would not do any more investigating on my own. It was a promise once again that I had no intention of keeping. He told me he would consult with Kojak, and they would put their heads together on the best course of action. Now that I knew for sure that Brett Willis, Arnold Willis' son, was involved, I didn't think I could trust him to credibly investigate the case. On the other hand, if I brought him evidence that proved his son didn't kill Max, maybe he would play ball with me.

Zack was right. "SHELL" in the note must be referring to the turtle shells. I had to figure out how the shells fit into the equation. Was there something inherently valuable about the shells themselves; were they not really going to a charity?

The whole situation was very complex. One thing that wasn't confusing to me was the fact that I finally had someone in my corner. It was obvious that Zack truly cared for my well-being. Other than Louise and Kojak, I didn't really have anyone in my life who I honestly believed had my back. After a brief departure from my feelings for him, I now believed that Zack was also one of those people.

I decided it was time to blow off some steam and look for the "Knot Guilty" boat in the marina. I liked, as my photographer Buster always said, *to bow up* against people when they did wrong. Adam always used to refer to the Shakespeare quote when he described me to others: "And though she be but little, she is fierce."

They wouldn't see me coming, the No Wake Zone scofflaws. If I couldn't catch a killer right now, the least I could do was to tell off a bunch of rule-breakers.

I loved everything about marinas: the subtle rocking sound of the boats as they brushed against the docks, the echoes of ropes and sails clinking against metal masts, the gentle creaking of the docks as they bobbed up and down with the tide. To me, a marina was a living, breathing thing, a place of possibilities, a place where at any moment, someone could jump on a boat and take off on a life-changing adventure.

I categorized the world into two camps, boat people and non-boat people. It wasn't so much about liking the water, knowing how to swim, or your immunity to seasickness; it was about your hunger for adventure, for something more than dry land offered.

I knew I was a boat person the first time my grandmother Belle took me to the Jersey Shore, and we went out on her friends' boat. As soon as I felt that wind whipping my hair back, the rumble of the motor pouring through me like an earthquake, saltwater spraying my face every time we dipped into a small wave, *I was hooked.*

Adam and I had talked about buying a boat, but like so many other things we never got around to, this was one of them.

"What's better than having a boat?" He used to ask me.

"I don't know, what?" I mocked, even though I knew the answer to the riddle.

"Having friends with boats!"

This always made me laugh, even though I had heard it a hundred times. He was right; we did have friends with boats who often invited us pre-children to join them on the water, and then later as a family. Some of my fondest memories involved the kids asleep in their life jackets curled up in damp beach towels on the bow of a boat, their faces sun-kissed, their wispy hair wet and matted. Adam and I would be nearby; his arm draped casually around my shoulder as we bounced along across the gentle wake. We watched the orange and pink sky radiating all around us as the sun slowly dipped below the horizon.

As this memory seeped into my brain, I almost forgot my mission. I stopped and blinked quickly to wash away the stinging tears that were starting to form at the corners of my eyes. I realized I hadn't been paying attention to the boats as I walked up and down the docks. I decided I would have to start over on "Dock A" and walk them again, looking for the offending boat.

By the time I got to the last dock, Dock D, I was hot, sweaty, and frustrated. I was about to give up when I saw a large pleasure boat, the kind of boat some people referred to as a yacht, tied to the far end of the dock. The stern was facing me, and as I got closer, I could clearly see the name: "Ripple in Still Water."

I did a doubletake to make sure I was reading the name correctly. I casually walked over to the boat and peered around the back into the glass doors that revealed a large sitting area and a kitchen. The lights were off, and it didn't look like anyone was inside. I walked around the side of the boat and tried to peek into a few of the round windows that most likely belonged to staterooms, but the glass was tinted, and I couldn't see inside. I could see that there was no one on the back or upper deck and no one in the bow area. Against all my better judgment, I decided to hop on and snoop around.

While I had been a journalist for twenty years, I wasn't a rule breaker and never a lawbreaker, but there was something about this case that I just couldn't put down. I had listened to podcasts where spouses of investigative journalists talked about how a case had become an obsession for their partners—such a great obsession it tore their families apart. I didn't think I was in *that* place, at least not yet. But here I was trespassing on Mark Maron's boat. Hoping to learn what? I didn't know.

The boat was in impeccable condition, thanks, I assumed to Captain Perry Spotz. It was so clean it gleamed in the sunlight. The deck was shiny, as were the well-polished stainless-steel handrails where I could see my reflection as I climbed the stairs to the upper deck. As I rounded the corner to the bow, I looked in the handrail and saw the reflection of someone else behind me, *Perry Spotz*.

"Can I help you?" A deep, husky voice said over my shoulder.

I turned around so quickly that I almost lost my balance, a move that would have sent me over the railing into the water.

"Oh, hello," I put my hand to my heart in a feigned moment of being innocently startled. "I was looking for the owner. Sorry, I didn't mean to overstep. I called out, but I didn't get a response."

"I've been here the whole time. I didn't hear anyone calling."

I tried to gauge Perry Spotz's true reaction to my presence, but I couldn't see his eyes through his blue mirrored reflective sunglasses. His voice was cool and unwavering.

"I apologize. I guess I wasn't loud enough," my mind was spinning, trying to spin a yarn I could sell to this hardened man who didn't seem willing to buy anything I was selling. I decided there had to be a grain of truth in my response, that total fabrication would come back to haunt me.

"No, you weren't. You said you were looking for the owner?"

"Yes. This is Mark Maron's boat, correct? At least someone here at the marina mentioned that to me."

"And who is asking?"

I could tell my ruse was falling flat on this man who was starting to creep me out with his deadpan voice and eyeless face.

"Maddie, Maddie Arnette," I reached out my hand, and he took it reluctantly, but when he held it, his grasp was so tight I felt like he might crush the bones in my fingers. "I'm looking for Mark, Mr. Maron, to thank him. I had a little accident Friday night, well, really, not an accident per se, but a *situation*."

"A situation?"

"I was almost hit by a boat on my paddleboard. I climbed up on his dock, and he and his wife were really kind. They took me into their home, made sure I was okay, got me some dry clothes, drove me back to my condo."

Perry stood very still after I gave him this information. I assumed he was looking directly at me, trying to assess me, but I couldn't see his eyes behind the blue sunglasses. After what seemed like a very long, awkward silence, he finally spoke.

"Mark is like that. He's a good guy. Always helping people."

I thought back to my original assessment of their relationship that Mark was Perry's sponsor in Alcoholics Anonymous. After all, Mark had helped him. Why wouldn't he help a stranger? It made total sense. Yes, he was rich, but rich people could be altruistic. It wasn't impossible.

"Yes, seems like that. Anyway, I won't take up any more of your time. I was just hoping to catch him. Will you tell him I came by?"

I turned around and walked quickly down the stairs. I could hear Perry's footsteps gaining on me at a fast pace.

"I sure will. But he doesn't come here much. It's a charter boat. He leaves things up to *me*."

I started moving faster in the direction of the dock after he strangely emphasized the word "me," sending a chill up my spine even in the oppressive heat. As soon as my feet hit the dock, I started fast-walking in the direction of the marina store, figuring at least there would be other people there and I would not be alone with this odd man, a man who inexplicably left Max Prince to drown. Or at least he *thought* he did, which was enough for me to dislike him and fear him.

As I got to the dock store, I was breathing hard. I lowered myself onto the bench in front of the building and watched the boats pulling out of the marina. Suddenly, I noticed Perry pulling out in a small recreational boat. I realized it must have been the boat I saw moored next to Ripple. He rounded the corner and pulled out in front of the store momentarily before gunning the engine. That's when I got a clear view of the boat's name—*Knot Guilty*. Perry was the No Wake Zone offender. I also got a clear view of something else, a quick vision of the boat coming at me Friday night. As it slalomed in the wake, charging at me, changing direction on a dime, I had caught a glimpse of the name on the side of the boat written in blue swirly letters. I didn't remember it until now. The boat that had tried to run me down, the boat that had cut my paddleboard in half, was the boat Perry Spotz was driving.

So, what did it all mean? I honestly didn't know. Was it Perry Spotz who tried to hit me, or even worse, *kill me?* Or was it someone else driving his boat? Maybe Perry went after me at the direction of Mark Maron. Or maybe Perry had his goons come after me—goons like Jason and Damien.

There were so many possibilities that my brain was doing cartwheels. Maybe Zack was right; maybe I was in over my head. Maybe I should just back away like he asked me to and let him and Kojak figure it all out.

I sat down on the seawall and let the sunlight bathe me in a warm glow. I closed my eyes for a moment and thought back to the morning I found the man floating in the water. It still didn't seem real to me. And now that I knew that it wasn't Max, it was even more frustrating because I had no name, no way to identify the man with the dark eyes staring back at me. I still hadn't received a return call from Officer Jackson at Camp Lejeune. I made a mental note to call him again.

I watched the boats cruising by and children hanging over the railings bundled in life jackets. Dogs stood at the bows like sentinels, displaying their sense of balance that kept them standing even when a rolling wake threatened to throw them off-kilter. I caught snippets of music pumping from speakers as they passed. With few exceptions, people always looked so happy when they were on boats. And why not? There was nothing more invigorating than cruising along on top of the water, feeling the warm breeze skimming across your face and whipping through your hair.

Max's death and the unknown man's death had cast a dark cloud over this beautiful place for me. I wondered if I would ever get over it, if I would ever be able to look at this place the same way again, seeing only its aqua blue water and foamy white waves outlined by vivid green marshes illuminated by the brightest sunlight.

I wasn't sure whom I could trust at this point to make everything right, but I knew that I had to do something. I couldn't just do nothing and pretend to go on with my life like the people who had watched Max fall into the water. Even though that's not what killed him, even though it was clear now that something else had happened to him later, that someone had put a bullet in his head, the people on the boat *thought* they had watched a man drown and did nothing. In my book, that was just as bad as if he had really drowned.

I wondered how people continued living happy lives believing that someone had drowned on their watch. The only person who seemed to be having a hard time with what happened was Stella Avery. Because of her obvious remorse, I believed she was the key to unraveling the entire mess. Somehow, I *had* to get her to talk to me.

I called Stella, texted her, and emailed her. When I hadn't heard back by late afternoon, I figured I had my answer. I would have to try another tactic to reach her in a different way.

While I didn't think Dawn Avery knew anything about what was going on, she seemed like a reasonable person. If I confided in her what I believed had happened, maybe she would reach out to Stella and try to get her to come forward. Whatever Stella was afraid of, it was clear she needed some protection. I knew taking this path was a big risk, but I didn't have any other great ideas. So, I headed for The Last Straw Cafe.

The brunch rush was over, and it was too early for dinner. The restaurant was quiet. Two couples sat at a table with empty plates finishing mimosas and coffee, while Dawn and two waitresses went from table to table, picking up dirty plates and wiping down the surfaces. When I first walked in, she didn't recognize me.

"Sit at any clean table; we'll be right with you," she said without looking up as she leaned over a table, wiping it down with a white rag. In her left hand, she had a stack of dishes perched delicately on her open palm.

I stood behind her and waited for her to stand up and turn in my direction.

"Dawn, it's Maddie Arnette. We met the other day."

At first, she appeared to bristle at the memory of me, this television reporter asking her strange questions about her daughter.

But then she must have realized the remaining diners were within earshot, and a forced smile spread across her face.

"Of course, I remember. Give me a second to put this stuff down, and we can chat over there," she nodded to a table in the far corner of the porch with a killer view of the ocean. "Can I get you anything?"

"No, I'm good; take your time."

I watched her head off towards the kitchen, and I slipped into a chair in the corner as she had instructed. Even at this moment, when I was about to have a difficult conversation with this woman, there was something so calming about looking out at the water. It was hypnotizing, watching the ebb and flow of the waves, hearing them crash along the shore in the distance. When I looked up again, Dawn was smoothing down her apron and sliding into the chair across from me.

"Stella told me you came to see her. She was *very upset* by it."

I hadn't expected this—Dawn knowing about my visit to Stella's office. I assumed that if she were lying to her mother about everything, she would not give her an opening to question what was really going on.

"I'm sorry that I upset her, but something very bizarre is happening here, and I think your daughter is involved, maybe not involved per se, but she knows something about it, and she's scared. I'm just trying to get to the bottom of it, to make sure whoever hurt Max doesn't get away with it. And frankly, to make sure they don't hurt her."

"Hurt Max? He drowned. It was a terrible, tragic accident. I don't know why you insist on making it out to be something else. These young people have been through enough. They need to be left alone to grieve."

Gone was the friendly, polite Dawn I had encountered when I first walked into the restaurant. She was gripping the edge of the table as if she might turn it over on me at any moment. I got it—she was protecting her daughter. But at what cost? What did she know?

"Dawn, I can't fill you in on everything, but I've learned some information about Max's death, that he actually didn't drown when he fell off the boat. Someone pulled him out of the water, and something else happened to him later. It seems like the whole thing may have been planned."

I watched her expression go from defensive to angry to confused in a matter of seconds.

"That makes absolutely no sense. The police said he drowned."

"I know this is going to sound crazy, but a man did drown that same night. It just wasn't Max. Someone passed off the other man's body as Max's at first."

"But I saw Max, at the wake, *that was Max*."

"True, you did. But the bodies were switched at the funeral home through a long series of events that I won't get into now. Ultimately, the real Max ended up in the casket at the funeral."

"But why would someone go to all this trouble?"

"That's a great question, one I don't have an answer to right now, but I'm trying to figure it out."

"So, why are you coming to me? What in the world does Stella have to do with this?"

"I'm not totally sure, but I do know one thing, Stella is the one who identified the unknown drowning victim as Max. She made it possible for this body switch to happen. She was his friend. She obviously knew what she was doing, that she was lying about the identification. She *knew* it wasn't Max."

"But why in the world would she do that?" Dawn had loosened her grip on the table and was now running her hands nervously through her wavy hair like she was trying to brush away the offensive idea with each stroke.

"I think she's scared of someone. I think someone threatened her. I honestly don't know if she's directly involved in what happened to Max, but for whatever reason, she was forced into making the false identification."

Dawn sat with my words for a moment. Her arms were limp; her hands sat in her lap as she stared out at the water, maybe looking for some of the calm I had enjoyed when I first sat down. When she didn't find it, she turned back to me.

"What do you want me to do about it?"

"I have some investigators who are working with the Attorney General's Office trying to get to the bottom of this. They can protect her if she just tells them the truth."

"She hasn't even told *me* the truth. What makes you think she's going to talk to some cops she doesn't know."

"Because it may be her only way out. Mrs. Avery, I think your daughter may be in real danger."

21

TEACH YOUR CHILDREN WELL

DAWN AVERY WAS STILL IN SHOCK when I left the restaurant. I wrote down Kojak and Zack's contact information on the back of a blank order form I tore off one of the waitress' pads. She told me she couldn't make any promises, that Stella had been so fragile lately, the last thing she wanted to do was topple the apple cart and send her even further down into the dark hole where she had lived since Max's death.

I told her I understood, but I reiterated that I thought Stella was in danger. I thought about telling her the details of my paddleboard mishap to reinforce the seriousness of the situation but then decided against it as the woman looked like someone had just dropped an anvil on her head.

In my experience, a mother could reach someone in trouble much faster than any investigator or journalist could. Years ago, I was getting harassed online by a registered sex offender in South Carolina. When I called the law enforcement agency in his area and told them he was in violation of his probation because he was court-ordered to stay off social media, they said they would see what they could do. I realized I wasn't going to get anywhere through official channels. After doing a little digging, I located his mother and called her. Once I told her what was going on, she told me she would take care of it. And she did. I never heard from him again.

I hoped Dawn would have the same power of persuasion over her daughter to get her to do the right thing, to come forward and tell investigators what she knew, even if it incriminated her.

Leave it alone—the same words from Stella, Damien, Kojak, and Zack. They were begging me to listen to them, but I was in too deep. I couldn't let this one go. I had created a checklist of paths that I could go down to try and solve the mystery surrounding this case. Stella was the first name on the list. The second name on the list was Major Arnold Willis. If I could give him a way out for his son, he might be less willing to sweep the investigation under the rug. There was a good chance that his son Brett and he had been victims in this situation, that they had been used just like Stella to help cover up someone else's mess.

When I called the detective's office, his secretary told me he didn't have anything new to share, but that he would be happy to meet with me briefly Monday morning. He only had a small window of time, fifteen minutes. I told her that was fine.

When I hung up the phone, the sun was just beginning to set. I laid my head back on the pillow behind me on the chaise lounge and watched the rich tapestry of colors blending together in the sky above me. I could hear the boats whizzing by on the water below, but my attention was solidly focused on the horizon as the glowing orange ball dipped slowly into the water and disappeared.

Just as I was beginning to doze off, lulled by the whir of the boat engines and the birds chirping in the marsh, my phone rang. I looked down and saw Janie's picture come up—she was dressed as Cat in the Hat for a Halloween party, holding a beer bottle in her "paw" adorned with a sock. I made a mental note to change her profile picture on my phone.

"Maddie, so glad I got you," Janie said breathlessly.

"Hey, Janie," I said with a little more ice in my voice than I had intended. I was still reeling from our strange lunch with Jason and Damien.

"Look, I know that lunch yesterday was super weird. I get it. I mean, I don't get it. All I know is that they're involved in some shady stuff, and they wanted me to warn you, that's why I arranged the lunch, but I know it probably just made you more confused than afraid. That's what I told them. I told them they needed to come clean with me about exactly what's going on, and Damien refused. He told me it was "above my pay grade." Whatever that means. It's no secret that Damien is not exactly Mensa. So, anyway, I just want you to know I'm done with him. I told him if he won't tell me the truth, we are over for good."

As Janie waited for my response, I sat there thinking about how many times I had heard these words from Janie before about leaving Damien. I had never criticized him to her because I always knew it would backfire on me. They would eventually get back together, making me *that friend.* You know, the one who talked junk about your partner when you were broken up and then became persona non grata after you got back together. But this time, things were different. This wasn't just about Janie dating an immature jerk who couldn't hold a job. This was about Janie being involved with someone who might somehow be involved in a person's death. I had to tread very carefully.

"Janie, I'm sorry to hear that. It sounds like you made the right decision."

"Thanks, I know I did. I mean, I'm still sad. We've been together for a long time, but this crap with Jason is where I draw the line. If he can't come clean with me, I just can't be with him anymore."

"How did he take it?" I asked, not really caring but wondering how we would get to the bottom of the mystery if Janie was no longer in Damien's inner circle.

"Not well. Actually, he took it badly. He threw my leather jacket off his balcony into a puddle. They're impossible to clean, by the way, leather jackets, that is. So, he was really trying to mess with me. But I took it well. I just scooped the jacket out of the puddle and kept moving. But then I tripped on a rut in the sidewalk; that kind of diminished the strength of my departure."

If the whole thing wasn't so sad, it would have been funny. I pictured Janie tripping, catching herself, and then regaining her composure, sauntering off like nothing had happened, holding the dripping leather jacket at arm's length.

"Janie, at the risk of offending you, I know that Damien isn't exactly a rocket scientist. You don't think he could be tied up in this guy's death, do you? I mean, he's done some pretty stupid stuff, but this would really take the cake."

"No, I mean, not directly. But I could see him making some bad choices and then getting backed into a corner. Truth be told, I don't know what to believe anymore. I just know I should have gotten rid of him a long time ago. I don't know why it took something this dramatic for me to cut him loose."

I bit my tongue as I listened. I wanted so much to chime in and tell her that Damien had never been good enough for her. That he used her for her apartment, her paycheck, her car, that she was worth so much more than this loser guy who had attached himself to her like a sycophant. But then I remembered my own rule—to be careful in case they decided to get back together.

"Janie, let me ask you something. What was all that stuff with the cigarette pack yesterday and the cagey note about a 'shell game?'"

For a moment, I thought maybe Janie had hung up. There was nothing but silence between us over the phone. Then she cleared her throat and started talking again.

"I don't have any idea what you're talking about. I don't know anything about a note."

For the first time in the history of our friendship, I didn't believe her. This made me more afraid for her than ever.

When I arrived at the police station Monday morning to see Major Willis, I realized that again, just like with Stella and Dawn Avery and with Janie, I was taking a risk. I had no idea what the detective really knew and how far he would go to protect his son if he thought Brett was involved in Max's death. I wasn't going to show him my complete hand, but I decided I needed to give him enough information to bargain with.

As the secretary ushered me into his office, I looked at the family photos on his desk and identified the son I now knew was Brett, Arnold Willis's mini-me. This time, instead of the casual and friendly banter that we had exchanged in the parking lot on Friday afternoon, he seemed tense. It appeared to me that I was a fly in Major Willis's personal space, continually buzzing around. He was done with being polite.

"Major, I'm not going to beat around the bush. I know your son Brett was the person who hit Max during the fight on the boat the night of the party. They got into a drunken altercation over something stupid, a girl, maybe. But what you probably don't know is that while that punch sent Max into the water, it didn't kill him. *Max Prince didn't drown.*"

I wondered if they taught cops to be stone-faced at the academy when they were training them to interrogate people. Maybe they even practiced their stoic faces in front of a mirror. Arnold Willis wasn't giving anything away with his expression, not even a twitch of an eye. After staring at me for a long while, he finally spoke.

"Go on. I'm listening."

"I really think your son was goaded into that fight, that someone *did* want to get rid of Max Prince, that they wanted to make it look like a drowning, a tragic accident. They used your son to make this story work. Baited him to pick that fight, plied him with alcohol. But you don't have to protect your son anymore. He's *not* responsible for Max Prince's death."

At this mere suggestion of possible impropriety, I got a reaction. Major Willis laced his fingers together at the edge of his desk like he was trying to stop himself from reaching across the space between us and putting those same fingers around my neck.

"Why would you think I would protect my son if he did something wrong?"

"Because that's a natural impulse for a parent. I'm not blaming you. I'm just saying I have credible evidence that Max Prince was pulled out of that water *alive* and that whatever caused his death happened later, at someone else's hands."

I didn't want to give away too much—the gunshot wound, the body-switching; it was so surreal, and I knew I would sound crazy if

I went into all of that now. *Keep it simple.*

"Well, if that is true, then we would definitely want to re-open the investigation and get to the bottom of what happened. But I'm going to need a little more from you to take that leap. Starting with where that information is coming from."

"I understand completely. So, I have a friend in law enforcement in Oak City; maybe you know him. He goes by Kojak; he's with Major Crimes, Oak City Police Department."

"I know the name. Hotshot guy, handled that case recently where the wife of the restaurant guy died."

"Yes, that's him. Anyway, I've been in touch with him and pretty much laid out everything I know. He thinks you need to get the Attorney General's Office involved, their investigators, to keep it clean. I'd be happy to put the two of you two together to figure it all out. The main thing is that I don't want to see it swept under the rug. Max Prince deserves justice for what happened to him; so does his family."

With the mention of the Attorney General's Office, I was sure Major Willis was going to throw caution to the wind, unlace his fingers, and leap across the desk to strangle me. But his expressionless face was intact. He paused again and appeared to be choosing his words carefully.

"I don't think it's necessary to involve a state agency in our investigation, but I'd be happy to speak with Kojak—what's his real name?"

"Flick, Major Tommy Flick. But like I said, everyone calls him Kojak. I don't think he even answers to Flick," I said with a small laugh, a poor attempt to give the intense moment a touch of levity.

"All cops have nicknames. It comes with the territory."

"I've heard that, so, what's yours?"

"It's Serpico."

22

CARDS ON THE TABLE

We shook hands when I left, and Major Willis promised to call Kojak. As much as he didn't want an Oak City cop meddling in his business, I think he knew he had no choice. He couldn't make it look like he had deep-sixed the investigation because he was protecting his son, which it appeared, at least on the surface, that he did do. And now that he had the opportunity to clear his son's name, I assumed he would take it.

The rest of the fallout would certainly be bad—the misidentification of the body of a mysterious drowning victim. It wouldn't reflect well on the Cape Mayson Police Department, no matter how things eventually turned out.

When I left Willis's office and started the short walk to my condo, I immediately Googled the name "Serpico." I had heard it before, and I knew by the way he had said it, with such relish, that it *meant* something. And I was right. Serpico was the name of a character played by Al Pacino in a 1973 movie of the same title. The premise of the movie was that Serpico went undercover in the New York City Police Department to root out corruption. What was Willis trying to tell me? Was he truly a good guy who was onto something? Did he know what was really going on with Max Prince's case and was just pretending to be in the dark so that he could continue to investigate it on the down-low?

I honestly didn't know. What I did know was that I needed Kojak and Zack to help me figure out the whole mess. I was exhausted, and I needed a break. I hadn't gotten the break I was hoping for in this beautiful place that was supposed to be a retreat from my stressful life. Instead, I was back in the thick of things—or maybe I had never left.

"Oh my gosh, it's so good to hear your voice. I thought you were dead. I've been texting you for days, and you've been ghosting me," Louise said with mock sadness in her voice. I had decided I owed her a call, probably more than one. So, I sat down on the chaise lounge, kicked off my shoes, and hit her number in my favorites list while the scorching midday sun was just beginning to creep across the balcony.

"I know. I know, and I'm sorry. Things have gotten a little crazy since you left."

"Do tell."

"I can't get into all of it in one phone call. But let's just say that guy Max, *he didn't drown*. In fact, I've confirmed what I told you at the wake. The body I found was not Max Prince. Confirmed. Oh, and someone tried to kill me."

"I think you kind of buried the lead. What do you mean someone tried to kill you?"

"Well, I was on my paddleboard the other night, and this boat just kept coming at me. Finally, I jumped off, and the boat hit my board, cutting it in half. I'm okay, though. I jumped just in time. Not a scratch on me, but my poor board is driftwood."

"That is so freaking scary. Why are you still there? You need to come home immediately! Have you told Zack about this?"

"He knows."

"And what did he say?"

"Pretty much the same thing as you did. He wants me to back away from this whole investigation."

"And?"

"Well, I've been trying to, but you know how I am."

"I do know how you are. And that's why you ended up with a gun to your head. Do you recall that, or did it just slip your mind?"

Louise always had a way of bringing reality right to my doorstep so that I could examine it and think about the choices I was making. She was a good friend in that way, in the way she made me see what I needed to see, not always what I wanted to see.

"I know. You're right. It's just driving me insane, not being able to figure all this out."

"I get it, but you're supposed to be recharging, not jumping directly back into the fire. And what about the kids? They need their mother even if they are temporarily out of sight at camp. You need to think about them when you go off on your wild adventures into the dark world of crime. Be sensible. I know that's not really in your wheelhouse, but at least try. Lord, I need a drink. I know it's early, but I may need to put some Bailey's in my coffee."

Louise always knew how to make me laugh, even in the darkest moments. I appreciated her for that more than she would ever know.

"I hear you."

"I sure hope you do. Now, more importantly—what is going on with Zack?"

"Believe it or not, I was completely into him, and then he pissed me off because I thought he had ulterior motives for wanting to get to know me. I recently found out I own my grandparents' property in Pennsylvania. The land, the house, everything. He wants to buy it to start a bed and breakfast. His intensity over this really freaked me out. So, I ghosted him and decided I would never talk to him again. And then I changed my mind. It's all good now."

"So, wait a minute, that all happened in the last few days since I left? That sounds like you have gone through every stage of the relationship. Things should be smooth sailing from here on out."

"Maybe, I don't know. I just don't know if I'm really ready to be in a relationship."

"*Ready?* That's like saying I'm ready to have a child, or I'm ready to get married. Nobody's ready for the big things in life. We just jump in. We do them, and we hope for the best. You will never truly be ready to move on from Adam. If you wait for that lightning bolt moment, it will never happen. You just need to be as ready as possible, hopeful, open to the possibilities."

"You know you missed your calling. You should have been a therapist."

"Tell Scott that. He'll get a big laugh about it when he's paying the bills for our marriage counselor."

I called Kojak and told him about my conversation with Arnold Willis. He wasn't thrilled that I had basically confronted the guy about covering up for his son, but he understood where I was coming from and agreed that a guy like Willis wasn't going to push this case forward on his own without some cajoling. Kojak told me again he had filled his buddy in at the Attorney General's Office on what we had uncovered. His friend continued to insist that the situation warranted some investigation by the state police, that there was no possible way Cape Mayson Police could be objective if Willis's son were involved. In fact, Kojak's buddy said that Willis should have recused himself from the case as soon as he learned his son was on the boat. The problem with this scenario was that in a small town, there simply weren't enough investigators to do the job.

I told Kojak my new hypothesis, that Willis really might be a good guy and was just trying to investigate the situation on the down-low without interference.

"Not likely," he snorted.

We both agreed that the body-switching situation was the most egregious part of the case, and that the unknown drowning victim deserved to be identified and returned to his family as much as Max Prince deserved justice for what had happened to him. But when it came down to who was ultimately responsible for Max's death, the list of possibilities was long and confusing.

I looked down and saw that there was someone calling me from Camp Lejeune. It had to be Officer Jackson. I said a quick goodbye to Kojak and told him I had an urgent call that I needed to take.

"Maddie Arnette," I answered, clicking over to the other call.

"Miss Arnette, this is Officer Jackson. We do have one AWOL Marine right now. He traveled to the coast on a forty-eight-hour pass with some fellow recruits and has not returned. The information we have from his group is that he was unhappy here and most likely left on his own accord. We have no information to suspect that anything bad has happened to him."

Right away, I realized that the drowned man's buddies were trying to keep themselves out of trouble. They couldn't exactly say *We lost him when he was drunk and then left town without him.* Without hesitation, Officer Jackson gave me the Marine's name—Ted Barton.

"Have you been in touch with the Cape Mayson Police to see if there are any reports that match your missing Marine?"

"No ma'am, like I said, from what we understand, he left of his own accord. He's not missing per se, just missing from his obligations."

I stared at the water and thought about the man who floated up to my paddleboard. Now, I had a name. I just needed to find Ted Barton's family.

When I saw Zack's name pop up on my screen right after hanging up with Officer Jackson, I could feel the smile spreading across my face. And then I immediately felt guilty for being happy. It was like the universe was conspiring to give me joy and make me a martyr at the same time. I took a deep breath before answering.

"Hey there," I said, trying to cover up the obvious excitement in my voice.

"Hey there. How are things? Are you okay?"

"Okay?" It took me a second to realize what he was asking me. He wanted to know if I was *safe.* I wasn't sure how to respond. "Yes, of course."

"So, I was thinking. The twins have several weeks left at camp, right?"

"Yes," I hesitated, not sure where this conversation was going."

"Well, then why don't you come up here, to Pennsylvania, for a few days? We could hang out. I could show you some of my favorite places here; you could learn a little bit about me. And it might take the heat off you down there if you disappeared for a few days."

The doubt was creeping back into my mind about Zack only being interested in me selling him my grandparents' land. I pushed the thought away as soon as it entered my headspace, refusing to entertain any negativity after I had worked so hard to reopen my emotional door to him.

"Sure. Yes, that would be nice; I mean *fun*." As soon as the words came out of my mouth, I felt like a tongue-twisted teenager agreeing to go to the school dance with a boy I had just met at the mall. Truthfully, I could use a break from this place and from Max's case. "Well, I do need to meet with Belinda Parsons, the real estate attorney. I need to tell her something about the property. Need to get the paperwork from the courthouse, see if it is all in order, and so forth."

I knew that I was testing Zack, baiting him by throwing out the topic of the land to see if he would bite. He passed the test. He said nothing.

"It's settled then. I have plenty of time off stored up. I rarely take my vacation time, so it's been piling up for years. How soon can you come?"

"Soon, I guess. I'll look at flights when we hang up, and hotels," as soon as I said the word "hotels," I could tell I must have offended him or hurt his feelings. I was met with silence on the other end of the line. "I mean, I don't really have any family there anymore to stay with, and my grandparents' house is certainly not habitable," I stammered.

He cut me off.

"You'll stay with me, at my house. I've got plenty of room. It's a three-bedroom. I have a guestroom and a study with an extra bed as well. I mean, you can have your choice of rooms."

I hadn't considered the fact that he might want me to stay with him. It all seemed too soon. But then again, we were adults. We weren't playing around, or at least I didn't think we were. His offer seemed genuine and respectful.

"Ok, if you don't mind. That would be great."

"It would be my pleasure."

After we hung up, I cradled the phone in my hands for a few minutes before grabbing my computer to search for flights. I laid my head back on the chaise lounge and let my heavy lids close, making a mental note that I should take my contacts out in case I fell asleep. I ignored the note and drifted in and out of sleep to the gentle sound of boats slicing through the water. I was thinking about Zack's face—*relaxed Zack*—the one I had met at The Last Straw Cafe, the one I knew from Cape Mayson—not *cop Zack*—the serious guy in the suspenders and a bow tie whom I had met in Pennsylvania in the spring. I wondered which Zack I would encounter when I got there. I liked *relaxed Zack* the best, but I needed *cop Zack* to help me navigate the situation with Roger and to help me unravel Max's case.

As I began to doze off again, another face popped into my sleepy brain. It was the watery face of the man I now presumed was Ted Barton, the man Stella had passed off as Max Prince to police, the man who could have ended up in a casket at another man's funeral. The dead Marine.

The only option was for police to get a court order to exhume Max's body, to prove that he had a gunshot wound, that he didn't drown. But this still left the question of why no one was missing Ted Barton. That's when I heard my phone vibrate. I looked down to see a text from the dog walker Gina Finkel with an attached link to a Facebook post by a person named Cammie Barton. I was immediately intrigued because Cammie's last name matched the name that Officer Jackson had given me of the AWOL Marine. I clicked on the link and read it.

"Missing: Ted Barton, Marine stationed at Camp LeJeune in Jacksonville, North Carolina. Last seen by friends in Cape Mayson on Friday, June 7. Please message me if you know anything at all. I promise to keep your identity confidential. No detail is too small. I am his sister, and his family is very worried about him."

I stared at the photo of Ted Barton. I was pretty sure Gina Finkel had found her Batman, and I was pretty sure I had found the man with the dark eyes I would never forget.

23

HOMEWARD BOUND

I DIDN'T WANT TO TELL ZACK about Ted Barton over the phone. I decided it was better to have the conversation in person.

I had reached out to Cammie Barton by Facebook Messenger and told her that I might have some information for her about her missing brother. I wanted to hold a little back at first to make sure I was right before I started sharing the whole bizarre story with a perfect stranger and getting her hopes up. She responded and told me that her brother had gone drinking with some buddies one night recently in Cape Mayson, that they claimed he wandered off in a drunken stupor, and they never saw him again. They said they thought he must just be on a park bench or the beach sleeping it off, but when he didn't come back to the hotel the next morning, they had to return to Jacksonville without him because they were only allowed a forty-eight-hour leave, and it was about to expire.

They reported him missing to their commanders, who chalked it up to the fact that Ted was not doing well in his training and was overwhelmed. They briefly looked into it, interviewing the Marines he was partying with that weekend and decided that Ted had probably wandered off on his own, that he was running away from his military service because he realized he was not cut out for it. Ted still owed them two years in return for his college education that they had paid for. Once the investigation headed down this path, everyone stopped talking about Ted as being "missing" and started talking about Ted as "running away" from his responsibilities.

Ted's friends at the base didn't buy it, but they were also scared of getting in trouble for losing track of their friend that night. Nobody wanted to contradict the outcome of the investigation because it would mean admitting they were all so drunk out of their minds that they lost Ted. Not unlike Max, Ted was a victim of a group of people who were reckless, who let their fear and egos stop them from doing the right thing.

Cammie wasn't buying any of it. She knew that Ted had been struggling with his training and wasn't sure he was cut out to be a Marine. But she also knew that he was loyal, honest, and had a strong sense of responsibility. She knew in her heart that something bad had happened to her brother, and she just wanted to know where he was. She was pretty sure he was dead. But she could handle the truth; what she couldn't handle was not knowing.

As I corresponded with this woman back and forth through digital messages, I realized that I was probably the only person who could give her the answers she was looking for. But explaining to her the intricacies of why this happened and then telling her the hard truth that her brother's body was likely a pile of ashes left at a funeral home was too much. I needed Zack's guidance for this one. Cammie would have to wait a little bit longer for justice. Still, I wanted to give her something to satisfy her in the meantime.

I told her that I was a reporter and I had seen a missing person's report about a man with a Batman hat who was stumbling down the street drunk that night with a buddy, presumably another Marine, and that police had responded to a 911 call but couldn't locate the drunk man. This was the easiest thing to share because it was all true. I just omitted the part about me finding a body that might be Ted.

Cammie messaged me back in all capital letters:

OMG, HE HAD A BATMAN HAT. THAT'S GOT TO BE HIM. I CAN'T BELIEVE I'M JUST HEARING THIS NOW. THANK YOU SO MUCH!

I told her I would work to find out more and would be in touch later. We exchanged cell phone numbers and agreed to speak in a few days. I hoped at that time I would be able to share with her the whole truth and give her the closure she deserved.

As the plane lifted into the air, I stared out the window, looking down as the shimmering blue ocean receded in the distance, becoming smaller and smaller as we ascended into the clouds. From the air, the ocean didn't look scary or dangerous, like a place that had the power to take lives. It was a place with another world living beneath the surface, a dark world filled with sea life and secrets. I knew the power of the ocean, and I respected it.

We were in the white fluffy clouds, surrounding us like pillows that made you want to jump into them from the plane's wing and land softly like an angel caressed by summer air, looking down at the world below. But not unlike the beauty of the ocean beneath us, I knew the clouds, for all their gentle appearance, would not hold a person who jumped from the wing. There were so many things in life like that—things that appeared to be safe from a distance, to be peaceful, welcoming, and uncomplicated—yet they held the capacity to destroy you.

It suddenly occurred to me that people were like that too. They could appear one way, a way that made you feel safe, a way that allowed you to let your guard down, but really, on the inside, they might also have the capacity to crush you. As the plane sped towards Pennsylvania, I silently prayed that Zack Brumson was not one of those people.

After much angst about staying at Zacks's house, given that we had only known each other for a short time, I rented an Airbnb just down the road from him. It was a converted barn made into two apartments. I was staying in the one upstairs that had a small porch and an amazing view across the rolling green hills of Andrew Wyeth country.

The property was owned by one of Zack's friends and former colleague, a retired officer. So, Zack reluctantly agreed to the arrangement because it was so close to his house, and it was his buddy's place, a place he deemed safe enough for me to stay at because it had an alarm, and his friend lived in a house on the property and was well-armed.

When I walked out of the terminal with my one small roller bag and saw people ahead of me meeting their family members and friends, embracing, and exchanging excited greetings, I had a sudden panic attack wondering if Zack might not show up. Maybe he would text me and tell me to get an Uber; maybe something came up at work, maybe he got cold feet.

"Hey, you," I heard a familiar voice call out to me. And just like that, there he was. He was *relaxed Zack* again in army green cargo shorts and a faded black graphic t-shirt. He was wearing white, slightly tattered Converse sneakers, which instantly put me at ease. He leaned in and gave me a kiss on the cheek. I felt a jolt of electricity run through my body. I could feel my cheeks turning red.

"Hi, thanks for coming to get me," I reached in for a slightly awkward hug. It was like our relationship had gone from friends to something else in just the span of a week, and neither of us really knew how to define it. I wasn't even sure if I was ready to define it.

"Of course—there are not a lot of Ubers in Dilltown." Zack smiled, draped one arm casually over my shoulder, and grabbed the handle of the roller bag with his other hand, taking charge of it without asking. I let him.

"It's good to see you. I have another incredible development to tell you about in this whole crazy mess."

"I want to hear all about it, I really do. But I'd like to put business aside and take you to one of my favorite places. Remember, this trip is about us getting to know each other better. Specifically about you getting to know *me*. There are many reasons I have stayed here for as long as I have, here in Dilltown, here in Pennsylvania. I want to show you a few of them."

As we passed people, they smiled at us. I'm sure they thought they were looking at a couple in love. I caught a glimpse of our reflection in the glass doors as we left the building, looking every bit the happy couple. I reminded myself that not everything was as it appeared.

We sat at a rustic farm table on the old stone porch of a house converted into a restaurant, drank red sangria full of pieces of fresh fruit poured from an etched glass carafe, and spread goat cheese on crusty chunks of brown bread that were still warm. There was also a cutting board in front of us laden with plump juicy vegetables cut into bite-sized portions. I was so seduced by the setting, the food, the man that I had to remind myself to pump the breaks, to not be taken in by the perfection of the moment. We had so many serious things on the table, besides food and good wine, that needed to be discussed. But maybe they could wait?

Adam had always been better at engaging in the moment than I was. I was always looking forward to what was next, thinking about what I might say in response to someone's story instead of really listening to the details of what they were saying. It was partially just how my brain worked—at warp speed, so fast that sometimes it made me dizzy—and partly because since I was a little girl, I always felt like I was running out of time, like there was a finite amount of time given to everyone, and for some reason I had been given less than others.

This most likely had something to do with losing my mother at a young age. Even though I didn't fully comprehend that she was murdered at the time, I knew she was *gone*. And it didn't take me long once I got into school to realize that this wasn't normal, that other girls had their moms around for the entire time they were growing up. It made me wonder if I, too, was going to die young. When I got nervous as a child, and my heart started to beat fast, and I got short of breath, I was sure it was the end, that my time was finally up, that I would never even get the chance to have children.

My grandmother, Belle, who raised me, put me into therapy at a very young age, given the tragedy I had experienced. Dr. Ginette Kincaid helped me work through my panic attacks; the name I now knew described what was happening to me. She called them my "anxious moments." We worked on deep-breathing exercises, meditation, and even a little yoga. It all helped, but nothing cured them until I met Adam. His advice was to slow down, to engage in the moment, not to try and control everything that came next. He said if I started to feel out of control, like I was about to have another "anxious moment," all I needed to do was to change something, to remove myself from the situation if possible. He was right. Free of charge, my husband had done what no high-priced therapist had ever been able to do—he taught me how to pull back from a panic attack.

And now, here I was, in this beautiful setting, watching Zack's lips move as he told me some animated story about the first time he came to this restaurant, and all I could think about was my mother, Roger, and Max. I stopped myself in mid-spiral and tried to focus on what Zack was saying.

"And I was like, so you make the goat cheese, but you buy the goat's milk from other goat farmers? You have all this land; why don't you have your own goats? And the guy, Francois, the owner, says: *Have you ever milked a goat? It's no fun.*"

I knew this was the point in the story where I was supposed to laugh, and so I did, a big hearty laugh, probably too big of a laugh for the quality of the story, but I was trying to make up for my lack of attention. Luckily, he was so eager to amuse me that he didn't seem to notice my over-the-top response to his story or my previous disinterest. It was this lack of awareness that almost made me feel bad for men. They were no match for us.

"That is too funny," I added, punctuating my raucous belly laugh with colorful banter.

"Hey, I can tell you are not one hundred percent here. What's on your mind?"

"It just feels weird being happy in the place where my mother died."

Zack reached across the table and gently grasped my hand. It felt natural. I let my hand sit there, feeling the weight and warmth of his fingers atop mine. Like his delicate kiss on my cheek at the airport, it was a soft touch meant to show me affection at a slow pace. I appreciated it.

"I get it. But you also need to remember this is where she *lived*. I'm sure she had many happy memories here from growing up, many more that outweigh the tragedy of her death. I think if you focus on that, then this place can eventually have some positive meaning for you."

I sat with this thought for a moment with my hand in his. Just when I thought he wasn't paying attention, he had surprised me again.

"I guess you're right. It will just take time."

"Of course, it will. And you know, whatever happens with Roger, if you find out for sure that your dad isn't responsible for your mother's death, it could go a long way towards your healing."

I knew he was right, but I didn't want to think about Roger right now. I wanted to think about these rolling green hills surrounding me and the sun glinting off our glasses filled with delicious red liquid and fresh orange slices. I wanted to use what Adam taught me about being in the moment. How ironic that my dead husband was tutoring me on how to be a good date.

"Right, let's get off this topic. Too dark. So, tell me something about you and Dilltown. Why do you love it so much? Why did you decide to make it your home?"

"Is home something you ever really choose? Or does it choose you?" Zack said, pausing to look out across the hills into the distance. "It's hard to say. It's just my place, that's all."

After a great farm-to-table meal featuring a beet salad, a thinly sliced chicken breast on multigrain bread with a spicy mustard marinade, and red potato salad, capped off with raspberry gelato, we walked into the revitalized part of Dilltown. It was a small strip of boutiques and cafes that emphasized the willingness of the little town to evolve against the odds being that it was more than an hour from Philadelphia, the closest big city. The last time I had driven through the town just a few months prior; all I saw were the empty storefronts and "For Sale" or "For Rent" signs in the windows, but Zack showed me this new version of the town, and I was hopeful for the community.

As we strolled down the street holding hands, I felt eyes on me. I knew that I was probably imagining it, but all I could think about was that people knew who I was. *There she is, the little girl whose mother was murdered in the Hartsell house, you know that old one up on the hill, the one that looks like a haunted house now? Husband did it. Went to prison for life—poor child.*

I knew it was insane for me to be thinking this way. It made no sense. Most of the people who owned these fancy boutiques and hipster stores were probably not from here. They were city dwellers looking for a kinder, gentler life. They had no reason to know the history of this place. But the voices in my head persisted. *What is she doing here? Why is she back? I heard she owns the house and the property. A big developer is interested. She will sell out for sure.*

Suddenly, I remembered that I had told Belinda Parsons I would call her, and we would get together while I was in town to talk about the house and the property. Selling it to a developer who would no doubt subdivide it and put up a cookie-cutter neighborhood for people wanting to escape city life would most likely be my best shot of making some real money. I suspected it would be enough to fill the twins' college funds and then some. I would finally be free of this place and could wash my hands of it forever. But as I looked over at this man, this man who was smiling confidently as we walked down the street holding hands, I wasn't sure I wanted to be done with it. I also wasn't sure about what to do with *his* offer to buy the property and turn it into a bed and breakfast.

"Hey, this has been awesome, but there are a few things I need to do while I'm here. One of them is to take a run after I digest that amazing lunch that made me gain about ten pounds on the spot."

Zack looked at me, a little unsure at first. Then he pulled his hand away and encircled my waist from behind as we walked.

"Dinner?" He said, still looking straight ahead as we ambled down the street.

"Dinner, *yes*, dinner." I was also looking straight-ahead too, but I knew we were both smiling.

I decided I would listen to what Belinda Parsons had to say before making my final decision about my grandparents' property. I met her at a coffee shop on the edge of town, hoping that I wouldn't run into Zack. She explained to me that the developer was indeed interested in subdividing the land and putting up single-family homes, as many as they could get it zoned for.

"People really want to live in the suburbs. I mean, this is still the country, but the way the city is spreading out, it's becoming part of the suburbs. No one can afford those fancy country club community prices closer to Philly, so this is the best of both worlds—close enough to access the city if you want to, but you can also stay right here and enjoy the beauty and the safety of a small town."

As soon as she said the word "safety," her hand went directly to her mouth, as if saying this to the child of a murder victim was the worst thing she could ever have done. I tried to gloss over it to make her feel less uncomfortable.

"How quickly are they interested in doing this?"

"As soon as possible. They've got the plans, and they are ready to clear the land and break ground. And they're willing to pay a premium because they're so sure it's going to be a success."

"What's a premium? I'm embarrassed to say I don't know much about property values are around here."

"Fifteen thousand an acre, one point nine million and change—that's for everything, the house, the acreage."

"But the house, they don't want it—it will be razed?"

"Correct."

I thought about the state of the old house the time I went to visit Roger in prison a few months back. It was a dilapidated farmhouse in grave disrepair from its sagging roof to the weeds growing through the sideboards, to its broken windows and the jungle of prickly brush that had overtaken the yard. Despite Zack's optimism, it was hard to imagine anyone resurrecting it to any semblance of normalcy. Plus, in homage to my mother's death, it seemed only right to wipe it clean from the earth.

"Wow, that's a lot of money—more than enough money for college and *then some*."

"How many kids do you have?"

"Twins, 12-year-olds, so I have a few years to go, but it will be exponential to have two in college at the same time. And frankly, much to my chagrin, one of them is even talking about boarding school. That will cost as much as, if not more than, college."

"No doubt. Selling this land would have you more than covered. If you invest well, you could probably even retire. Make your money work for you."

"I hear you. But it's also very emotional for me. This has all happened so quickly. I need some time to think about it."

"I understand. Take the time you need. But don't take too much time. These developers have a way of flipping farms for cash very quickly. I don't want you to miss out on the opportunity."

I had worn my running clothes and walked to the coffee shop from the Airbnb so that I could take a much-needed jog after the meeting and process everything. Running was my therapy, my getaway, a way to clear my head. It grounded me like nothing else could.

I listened to my breathing and the sound of my sneakers hitting the pavement as I headed up a steep hill in the sweltering afternoon heat. Pennsylvania wasn't nearly as humid as North Carolina, but it was still summer, and the mugginess was a little like a wet blanket I couldn't cast off.

I hit my stride despite the less than optimum conditions. I saw the edge of a concrete building peeking out from the brush at the top of the hill on the right. As I got closer, I noticed a rusty sign on a bent post swaying in the minimal breeze next to the old shack with tiny broken windows. It sat in what used to be a parking lot, but the weeds had grown up through cracks in the pavement, and now soft green moss-covered most of what used to be asphalt.

As I got closer, I could read the sign, which was upside down on the ground. In swirly red cursive, it read: "The Blue Moon." It took me a second to realize why I knew this name. It was the place where my father, Roger, had met Clifton. I stood and stared at the rundown building for a moment, catching my breath, my hands on my hips, sweat rolling down my back. Clearly, it had been closed for many years. The cinder blocks were crumbling; the roof was caved in, and the red scratched metal front door stood ajar. Darkness loomed behind it.

I wasn't interested in going inside. I wasn't interested in the history of this foreboding place or the secrets it held. I was only interested in the truth. I wanted to know why this stranger, this associate of my father, had taken it upon himself to kill my mother.

Suddenly, a chill went down my spine. I wrapped my arms around my body to warm up; there was no way I could be cold on such a hot summer day. It occurred to me as I looked at this trash heap of an old bar that this place had probably destroyed many lives—not just my family's. Maybe the house where my grandparents lived, the house where my mother was raised, the house where my mother died, didn't deserve to be torn down. Maybe *this place* should be bulldozed instead.

I glanced at my watch and realized the day was getting away from me. If I was going to finish my run, shower, and get ready for dinner, I had to get a move on it. I glanced back one more time at the old bar making a mental note to research who owned the property and to find out why it had never been torn down.

I continued up the hill. I knew where my feet were taking me even before I rounded the corner—my grandparents' falling-down farmhouse greeted me with a wink and a nod, like a sad, sagging cartoon character out of a fairy tale. It had only been a few months since my last visit, which had been my first visit since childhood. Instead of darkness like the aura that surrounded the bar, this place was encircled in light reflecting off the bright green rolling hills that seemed to skim the roof and slide over the edge, illuminating the old wraparound front porch.

It has potential, a voice in my head said out of nowhere. Was I crazy to think that this was the right course of action—to walk away from nearly two million dollars just to preserve this piece of my family's history? I was leaning against an old oak tree, enjoying the shade, and taking a sip of water from the bottle on my runner's belt when I smelled it. There was no denying it. I knew immediately what it was: *Smoke.*

With my violently shaking fingers, I somehow managed to call 911. Within seconds of smelling the smoke, I started to see the flicker of orange flames shooting through the roofline. I stood there helpless, knowing there was nothing I could do, and that an old wooden house like this was likely to be devoured quickly. Maybe this was a sign; maybe the fire was making my decision for me.

I heard a piece of burning wood fall to the ground at the edge of the house, crackling with hot embers. I turned away and decided to call Zack as I heard the welcome sound of the fire engines in the distance screaming my way.

"The house, my house, it's on fire," I said, barely able to get the words out, surprised by my own emotional attachment to the place.

"I'm on the way. Did you call 911? Is the fire department there yet?"

"Yes, they just got here."

I stood there feeling even more helpless as three ladder trucks screeched into the overgrown front yard. The firefighters jumped out, pulled the massive hoses from their trucks, and began immediately dousing the now intense flames with heavy streams of water. The firefighter in charge, the man I later learned was the captain, walked over to the tree where I was standing.

"You must be the Hartsell's granddaughter," he said.

"I am. How did you know that?"

"Small town. Heard you were back. Anyway, any idea how this started? Did you see anything?"

"No. I was out for a run, and I just stopped here for a moment. The next thing I knew, I smelled smoke, and then I saw the flames."

"So, you just *happened* to be jogging by here when the fire started?"

I didn't like the accusatory tone of his voice. What incentive would I have to burn down my grandparents' house, *my house?* I already had a major offer on the table that involved razing the house. There was no need to destroy it. It was absurd that he was even implying this. I tried to keep the emotion out of my voice.

"Yes, that's how it happened. I'm trying to decide whether to sell it and sell the land or whether to restore it. So, I wanted to take a look at it."

The fire captain turned and looked up at the house that was now a wet, smoky mess. The water had finally beaten down the fire.

"I guess your decision is made now. Not much to save here."

I didn't like his tone. And as far as I could see, the fire damage was superficial. The roof was severely compromised, but the structure of the house was intact.

"I don't think that's true. I will have to get someone to look at it. I think it could be saved."

He looked at me and shook his head. He walked away in the direction of his crews, who were, for the most part, standing down now. A handful of firefighters continued to spray the hotspots that were popping up across the top of the roofline.

My phone vibrated. I thought it might be Zack telling me he was on the way. I looked down. It was from a blocked number. It read:

Mind your own business. You are playing with fire.

24

PLAYING WITH FIRE

ZACK HELD ME FOR A LONG TIME as we looked up at the steam now rising off the hot, wet roof. I was sweaty from the run and sooty from standing so close to the fire, but I didn't care. I knew from my experience covering fires for the news that my clothes, including my running shoes, would most likely have to be thrown away. It was a smell that never came out, no matter how many times something was washed. I felt safe in his arms, safer than I had in a long time. My concerns about Zack's motives evaporated the more I peeled back his layers, and he revealed himself to me.

I remembered the first fire I covered. I was fresh out of college, working at a little television station in New England. I awoke to my editor's phone call telling me to look out the window from my apartment. I pulled myself together, put my glasses on, and pulled up the shade in my bedroom. The light blinded me at first, but once my eyes adjusted, I could see the massive orange plumes of fire shooting into the air like rockets from the roof of the apartment building down the hill. And that's when I saw the people, little black dots jumping from windows—six, seven stories up. From my vantage point, I couldn't see where they landed, but I knew it was a very bad situation. Four people died that day jumping from those windows.

From that moment on, I always checked and double-checked that my toaster and hairdryer were unplugged before I left the house. Sometimes, when I wasn't sure, I came back before I had even driven a block down the road just to check on everything one more time. Fire was my worst nightmare.

"Wow, so glad you're okay and so glad you happened to be jogging by just at the right moment," Zack said into the top of my head as he held me. I could feel his lips lightly brushing the top of my head.

"Captain jerk over there tells me it's a total loss, that it can't be saved—I mean, that is if I *wanted* to save it."

"Don't listen to him. We need to get a structural engineer in here and an architect to look at it. That guy doesn't know what he's talking about."

I pulled away and held Zack at arm's length. I wanted to tell him that I had decided to keep the house, to keep the property, to make it into a bed and breakfast like he'd talked about, and that maybe we could be business partners. But first, I needed to tell him about the frightening text. I wanted to let him know that this was *arson*, and that before we went ahead with this project, I had to figure out who was after me and why.

"There's something else. A text."

"What kind of text?"

"A text telling me to butt out. A text that made it clear this fire was intentionally set to scare me. Zack, someone followed me all the way to Pennsylvania to give me this message."

I pulled up the text and held up the phone in front of him so that he could read it. After staring at it for a moment, he took the phone from me and reread it again.

"I can get this traced."

"It's from a blocked number."

"I've got guys. Let me see what I can do."

He draped his arm over my shoulder and pulled me in towards him again. We stood there quietly, watching the firefighters as they continued to douse the roof with a steady stream of water, creating steam that was now rising in front of the sun as it sank into the horizon. If it wasn't so tragic, it would have been beautiful. But a lot of things in life were like that—tragically beautiful.

The rest of my visit with Zack was like something out of a romantic comedy. We had a few great meals, laughed at each other's nuances, and mostly stayed away from the serious topics that were orbiting our shared universe.

I did agree that I would go to Roger's hearing. He promised to go with me, which I knew was the only way that I would be able to handle it. It was not something I could do alone.

He told me he would get some experts to look at the house and see what could be done. I put Belinda Parsons off again despite her insistence that I might miss out on the deal of a lifetime. I told her I just needed more time to think about it, which was the truth. Although I had pretty much decided that if Zack's engineer and architect said the house could be saved, I was headed in the direction of restoring it.

The final piece of our tumultuous few days was not as easy to navigate. Zack's "guy" was able to trace the threatening text to a burner phone. It was purchased with a certain number of hours on it and then it was thrown away when those hours expired. The one thing he could tell me was that the call was initiated from an area code in Cape Mayson, North Carolina. That sealed the deal—the fire *was* related to the Max Prince investigation, and it was meant to scare me. Zack said under no circumstances did he want me going back there. He said my near miss on the paddleboard along with the fire meant that I was, without a doubt, in danger.

"I don't think you understand. I *need* to go back. I can't allow their threats to keep me from getting to the truth."

"This is not something to be messing around with," Zack said, shaking his head as we sat on a bench outside of airport security. It was time for me to go, and this would not be resolved before my flight.

"Look, I know you're worried about me. But I will be careful. *I promise.*"

"Isn't that what you told Kojak before you ended up with a gun to your head?"

"This is different," I said, standing up and grabbing the handle of my roller bag to signal that I was, in fact, leaving.

"How? How is it different?" His eyes were pleading with me to stay. He grabbed my free hand.

"Because I'm in control this time. I'm not going to be blindsided. I just need a little more time to figure this thing out."

Reluctantly, he let my hand slip out of his. He stood up and silently embraced me. He gave me a long soft kiss on the cheek and then pulled back, cupped my face with his hands, and kissed me on the lips. As much as I wanted to stay there, frozen in that moment, I didn't let him linger. I pulled away and turned toward the security line, giving him a half-wave over my shoulder. It was nice to have someone worry about me again. It had been so long. But it also felt a little suffocating for someone to be telling me what to do. I would deal with these dueling feelings later. I had a murder case to solve.

I got back to the apartment in Cape Mayson well after dark. In a strange way, this little summer rental was starting to feel like home—a cozy respite from my everyday life in Oak City.

I checked my voicemails—calls that no doubt came in while I was in transit. One was from Zack making sure I got home all right, his voice laden with worry. One was from Kojak telling me he and his buddy at the Attorney General's Office had made some progress on the investigation. And then there was a message from Jason asking me to meet him on a small island across the waterway from my building the next morning.

I still hadn't replaced my paddleboard, but I knew the marina had an assortment of kayaks that people who stayed there could borrow. I decided that would be my mode of transportation. I paused, imagining what Zack would think of this plan—meeting a practical stranger who might be connected to a murder case on a deserted island. He would not approve. As a result, I had no plans to tell him about it. While the whole Jason-Damien-Janie situation had been bizarre, I still felt Jason's motives were about wanting to get justice for Max. Nothing about my hypothesis had any basis in real facts. It was just a gut feeling.

I crawled into bed, exhausted from my trip and from all the drama that had happened in just a few short days. As I drifted off, I thought about the farmhouse, not on fire, not falling apart, but restored to its former glory, glistening amongst the green rolling hills. I pictured guests in rocking chairs on the long porch holding glasses of wine or iced tea. I imagined a flagstone path lined by wildflowers leading up to the front steps, now painted a barn red. Above the steps at the edge of the porch was a white clapboard shingle hanging from a rustic wooden frame. In red cursive lettering, it read: *Patty's Place.*

The short kayak ride over to the small island the next morning was a welcome distraction from all the stress that was weighing me down. Unlike paddleboarding, where my legs and core bore the brunt of the work, in a kayak, I could relax a little and let my arms lead the boat gently through the water. I smiled as I was back in my happy place, on the water with the sea spray dousing my legs and tickling my nose as I paddled through the No Wake Zone over to the thin slice of white sand. The middle of the island was full of wild vegetation, but there was a clear area cut out where people often pulled up their kayaks and took a break.

As I approached, I could see that Jason was already there. I spotted him immediately—his tall, lanky frame jutted awkwardly out of the top of the sea kayak. He was running his hand through his tufts of almost white-blond hair atop his tanned face.

"Hi there," I said, trying to sound casual as I slid my kayak up on the shore next to his. "So, what's with this clandestine meeting?"

At first, he looked at me like it was inappropriate for me to be saying something so flippant, given the probable nature of our conversation. But then, some brief understanding seemed to pass over his face when he realized I was just trying to lighten the moment.

"I have a video I need to show you. I didn't tell you about it earlier because I was scared to reveal too much. But the video is how I know everything I do. Perry liked me to take video of parties that we could post on our social media to entice future customers. There was also a girl on the boat that I was sort of crushing on. She was dancing, so I was trying to get some video of her, too. I know it sounds super creepy. Please don't judge."

He turned away from me for a moment, seemingly to get his nerve up for what was about to come next.

"I have it all. The fight between Brett and Max. Max falling into the water. The other boat in the distance. It's all in the background. But the thing that I think is the most telling is what Perry does. He says, and it's real clear on the video, *we're out of here.* I will show it to you, but I am afraid to send it. I don't want there to be a trail leading back to me."

I looked at Jason as he said this, trying to assess his sincerity. I had been wrong about people before, but at this moment, I believed him. I believed that he didn't know what this was all about and had been an unwitting player in this tragedy.

"Look, I know you *knew* Max more than you're letting onto. I saw the photos of you and Damien and him volunteering at the turtle rescue, loading the shells into the trucks. Why didn't you tell me you hung out with him?"

"I don't know. I was scared. Damien told me I could trust you, but he also told me not to say too much. Look, I worked for Perry and I guess, indirectly for Mr. Maron. But I don't really know anything about them or their business. I just try to keep it in between the ditches, and keep my nose clean. After I got injured in that land mine explosion, well, I thought my life was over. Believe it or not, I had planned to have a career in the military. I know that sounds weird, but it was the only thing that ever really made sense to me. It gave me a purpose. It gave me structure. It made me feel like I was contributing to something greater than myself. After I came home, I was lost. I didn't know what I was going to do. Perry hooked me up. Instead of just pumping gas at a marina for the rest of my life, I was somebody's right-hand man. I did whatever he asked me to do, and I didn't ask questions. I figured the best way for me to get along with the dude was to be quiet and do my job, so that's what I did. But this—*somebody dying?* I didn't sign up for this. It's not who I am."

"Okay, I get it. Perry gave you a chance at something more, something better, and I'm assuming he paid you well."

"He did, and he always implied that he had bigger plans for me. So, I just hung in there."

"Do you think he's responsible for what happened to Max?"

"I have no idea. Like I said, I didn't ask questions. Sure, he's a weird dude, kind of cold. But I got the sense he's been through a lot, and just like he gave me a shot, Mr. Maron gave him one, and he was determined not to screw it up."

"So, he could have sped away that night because he was scared of the ramifications of having a guy fall off the party boat he was in charge of, and he just knee-jerked and took off without thinking it through."

"Correct."

"Or, he could have been in on some elaborate plan to get right of Max for some unknown reason."

"Correct."

Our kayaks were now bobbing slightly in the surf as boats cruised by in the waterway behind us, ignoring the "No Wake Zone" signs. But our bows were still stuck firmly on the edge of the little island in the sand. All around us, life was swirling—birds dove into the water looking for fish and the wake rolled up on the shore in front of us, unmooring our bows a little with every ebb and flow. There was a stillness at the moment as Jason and I sat quietly, trying to figure out where we should go from here.

"So, why tell me all of this? Why not tell the police and let them investigate properly?" I said after a long moment of silence passed between us.

"Because I just can't. I really don't know what's going on here, who is involved in what. I can't risk pissing them off, and I also don't want this to define the rest of my life. Plus, with that cop's kid involved, I don't trust them to do the right thing. I figured you could get the information to the right people and make it right. Maybe someone above the local police, with more power. Someone with no dog in the fight."

"Okay, well, let me ask you this: Who got you involved in the turtle rescue? Did Perry have anything to do with that?"

At this, he threw his head back and laughed like I had just said the funniest thing he had ever heard.

"Hell, no. Technically, it was a volunteer thing, but we got paid."

"Did the group pay you?"

"No, Max asked us to do it. He volunteered there for years. But he said they just needed some extra hands loading a truck. A donor to the organization would pay us on the down-low to do it. The dude paid for the whole thing—the trucks, the shipping, the loading. So, we said *sure*. We did it a couple of times. It was good money. No big deal."

"So, was Max the connection between the turtle rescue and the museum in Florida that took the shells?"

"No, it was his friend from high school. You know, the girl who had the party on the boat. She was the one who set it up. He just made it happen."

"You mean *Stella?*"

"Yes, Stella."

I sat still for a moment, thinking about how all roads seemed to lead back to Stella Avery.

As I paddled across the waterway to the marina, all I could think about was the fact that someone was lying. Since the beginning, Jason and Damien had seemed sketchy to me, the most likely people to be mixed up in trouble. I was now seeing Jason in a different light. He had been honest and vulnerable with me. I hadn't asked him about the note in the cigarette pack because I was starting to believe that *he* hadn't put it there. I didn't want to tip my full hand just yet.

For some reason, it felt prudent to withhold this detail from him.

Perry still seemed like a big question mark, especially after my uncomfortable interaction with him on the Ripple. And I now knew for sure, based on seeing Jason's video, that he had sped away from the scene knowing Max had fallen into the water. If nothing else, he was guilty of *that.*

Jason showed me the video on his phone as we sat side-by-side in our kayaks. He let me watch it three times to make sure I saw what I needed to see. I wanted a copy so badly, but I didn't want to push my luck.

He held up his phone to me and tried to tilt it out of the sunlight so I could see the tiny screen. I shielded it with a cupped hand as he pushed the triangle in the center of the video, and it began to play. With all the powerful lights on the boat, I could clearly see the dancing girl that Jason was focusing on, but then, suddenly, comes the sound of two men's loud voices off-camera above the din of the party. Then, Jason widens the view, maybe because he heard the voices or because he didn't want to make it look like he was focusing on the girl. After a few seconds, the man I now know is Brett stumbles backward into the frame with his arms extended, his fists clenched. Max falls into the frame behind him and grabs the material of Brett's shirt with both hands. That's when Brett punches Max with a right hook, and Max slides like an acrobat doing a backflip over the metal railing into the water.

The music is so loud; people are still drinking and dancing, raising their glasses, singing along to the lyrics. They probably didn't even hear the splash. But then, as soon as Max goes into the water, everything goes silent. The music is turned off abruptly, and everybody freezes in mid-motion like they're playing a game where they're not allowed to move when the music stops. At this point, Jason has the phone down at his waist, but the video camera is still rolling. It is tilted at a funny angle and aimed sideways at the waterway at the stern of the boat. You can see a small motorboat approaching someone, presumably Max, who is flailing his arms above his head in the water. Someone on the boat has a small spotlight on him. The boat pulls up next to the struggling man, and a life preserver is thrown to him. Then hands reach down and yank the person and the life preserver out of the water just as Ripple is pulling away. Through the silence, you hear: *We're out of here.* After that, the camera cuts off.

It made sense to me now that Jason knew what he did from viewing this video, not from seeing it with his own eyes. There was so much chaos at the moment; it's easy to imagine that Jason was not focusing on what was happening in the distance with Max and the boat that pulled up next to him. Luckily, the camera was focusing on it and created a permanent record of what happened as long as Jason didn't erase it.

I kept replaying it over and over in my head, trying to pick up new details, something I may have missed. I wished that Jason trusted me enough to send me the video so that I could save it on a USB and give it to Kojak to give to the Attorney General's Office. Whatever was happening here was bigger than Jason and Damien. It was also way bigger than me.

The one thing I couldn't wrap my head around was Stella's involvement. Maybe it was just a coincidence that she brought Jason, Damien, and Max together to help load trucks at the turtle rescue. Maybe this had nothing to do with what happened to Max. *Or maybe it did.*

I got to The Last Straw Café after the lunch rush. A hostess took me to a table with a perfect view of the water. I couldn't help but think about the juxtaposition between the beauty of the place and the tragedy that had happened here. I wasn't sure how Dawn would react to my third visit. At this point, I really didn't care. It was clear to me that Stella knowingly misidentified the missing Marine, Ted Barton, as Max, and that she was somehow involved in this turtle rescue project that brought together several of the key players in this case. She was afraid of something, and I needed to know what that something was.

In addition, the strange note referencing "SHELL games" clearly had something to do with the turtle shells being loaded onto that truck bound for Florida. But what was the connection? That's what I had to find out.

After I studied the menu for a moment, I ordered a piece of quiche, a side salad, and a sparkling water. Dawn eventually came out of the kitchen to bus the dirty tables left over from the lunch rush. After a minute or so, I caught her eye. She hesitated but then put down the stack of dishes she was holding and came over to my table.

"Hey, Dawn, how are you? Thought I'd come back. I enjoyed it so much last week," I said, trying to keep things casual. But I knew I sounded lame after the difficult conversation we had just a few days ago when I confronted her about Stella's involvement in the case.

She eyed me warily and wiped her wet hands on the front of her apron.

"Look, I'm not sure what your deal is, but my daughter is a mess. I have no idea what's going on. Like I told you the other day, I can't help you. She won't even talk to me, let alone the cops."

Despite her defensiveness, I sensed an opening. I had already told her when I visited the restaurant Sunday that I thought Stella might be in danger. I knew that this had tugged at her heartstrings. I just needed to pull on them a little tighter now.

"Well, I've learned a few more things that might help *us* figure out what's going on here."

Mother to mother, I thought. It was my way in. I motioned for her to sit in the empty chair across the table from me. Reluctantly, she pulled out the chair and sat down.

"Go on."

"Well, did you know she was involved with the turtle hospital?"

"Yes, she and Max both started volunteering there in high school and then continued. Of course, she was in college and graduate school out of state and then got the job in Oak City, so she was less hands-on in the past few years. But she was still involved."

"Specifically, I recently learned that she was involved in getting the shells of turtles that died donated to a museum in Florida; she organized the shipping. And she got Max and two other guys to help load the trucks."

"And?"

"Well, it may mean nothing. I don't really know what it means."

"So, why bring it up?" Dawn said, sounding exacerbated already by our conversation.

"Apparently, there was some anonymous benefactor to the organization who paid for the whole thing—for the trucks, for the shipping, for the guys who loaded it."

"Okay, so big deal."

"Did Stella ever mention who the big donors were to the group?"

With this, Dawn got very quiet and looked out at the ocean as if the answer might be there, floating on the crest of an incoming wave. I waited patiently. I had a feeling that she was on the precipice of telling me something important, even if it wasn't the exact answer to my question.

"Look, Stella has secrets. There's *a lot* she doesn't share with me. All I know is that she had a boyfriend, an older man. She didn't like to talk about it. I never met him. It could have been *him.* He could have been the donor. She never told me his name. She slipped once and said his nickname, but I can't remember it. It had a nautical angle to it. It was corny."

I considered this revelation for a moment. *Stella Avery had a secret boyfriend.* So, maybe whatever was going on had to do with him? But why in the world would he have a beef with Max? A beef so intense that it led to his death. Something about this whole thing wasn't adding up. One thing that I did know for sure was that I had pushed Dawn as far as I could. I reached across the table and put my hand on hers.

"Will you let me treat you to a glass of wine? Let's stop talking about this stuff for right now. Neither of us really knows anything for sure. But I do know what it's like to be a mom and to worry. I have a very anxious 12-year-old son who is at his first sleepaway camp. I'm trying not to think about it."

With that, I was no longer the journalist digging for information; I was just a mom sharing a moment with another mom.

25

SECRETS AND LIES

THAT NIGHT OVER THE PHONE, I told Kojak everything I had recently learned. He agreed with me that Stella was a key player in whatever was going on. Unlike me, he wasn't willing to write off Jason and Damien as bit players yet. He promised me he would talk to his guy at the Attorney General's Office again the next day and see where everything stood with their investigation.

Almost as soon as I hung up, Zack called. I briefed him on what I had told Kojak, but in far less detail. I was exhausted and not in the mood to share every gritty nuance of the new developments. But he got the gist of it, that Stella appeared to be in on it with at least one other person, if not multiple people.

"I don't like you being there all alone. I don't like it at all. I think I should come down there."

There he was again, showing up for me. Even if he didn't really mean it, it was sweet that he wanted to play my white knight and rush to Cape Mayson to protect me.

"I'm good. Seriously, this isn't my first rodeo."

"I get it. But someone tried to run you over with a boat and tried to burn your house down. It seems pretty serious to me."

"There is that."

"So, it's settled. I'll get on the first flight in the morning."

"Nope, honestly. I promise I won't take any more chances. I will keep a low profile until this whole thing shakes out. Kojak is on it. There's nothing to worry about!"

"You are stubborn."

"You're just figuring that out?"

I made a decaf coffee and settled down at my computer to take care of a lot of unfinished business that had been piling up. First, I sent an email to Kai about the podcast and apologized for being out of touch. I told him that I was caught up in a possible murder investigation, but I hoped to be at one hundred percent by next week, ready to focus on *our* project.

As I scrolled through the long list of emails, one caught my eye from the twins at camp. *How had I missed this?* I was nervous as I opened it, hoping they weren't telling me something was wrong. But as soon as I read the first line, I knew everything was okay.

Dear Mom:

We just wanted to let you know we are having a really great time at camp. Both of us are making a lot of friends. I learned how to kayak, so maybe you can take us to Cape Mayson before we go back to school. Miranda is very popular with the boys. She keeps getting asked to the dances by guys in my cabin, which is a little creepy, but I'm learning to deal with it. The music program is really good here. I like the teacher a lot. I am writing a new song that I think you will really like. I hope you're having a great time and not working too hard, as usual. And by the way, the reason I am on email is that I'm taking a computer class. If you write back, they will print it out and give it to me, so don't say anything too weird because other people might read it. Can't wait to see you in August!

Love always, Blake

Suddenly, I was tearing up—my sweet boy. I hadn't realized how much I missed them until this moment. Parenting was like that. One minute you were counting the years until they left for college; the next, you were sitting on the end of their beds, crying into their comforters. I had been so caught up in the investigation that I hadn't given myself time or permission to miss them. I needed to hold onto this feeling so that when they came home and left dirty clothes on the floor or dishes in the sink, I could remember how much I wanted them with me, even when they made my life exponentially more complicated.

After Adam died, having to be both mother and father was exhausting in ways I couldn't have imagined. There is no time off when you're a single parent. This sabbatical and their time at camp was the first time I had been truly alone since Adam's death. It was good to have a period of self-reflection, but I also knew I was better off with my kids than I was without them, no matter how hard it was parenting them alone.

I wrote a quick email back to Blake that the camp could print out and he could read without being embarrassed. I tried to make it upbeat without any trace of worry hidden between the lines. My heart was simultaneously full, knowing that my babies were growing up and empty, knowing they would eventually leave me for good.

I finally closed my laptop and headed for bed. I lay there, unable to turn my brain off. I wondered if I had confused the decaf and the regular coffee. Dawn's words about Stella were bouncing around in my brain—*secrets, older man, nickname, nautical.* It was something about the nickname that was keeping me up. Each time I was about to fall asleep, I started to run through a list of possible nautical nicknames, playing on words, the same type of wordplay that people used when they created boat names like "Knot Guilty." Just as I was dozing off for the third or fourth time, I heard one word clear as a bell. It was as if someone were standing next to the bed talking. I sat up quickly and scanned the room. I was alone. I got up and double-checked the deadbolt and the chain on the door. It was locked.

As I slid back under the covers, I turned the word over in my mind. *Cappy.* That was the word I heard alone in my bedroom as I drifted off to sleep. It had to be short for captain. But there were a whole lot of captains in a beach town. Which one was Stella's captain?

26

CONNECTING THE DOTS

I SLEPT HARD AFTER THE MIND GAMES and awoke the next morning to a knock on my door. I was so sleep-deprived that I was sure the knock was part of my dream. But then it got louder, and I realized someone was truly there.

I threw on my robe and stepped into my flip-flops. After my scare overnight, imagining that someone had been in the apartment whispering in my ear, I wasn't eager to answer the door when I wasn't expecting anyone. Not unlike answering phone calls from unknown numbers, I felt no obligation to ever open my door to strangers. On the rare occasions when the twins were home alone, I told them to never answer the door if they didn't know the person. This was the moment when I needed to take my own advice.

I shuffled to the front hall and peered through the peephole. I had to rub my eyes and refocus before I looked again to make sure he was really standing there. It was *him.* I couldn't believe it. I quickly released the chain and unlocked the door, almost thinking he might vanish when I opened it, that I was just imagining him, that it was an extension of my dream. But when I flung open the door, he was still there, looking sheepish with a small backpack slung over his shoulder.

"You should know I'm not a good listener," he said, obviously referring to me telling him not to come.

Surprising both of us, I threw my arms around Zack and held on. In the same way, missing the kids had hit me when I read Blake's email from camp; Zack's presence in my doorway confirmed my need for him in a way that blindsided me. We stayed that way for a long time, me on my tippy toes in my furry robe, hugging him, holding on tight as if I hadn't seen him in years when it had only been two days.

As I pulled away from his embrace, Zack cupped my face with both of his hands and gave me a real kiss on the lips, not like the ones he had previously given me. This was not a peck but a serious kiss that told me exactly how he felt about me. I didn't pull away.

"You're crazy; you know that?" I finally said, standing back to look at him there in my doorway with his backpack and his disheveled hair like he had just hiked hundreds of miles to get here. "Come in. I'm guessing you want coffee?"

I was trying to stay cool.

"That's what I came for. My Keurig is on the blink at my house, and the coffee shop down the street from me is a little overpriced. Figured this was a better deal," Zack grinned.

I led him into the kitchen, and he sat at the table watching me as I made coffee and scrambled eggs and cut up some fresh fruit for us. While the eggs were cooking, I walked around the apartment, opening all the shades and windows to let the sea air waft in and mix with the strong aroma of breakfast.

"I can't believe you're really here."

"I told you I was coming. You just didn't hear me. I'm not easily deterred."

"I can see that. It's weird because I had a dream, or something like a dream, last night where I was working out some of the investigation in my head. I heard a voice, a voice that sounded like it was coming from someone standing right next to my bed. Anyway, it was creepy. But my takeaway is that I think Stella was involved with an older man who went by "Cappy." So, now I just need to figure out who that is."

"Interesting. Well, I did learn that little runaround boat, Knot Guilty, is registered to Mark Maron's son, Phil. I mean, obviously,

Perry has access to it, but it does add another layer to this whole thing. Phil could be the guy who tried to run you down on your paddleboard."

I pictured the framed photo of Mark Maron and his mini-me that I had seen in his bathroom the night of the paddleboard incident. *Phil.*

"But why? What did Max do that made someone so angry?"

"Maybe it wasn't what he did; maybe it was what he saw. Maybe he learned something, some dirt that could hurt the person or persons who ultimately killed him."

I thought about how long it had been since I had someone to talk through cases with. Even though Adam wasn't a journalist, he had listened to me patiently many nights when I tried to unravel the details of a complicated case. Often, he offered theories or suggestions. They were usually spot on.

Zack had the added benefit of being an investigator. His brain worked a lot like mine, pulling apart the small kinks in a case like one might pick at the stubborn knot in the chain of a thin necklace with a safety pin, working at it until it finally came loose.

Our phones were on the table between us. Mine was on vibrate, but when it started bouncing up and down, I turned it over and saw that it was Kojak calling. I hit answer and put him on speakerphone.

"Hey there. You're on speakerphone. Zack is here with me."

"Of course, he is. That's good. You guys sitting down? Hold onto your hats."

Kojak always talked this way, in cliches from throwback television crime dramas. But he was no actor. He was the real deal.

"What's up?"

"So, apparently, your little friend Stella has been using her prescription pad pretty liberally to write prescriptions for opiates for fake patients. She's been amassing a huge amount of the stuff and then funneling it to an individual or individuals in Cape Mayson who are transporting and selling them. We think Max found out about this and threatened to go to the police."

I sat quietly with this news, feeling an immediate sadness for Dawn. In the short time I had known her, the one thing I was sure of was that she loved her daughter and wanted what was best for her. This would be devastating news.

And then it hit me—*from one Cappy to another.* That was the caption of Perry Spotz and Mark Maron in front of the Ripple. It stood to reason that Phil Maron was also a "Cappy," so he was most likely the older man Dawn had referred to as Stella's secret boyfriend. He was at least ten years older than her. It was all starting to make sense.

"So, now the AG's Office has officially opened an investigation into her and her possible involvement in Max Prince's death. And that's not all. My buddy told Arnold Willis they would slap him with an obstruction of justice charge for deep-sixing their investigation on account of his kid's involvement if he didn't start helping. Willis is now wisely playing ball. Turned over everything they got and more. Kid, thanks to your intuition that something didn't smell right, this thing might just get solved."

"Kojak, there's one more thing that I've figured out. I think Stella was involved with Phil Maron, Mark Maron's son, the guy who owned the boat. My guess is that he was the one in charge of transporting the opioids out of state. And I'm pretty sure I know how they did it—in massive sea turtle shells in the back of a truck bound for Florida."

I could see the relief on Zack's face. It was a subtle shift in his expression like he was releasing a mask of tension that he had carefully designed to hide his concern for me. Now, there was light in his eyes. State investigators were involved. They would get to the bottom of it with help from all the groundwork I had laid. I could bow out, or at least that's what he probably thought, that I would walk away now satisfied that the case was in good hands. He obviously still didn't know me that well. For me, it wasn't over yet. I needed to make sure justice was served for both the dead men.

"That's great news, Kojak. Thanks for everything you've done to get this to the right people. What about the missing Marine, Ted Barton?"

"They're looking into that, too. Seems like the employee Zack found out about, the guy at Windstream who cremated the Marine, is suddenly singing like a canary. He admitted to being part of the scheme to switch the bodies. Zack's buddy with the good intentions, figured out that what he initially thought was just an innocent mix-up was a cover-up. He put Max in the casket for the wake once he learned his true identity. The inside guy who was part of it, he's been to prison for drugs before, and he does not want to go back. There's no way he's going to get out of this blameless, but if he keeps talking, he'll get the best deal possible. Zack's buddy is pretty much off the hook. He did the right thing, returning Max to his family. He will have to testify about how everything went down, but he's fully cooperating."

"Wow, it's all coming together. That's amazing. Hopefully, there will be justice for both Ted and Max."

"Right on, kid, thanks to you."

I hung up, feeling a huge weight lift from my shoulders and evaporate into the early morning salty air that was now flowing through the apartment.

"What now?" I asked Zack as I eased onto his lap.

"I got you a present."

"Really? You didn't have to do that."

He took my hand and pulled me onto the balcony. He handed me my binoculars and pointed to the lawn by the pool area. With a head nod, he instructed me to look through them at the spot where he was pointing. When I finally focused on the spot, I saw a bright blue paddleboard with a large yellow bow in the center. Then we shared our second real kiss on the balcony. This one lasted a little bit longer. I felt lighter somehow, and giddy, like I was a teenager.

"What do you think?" He asked, pulling away from the kiss and putting his hand on the small of my back. At first, I thought he was asking me how the kiss was. Then I realized he meant the paddleboard.

"I think it's perfect." I felt the redness creeping up my neck into my cheeks. What if he thought *I* was talking about the kiss instead of the paddleboard? "Why don't you give it a spin?"

"I think I will."

This was a moment I would later replay in my head for months to come.

27

KIDNAPPED

THE WATERWAY WAS LIKE A FREEWAY—recreational boaters full of families and college students headed out for a day of fun, fishermen returning from a morning on the ocean, sailors, paddleboarders, kayakers—everyone trying to make their way through crisscrossing wakes.

Despite the unsettled water, my new board was sliding gracefully across the surface like butter melting across a hot frying pan. Still, I wanted to be away from the chaos. So, I decided to head out into the marsh. While there were no docks to provide a safety blanket, the water was relatively calm and shallow. Few boats could pass through the marsh at low tide, and there were many short tributaries for me to explore. Plus, the marsh was the best place to observe wildlife, especially the birds that tended to stay away from the more high-traffic areas.

I knew I had a perpetual smile on my face. My entire body was smiling. Here I was on a new paddleboard courtesy of Zack. He was continuing to surprise me with the way he paid attention. Zack seemed to know exactly what I needed and when I needed it. When I opened the door and saw him, I realized that when it came to him, my walls were officially coming down.

The marsh was deliciously quiet. I could still hear the din of boats rushing by in the distance behind me, but the harder I paddled, the farther the sounds drifted away. To my left, a blue heron stood regally at attention on a black oyster bed. Round, red jellyfish with ghost-like tentacles flowing behind them bobbed in the water just beneath the surface near the edges of my board. The sun warmed my face and shoulders. All was right in the world.

I had been so busy with my own personal drama that I hadn't been paying close attention to the news. Janie had left me a message saying there was a hurricane screaming up the coast. One of the weather models had it hitting Florida and then cutting across the state into the Gulf. Another model had it skirting Florida and then directly hitting North Carolina. A third model had it missing land altogether and heading out to sea. Basically, it was too early to tell, but she wanted to know if I might be available to be on standby in case it started to look like North Carolina was in the storm's direct path.

I had covered every hurricane since I started at Channel 8. It was so different from crime reporting, but it was a good different. There was nothing like the rush of standing out in one-hundred-plus mile an hour wind, holding onto a tree, ducking flying pieces of metal siding or roof shingles, and getting pelted with rain and sand to get your adrenaline flowing.

As I paddled into the rays of what seemed like perpetual sunlight and an endless blue sky, it was hard to imagine a storm could be on the way. But it was always like this just before a storm—stunningly beautiful, *until it wasn't*. The roar and intensity of a hurricane were like nothing else I had ever experienced. And while most people ran from them, evacuating the island, journalists ran right into them. I reminded myself to call Janie and let her know that, of course, I was available to help if they needed me.

The thought about calling Janie was the last thing I remembered before the pain. It's one thing when you know what's causing the pain, but when it comes out of nowhere, it's not only physically jarring but mentally destabilizing. I felt a sharp blow to my back. I immediately fell into the water. Somehow, I managed to pull the inflatable cord on the compact life jacket I wore on a belt around my waist. *Don't drown; I* heard a voice say. It was a woman's voice, not my own, yet familiar—my *mother*. Patty was speaking to me. But she was dead, so I knew this had to be a terrible sign.

I woke up in the darkness. I could feel that my ankles and wrists were bound together. There was something over me, a light blanket, and the smell of fish. I was rocking not-so-gently, and I could hear water sloshing and a line clanking against a pole. I had to be on a boat. A sailboat? How long had I been here? Hours? Days?

Based on the almost complete darkness, I assumed the boat was anchored out in the middle of the waterway, not in a marina. Often, sailboat owners dropped anchor in the center of a protected channel during a storm. It was safer than putting a boat in a marina and risking that it might come loose and hit the docks or other boats.

My back ached from where I had been hit by some blunt object. It didn't feel like anything was broken, just severely bruised. I was still in my bathing suit, which was dry now. I felt around my body the best I could with my bound hands to see If I still had on the dry pouch that I wore around my neck that carried my phone. Predictably, it was gone.

My mind suddenly started racing as I fully took in my predicament. Someone had put me here. Someone who wanted me out of the way. But who? Who would do this? Then, horrified, I thought of Zack, alone in the apartment, waiting for me to come back. When I didn't return, he would surely panic, blame himself, and probably come looking for me. Hopefully, he would call the police and get some help. But how would they find me here?

I thought about Blake and Miranda. They had already lost one parent; they didn't need to lose another one. These were the same thoughts that went through my head a few months earlier when a killer had held a gun to my head. At that time, I promised the universe I would get off this dangerous path of investigating violent crimes and concentrate on raising my children. My promise clearly hadn't lasted that long, and now, here I was.

I took a few deep breaths, pretending that I wasn't being held captive and that I was really in a yoga class. I knew panicking would not help me come up with a solution. I had to have a clear head. I realized that while my ankles seemed to be bound with plastic zip ties, my wrists were bound only with duct tape. Whoever did this did it quickly and haphazardly. The tape was wrapped multiple times but in a hurried fashion so that it bunched in several places. I decided that if I could free my hands, I could then surely find something to cut the plastic ties from my ankles.

I remembered an experiment from science class in high school about how much heat duct tape could handle. Part of the experiment was testing the different grades. In short, not all duct tape is created equal. We put a variety of tape through a series of experiments where we used different brands and applied variable intensities of heat to see if the tape would still stick. Not every brand withstood the heat. Some of them failed.

I took my bound wrists and put them in between my thighs. I was already sweating in the closed cabin with no air conditioning. I knew there was a chance someone was on the boat, guarding me. But I had listened carefully for a few minutes and didn't hear anything; I prayed that I was alone. There was a chance someone would be coming to check on me. I had to get away before that happened.

As the sweat dripped down my legs, I continued to press them into my wrists. Slowly, I could feel the poorly wrapped layers of tape beginning to shift, to slide up and down on my wrists. I then started to visualize the duct tape slipping away from my arms. In yoga, the teacher always told us to "Visualize the life you want" or "Visualize the world you want to live in." I figured why not visualize the outcome I wanted.

While I could feel the duct tape loosening, the movement had plateaued. I had managed to get it off my wrists and into the middle of my hands, but now, it would not budge. There were so many layers. I thought about what you do when you're trying to open something, and you don't have scissors or a knife. Then, it came to me—*teeth, use your teeth.*

I brought my hands and the sticky mess up to my mouth and started tugging at the layers with my teeth. At first, nothing happened; then, I could begin to feel them release. The layers began to slowly unravel as I gnawed at the frayed ends where the pieces had been sloppily secured. Finally, having done as much as I could with my teeth, I bent my knees, placed my hands below my bound feet, and with one huge push, I forced the failing ring of tape away from my hands.

I stopped and listened again, making sure I was alone. I sat up and looked around. Through a small porthole window, I could see lights in the distance. This confirmed that I was moored in the waterway, far from land. I couldn't risk turning on any lights in case someone was watching. So, I crawled on my knees, dragging my feet behind me, opening drawers in the cabin as I went. Finally, my hand felt what I was looking for, the smooth rubber handle of a small knife, a paring knife. I rolled back over onto my back and touched the blade to the plastic zip ties, and started sawing.

The boat was really rocking now, and the wind was beginning to pick up. I had to be careful not to cut myself as I gingerly sawed through the plastic holding my ankles together. It suddenly occurred to me that maybe there really was a hurricane on the way. Even days out from a storm, the outer bands started to kick up the surf and the wind as it approached. I didn't need a hurricane to make this situation any more complicated.

After a few seconds of sawing, the plastic fell to the ground, freeing me. With the tiny fragments of light coming in through the porthole, I was able to see well enough to crawl to the ladder that I believed would take me to the deck. I knew it was a risk to climb the ladder and push the door open, hoping no one would be there, but it was a chance I would have to take if I wanted to escape.

Now that I was no longer lying supine, the pain was beginning to radiate from my back throughout the rest of my body, floating down my limbs like a river of hot lava, making me wince with each movement. I grabbed the first rung of the ladder and decided it was going to take everything I had in me to climb it. Suddenly, faces started appearing to me—the twins, Zack, Louise, Kojak, my mother, even Roger. I knew that I was hallucinating, that they were not there with me, but it was like they were silently pulling me through, telling me I could do this.

With my ghostly cheering section on my shoulder, I scaled the ladder and forced open the door. I was greeted with an empty deck and a sail whipping furiously in the wind. I quickly scanned the length of the sailboat. *I was alone.*

I looked at the shoreline and tried to figure out how far I was from land, but at night it was much harder to assess. The pain was starting to radiate throughout my body again from the nexus on my back. I surveyed the dark water. It was too choppy. I would never make it if I tried to swim to shore.

I walked to the bow and then to the stern, looking for something, *anything,* that I could use as a flotation device. There was a life ring but allowing my legs to dangle in the ocean at night with the potential of sharks lurking beneath the black water didn't seem prudent. I silently wished I had taken Belle up on her offer to send me to sailing camp at the Jersey Shore when I was a teenager. But even if I did know the rudimentary components of sailing, chances are that I would not be able to captain a boat of this size safely to land.

I was sitting on a padded bench at the rear of the boat stewing over my situation when I saw a long, large, zipped canvas bag attached with bungee cords to the railing. I jumped up, wincing in pain, and unzipped the bag. Inside, there were two paddleboards and two paddles. Just like that, I was back in business.

I found a life jacket stowed beneath one of the padded benches and put it on. I knew what I was about to embark on was dangerous at best, but I also knew that staying here in the place where the kidnapper, or kidnappers, had ditched me was even more dangerous.

I climbed down to the swim platform at the stern of the boat and gently slid the board into the water. I had already attached the rubber leash to my ankle to tether me to the board. Given the height of the surf, I realized that standing up would not be an option. I would have to stay crouched on my knees for balance. I struggled to get into a strong position for paddling, one that wouldn't make the pain in my back worse than it already was. I pushed away from the sailboat with my paddle and headed toward the light.

I decided I would head straight for land. Just like I had ended up on Mark Maron's dock after the near-miss with the speeding boat, I would end up safely on someone's dock. But this time, I would not go inside and get on cozy clothes and drink a glass of water; I would ask them to call Zack and 911, in that order.

I was struggling to stay on the board as the waves cascaded over the top of my legs, threatening to throw me off balance. The night air and the water were warm, but I was shaking from the constant pain in my back that kept shooting up my spine. The water was dark and angry. It looked like it might just swallow me whole. I wondered if I had made a poor decision. Maybe I should have stayed there until it got light and tried to flag someone down. Maybe I should have looked for a radio to call the coast guard for help. But the time for maybes was gone. I had made a decision, and now I was executing my plan, paddling in the direction of safety.

I felt like I was in a washing machine—three strokes forward, two back. The faces of my helpers appeared again like spirits swirling in the air above my head. And there was that voice again, my mother's voice. As clear as a bell, I heard her say: *You can do this.* And so, I did.

As I got closer to the shoreline, the homes were starting to come into focus. It was a familiar group of fancy houses in a row along the waterway. Harbor Light. I could see the long, elegant docks, manicured lawns, and floor-to-ceiling windows. It was the part of Cape Mayson that had been gentrified—old homes were torn down, and big, new modern ones were built in their place. There was no pretense to make these houses look old to fit in with the classic colonial architecture of the original town. They represented a new beginning and new money.

I was losing steam, but the sight of the homes gave me renewed hope that I was indeed going to make it. I focused on the closest dock straight ahead of me and started to paddle furiously, using the last bit of energy I could muster to get me there. My legs were numb now after having been folded beneath me for a good thirty minutes or more, but their numbness was nothing in comparison to the pain which had now permanently settled in my entire core.

Ten more strokes and I would be there. I was looking down, concentrating on my labored paddles, willing myself to make each one smooth and strong despite my weakened state. I looked up just in time to realize that I was about to glide right into a dock, and it wasn't just any dock; it was Mark Maron's dock. How could this be happening to me again? What were the odds? And then I realized they were very good. If the Marons were responsible for kidnapping me, it made sense that they had put me in a moored sailboat in a straight line from their house so they could keep an eye on me.

I caught the edge of the dock with my right hand and continued to hold onto the paddle with my left hand. I knew that I needed to get out of here, but at the same time, I needed to know what was going on.

Shaking, I grabbed the ladder at the side of the floating dock. I kicked the board away into the surf along with the paddle, letting them float out into the darkness. At this point, worrying about the property of my kidnapper was not my concern. I crawled up onto the deck and crept behind a lounge chair. As I peered around the edge of the chair, I could just make out through the massive glass windows two men sitting at a table in the kitchen. Although they were far away, I could tell that one of the men was Mark Maron, and the other one looked just like him but much younger. It had to be his son, Phil.

What now? Mark had been so kind to me when the boat almost hit me. Was that all an act? If I believed in that version of Mark, I would run down the dock to the house, tell him what had happened to me, and ask him for help. But something in my gut told me that was not wise. I didn't know Phil; maybe *he* was the bad guy, and his father was clean. Or maybe, they were both bad guys.

I couldn't risk being wrong this time. There was no way to get away from the house except to go down the dock and cross the lawn to the road. But how in the world would I be able to travel the length of the dock in full view of the glass house without them seeing me? I decided I would have to crawl and hope for the best. I prayed that they would continue to be so wrapped up in their conversation and their drinks that they wouldn't notice me.

Drinks? There were several beer bottles sitting in front of the men. That's when I remembered that Mark Maron was supposedly a recovering alcoholic who had presumably met Perry Spotz in Alcoholics Anonymous and sponsored him. He had even set him up in business with the charter boat. Clearly, Mark was not the person he pretended to be.

As I made my way along the dock, I tried to stay as low as possible. Spray from the rising surf was pelting me in the face, stinging my skin like small needles being thrust into my cheeks. I did the fireman's crawl that we learned in grade school to get out of a burning house and stay below the smoke. The pain in my back was still there, but it was way down on my list of problems. When I got midway down the dock, I took a deep breath, realizing that I was almost there. Once I got to the lawn, I would sprint behind the bushes, out to the street, and then run as fast as I could to another home for help.

That's when the security lights came on. Floodlights on the front of the house suddenly lit up, blinding me, illuminating the entire dock in a wave of crushing light. There was no way they didn't see me now. I had two choices—go over the side of the dock back into the dark, choppy water, or face my demons and charge ahead through the yard. I chose the latter, giving myself better odds at running in the dark than swimming with sharks.

I jumped up and sprinted down the dock, my bare feet slipping on the smooth boards. I could see that the table was empty now. They must be on their way outside. I didn't let this break my stride. I would go left through the bushes and out to the road. As I neared the end of the long dock, I saw both men standing there stoically. Mark's arms were folded across his chest. The younger man had a hand on his hip. I thought for a second that maybe I had misjudged the situation. Maybe they were not the bad guys after all, and they thought some wacko woman had climbed up on their dock and was now running full speed in their direction for no apparent reason. That's when I saw the gun in Phil's hand and realized I had been right all along.

My cop friends always told me to run in a zig-zag pattern when faced with a gun. This was because most shooters weren't good enough to hit a moving target. Sure, they might catch you in the leg, or in the arm, or even in your butt, but chances are they won't hit your head or your heart. I had nothing else to go with at this point, so I charged right through the middle of the two men, to their great surprise, and then zig-zagged through the bushes out to the road, never looking back.

I heard shots in the distance, but I just kept running, adrenaline pumping through my veins. This was not a marathon but a sprint to safety. Nothing was going to stop me. My mother was on my shoulder again, whispering in my ear. *Run!* As I rounded the corner at the end of the street, I saw blue lights coming in my direction. Their sirens were a dull wail, getting louder as I moved closer to them. I stopped and waved my hands above my head. One police car screeched to the side of the road skidding into the gravel right-of- way as the others swerved around him and passed us, heading in the direction where the sound of the gunfire had come from. The passenger side door of the patrol car that had stopped flew open. It was Zack. Not a ghostly floating head hallucination of Zack, but the real Zack. I collapsed into his arms again, and that was the last thing I remembered.

28

TRUTH

I RUBBED MY EYES, wondering if I had slept in my contacts again because they were so fuzzy and agitated. Reluctantly, I reached in each eye and pulled out a gummy contact that had indeed been in there all night. I looked around, and it took me a minute to realize that I was back in my beach condo, in my bed, in my fuzzy white robe.

The events of the night before were starting to come back to me in drips like pieces of a long-ago memory I was trying desperately to hold onto. Did it all really happen? Or was it a dream? Then, I heard a noise. I shuddered and pulled the covers up to my neck. Was this some sick game? Were the kidnappers here with me in my house?

That's when I saw him in the doorway—*Zack.* His hands were full, and he had a bashful smile on his face.

"Just what the doctor ordered. An ice pack for your back, Advil for the pain, and hot tea for your nerves."

"Not sure any of that is going to be enough. I feel like I've been hit by a truck," I groaned, pushing up to my elbows, trying to take him in without the help of my contacts.

"Actually the paramedic we saw last night wanted to bring you right to the hospital, but you insisted on coming home and promised you would see a doctor today. Your back is just one big bruise, and your ankles are all cut up."

"Paramedic? I don't remember any of that."

"You pretty much collapsed and were in and out of consciousness. Severe dehydration. They gave you fluids in the ambulance last night and let me bring you home. Today, we need to get you to the doctor and to the police station to do an interview with investigators about what happened."

"What did happen?"

"Well, it appears that the guy that owned the charter boat, Mark Maron, and his son Phil, were moving drugs to Florida, opiates. You were right. They were using the turtle shells to do it. The guy that died, Max, he found out about it—threatened to expose them. They decided to have him killed, but they wanted to make it look like an accident. So, they staged the thing on the charter boat, got Brett drunk and fired up so he would pick a fight with Max. But they didn't want to take any chances—that's why they picked Max up, plucked him out of the water, and shot him."

"But then they didn't have a good plan for how to make it look like a drowning with a bullet in his head."

"No, they didn't, but they lucked out when you found the dead Marine. That's when they came up with the idea to use the guy at the funeral home to switch the bodies."

"So, I'm guessing Perry was involved too?"

"Investigators don't think so. They think he was an unwitting pawn in the whole thing. Just worried about the liability of losing someone on a charter boat trip; that's why he freaked out and bailed. It wouldn't have mattered if he had stayed. The Marons plucked Max out of the water quickly and took off."

"So, who encouraged Brett to pick the fight with Max?"

"Stella Avery."

"Why would she do that?"

"I'll get back to that in a minute."

"Okay, so, this drug thing, how did it work?"

"They're still trying to figure out all the details, but it looks like they were moving prescription pills in those shells through the turtle rescue place. That's how Max found out about it. He told

Jason. Jason was totally freaked out. Jason eventually told Damien, who told him to stay out of it, but then when Max died, both Jason and Damien wanted some justice for him. They were too scared to go to the police; that's why they came to you with their weird little head games, like the note in the cigarette pack, which apparently came from Damien, by the way. Jason didn't know about it."

"Damien has watched way too much Netflix."

"For sure. So, Stella was obviously bringing in the drugs since she had access to them?"

"Stella had connections as a physician's assistant. First, she was just writing and filling bogus prescriptions; then she hooked up with a pharmaceutical rep who was feeding them to her in large quantities in return for a cut of the profits."

"Wow, that's pretty messed up. Why would a young woman with a good job and so much promise do something like that?"

"It's the oldest reason in the book—*love.*"

"Phil!"

"Nope. That's what we assumed at first, but it was *Mark*. She was having an affair with Mark Maron."

I silently remembered Dawn Avery's words, that her daughter had a "secret relationship" with an older man, and that it had "changed her." *Cappy.*

"Okay, so now I know the rest of the story. What about me? What happened to me?"

"Well, that first attack on you when you were on your paddleboard, that was a warning from Phil. They had it all set up to happen in front of Mark's dock so he would look like a good guy, and you would not suspect him of anything. But then they decided things were getting too hot; you were asking too many questions, threatening to blow their cover. They had to get rid of you. But it wasn't going to be that easy. Your body—the body of a television reporter—couldn't exactly just float up on the beach without anyone asking major questions. So, they nailed you with a baseball bat, took you to the sailboat, tied you up, and they were working on their next move."

"What was their next move?"

"Good question. We'll probably never know."

"I don't think I want to know."

"Me neither."

"This is a lot to take in," I said, sinking back down into my bed, exhaling into the soft comfort of my pillow.

"I know it is. But you deserve to know the truth. Without you, none of this would have been revealed. You gave investigators all the pieces; they just arranged them until the puzzle fit together. Remember this case was closed, ruled an accident, until you got involved and started pushing."

Zack was sitting on the edge of my bed now, brushing errant strands of hair from my forehead. He reached down and kissed me on the top of my head like I was a child. He cradled my hand with his free hand.

"I'm just so glad you're okay," he said, his eyes filling up with tears. "I'm so mad at myself for letting you go out alone yesterday. What was I thinking?"

I reached up and stroked his shoulder, taken aback by my own show of raw emotion.

"You can't blame yourself. You should know before we go any further that I am someone who makes my own decisions, good and bad. I'm not very good at listening to what other people tell me to do."

Zack smiled and nuzzled his head into the pillow next to me, cradling my head with his hand.

"Okay, missy. Need to get you in the shower and dressed. I lined up a doctor's appointment for you at eleven, and then we need to go straight to the police station for an interview. The State Bureau of Investigation has temporarily set up shop in a conference room at the Cape Mayson Police Department. They need a full statement from you about everything—last night and all the things you have uncovered along the way."

Zack reached down and helped me out of bed, his hands around my waist, as I walked with great pain in the direction of the bathroom.

"You are not going to help me shower. I can do that myself," I said as I shuffled towards the stall.

"Okay, suit yourself. I'll just get busy in the kitchen making you some breakfast. You can't take Advil on an empty stomach. By the way, did I mention there's a hurricane heading this way? They're evacuating the island tonight. So, we kind of need to get a move on it. I've already packed you a bag. We'll need to head to a hotel inland after we speak with the investigators."

Zack's voice trailed off as the rushing sound of the hot water sprang from the tap above me. It trailed down my injured back like a bandage, temporarily wrapping my pain with its intense heat. Outside, I could hear the wind wailing, rattling the small window in the bathroom. Even knowing a storm was on the way was not enough to dampen my spirits. Max's murder case was solved, and for the first time in a long time, I knew I was right where I was supposed to be, with this man, on an island weathering another storm.

29

THE PERFECT STORM

As EXPECTED, THE DOCTOR TOLD ME my back was severely bruised, but luckily no ribs were broken, and I had no obvious injuries to my organs. He told me to alternate using ice and heat, to take Advil, and maybe have a good stiff drink before bed. He gave me cream for the cuts around my ankles and told me how lucky I was that I hadn't been injured more severely. He also told me to take it easy for a while, which he said with a twinkle in his eyes, fully knowing even from his brief meeting with me that this was not likely to happen.

I left the doctor's office feeling like it was a major waste of time, that I could have gotten the same information online, but Zack left feeling like he had done what he needed to do to make sure I was okay. So, for this reason, I wasn't annoyed about the wasted time.

When we got to the Cape Mayson Police Department, Major Arnold Willis greeted us in the lobby, sheepishly, knowing this was an I-told-you-so moment. But I was exhausted, in pain, and a violent storm was brewing outside. I was in no mood to chastise Willis or anyone else.

He led us to the conference room where a long wooden table sat surrounded by industrial chairs with hard, plastic bucket seats. Willis brought me a padded armchair and a stool for my feet. He could clearly see how much pain I was in. Obviously, the state investigators needed as much information from me as possible since I was the one who had basically solved the case and then became a target for the bad guys. Willis had been warned to play ball or risk an obstruction of justice charge.

I tried to tell them everything I knew from the very beginning. Luckily, my detective boyfriend had taken notes during several of our conversations about the case and was able to fill in the holes and remind me of things when my mind went blank. Willis made sure I had water and asked me multiple times if I wanted a Coke or a cup of coffee, which I politely declined.

While I told the investigators everything they wanted to know, including all the details that I could remember about the kidnapping, there were a few things I wanted to know, too—loose ends that I wanted them to tie up for me so I could wrap my head around everything that had happened.

They told me that Mark and his son Phil had been arrested and that federal authorities were on their way here to open their own investigation into drug trafficking across state lines. Stella had also been arrested, but if she testified against the men, she would likely get a deal and a reduced sentence.

The investigators let it slip that Stella was the one who allowed Max to find out. He saw an email from Phil on her phone that referenced drugs when they were planning the party together. This is when "the Max problem," as Mark apparently referred to it, started. Because it was basically Stella's fault, Mark told her to handle "the Max problem." She came up with the idea of goading Brett to punch him so that he would fall overboard. But Phil didn't trust that Max would drown, so at the last minute, he followed behind in his own boat and scooped Max out of the waterway to finish the job with a bullet.

To my great relief, the Marine's family had been officially notified. Ted Barton's ashes were still at Windstream, and Arnold Willis was planning to personally deliver them to his relatives in Virginia after the storm passed. Of course, they were horrified that he had been cremated without their knowledge and said they intended to sue the Windstream Funeral Home for their role in the debacle.

As we talked, I could see the sky outside getting progressively darker. The wind was furiously rattling the windowpanes, and detached leaves and branches from nearby palm trees were starting to swirl in frantic circles inside the gusts that were blowing by. I felt like the investigators were so entrenched in what they were doing inside the building that they didn't even notice what was going on outside. But I did, and I could see Zack did, too, as he glanced nervously over his shoulder every few minutes to check the deteriorating conditions. Eventually, he stood and put his palm respectfully up in a stop motion in front of the investigator who was interviewing me.

"Detectives, we've been here for three hours. I think it's time to call it a day. She's in a lot of pain, and it looks like all of us need to get off the island as soon as possible. We can resume this after the storm has passed."

The three state detectives, one woman, and two men, collectively glanced out the window at the same time as if they were seeing the weather conditions for the very first time. That's when Willis, who had been in and out of the room the entire time, burst in.

"Folks, apparently the storm has sped up. They've halted the evacuation. If you are here already, you need to shelter in place and ride it out. The drawbridge is closed."

The drawbridge was the only way on and off the island. We were officially trapped.

"You're welcome to stay here. This old building has weathered a lot of storms. Or I'd be happy to get one of my guys to take you back to your place. *But you need to go now.*"

Zack and I looked at each other and nodded in agreement. We would leave the car in the garage at the police department and get it later. It would be safer there than in the open parking lot at the condo. The building I was staying in was a concrete fortress. It was built in 1973 and had never had any major hurricane damage with the exception of some minor flooding in the first-floor units. I was high enough up that I wouldn't need to worry about flooding or flying debris, just wind. And because it was early in hurricane season, I wasn't too concerned about the severity of the storm. But I knew Major Willis was right—we had to go now, or we'd be trapped here at the Cape Mayson Police Department for the duration.

I sat in the backseat of the young officer's car, and Zack jumped in the passenger seat for the quick four-block ride to the condo. As I watched the foreboding dark sky and the wind nipping at the edges of loose roof tiles and siding, I was reminded of the power of mother nature. She had the ability to derail all things human, including a murder investigation. But even as I watched the storm approach, I was calm, knowing that the people responsible for Max's death were finally behind bars and that eventually, justice would be served.

At this moment, facing a hurricane didn't seem so bad compared to everything else I had weathered: my mother's murder, Adam's death, having a gun pointed at me—make that two guns now—almost getting run over by a boat, getting kidnapped. A hurricane seemed like a walk in the park.

As we pulled into the parking lot of the condo, I could see that the power was out. Emergency lights fueled by the building's generator were on, but we would have to take the stairs as the elevator would be out of service. We thanked the officer for the ride and urged him to get where he was going quickly so that he would be safe.

"I'm thinking apples, peanut butter and crackers, and red wine for dinner," Zack said as we huffed and puffed in tandem, climbing the stairs, his palms flat on my back to support me in my painful state. "We can't open the refrigerator, or your food will go bad. It will probably still go bad, but you have a better shot of keeping it if it stays closed and hope the power comes back on sooner rather than later."

"What do you know about hurricanes living in Pennsylvania?"

"I've been through a few, but I've been through even more snowstorms. Losing power is losing power. Just wait until you visit me in the wintertime—you'll see."

I thought for a moment how far away winter seemed right now, yet time with Zack seemed to move so quickly, like we were meant to be here in this humid, concrete stairwell with the wind howling outside, taking each step like we were climbing a mountain.

I looked at my phone, which would surely not last the night

given its forty percent charge. There were several missed calls from Janie, presumably asking me to work. Clearly, no one had filled her in on what was going on. I sent her a quick text telling her I was not available to work and left it at that. I would explain later.

Zack and I placed rolled up towels on the windowsills and at the bottom of the sliding doors to the balcony to keep the rain out. We closed all the shutters on the off chance the wind was strong enough to break the glass. There was one interior bedroom with only one window. We decided this would be the safest place to weather the storm. I gathered candles and matches and filled several jugs with water in case the island cut off the water service. I had never gone through a hurricane as a civilian before, only as a journalist, but I had done so many stories on what to do to prepare that I felt confident I knew the drill.

Zack's iPad had a full charge, so he was monitoring the weather conditions. It was forecast to come ashore at the South Carolina-North Carolina line and then follow the coastline up through Virginia. It was currently a category three storm but was expected to come across as a category two and then weaken to a category one when it hit land. I knew better than to look at categories. I had witnessed devastating category ones and seen threes that barely took a tree down. It was all about the direction it came in and whether it was more of a rain event, a wind event, or both.

"Are you worried?" Zack asked me as we snuggled on the small daybed we had dragged into the bathroom by candlelight, sipping red wine and eating apple slices with peanut butter. We decided this was even safer than the bedroom because it had no windows.

"Nope. Not at all."

"Good," he said, drawing me in closer. "Everything is going to be all right."

He was right.

EPILOGUE

CAPE MAYSON SURVIVED the hurricane with minor damage. There was flooding in low-lying areas, scattered limbs, roof tiles, and pieces of siding littering the streets. But it was all just cleanup. Homes, for the most part, had fared well, and no one was hurt, not even the handful of reckless surfers who got caught in the violent storm surge and had to be rescued by the U.S. Coast Guard.

Zack and I decided that I would finish the summer in Pennsylvania living at the Airbnb I had rented when I visited him. He offered for me to stay with him, but I still needed my independence to see where this was going. Plus, I decided to have the twins come to Pennsylvania as soon as camp ended. We would stay there together for a few days before heading back to North Carolina so they could learn more about their roots. I planned to take them to their great-grandparents' house and tell them happy stories about my mother growing up there.

Zack and I were also working on the plans to renovate the old farmhouse and turn it into a bed in breakfast that we would own together, but he would run. We both agreed that I needed to stay in North Carolina until the twins graduated from high school. They had had so many disruptions in their lives. They needed to be in their own home, where they felt comfortable, with the friends they had grown up with.

While six years seemed like an eternity, I knew it would go by in the blink of an eye. I also knew it would give me plenty of time to really assess what this thing with Zack was. Was it just a business partnership *or a real partnership*, one that had the potential to last a lifetime? I honestly didn't know yet. I still wasn't ready to define it.

This decision not to sell the property was to the dismay of Belinda Parsons, who called me repeatedly and told me how much money I was missing out on. I respectfully told her that if I could make money now, it would still be there in two or three years if I changed my mind. This was what my gut was telling me to do. She didn't like my answer, and I didn't care. Living through tragedy gave me the ability to not care about the opinions of people who were not important in my life. Post-traumatic wisdom, I had heard it called.

With Roger's hearing coming up soon, I decided it was time for me to visit him again. I had last seen him in the springtime. That had been my first visit with him since I was twelve. I was so overwhelmed by my conflicted feelings for him at that time and his continued love for me after so many years that I left even more confused than ever. But this time, I was ready.

I borrowed Zack's car and drove to the Penn State Grove Correctional Institution in Inverness, Pennsylvania, about an hour from Dilltown. Zack wanted to go with me, but I insisted on going alone. I needed to do this on my own. If there was any chance that Roger was going to be released from prison, it was important to me that I establish the ground rules of our relationship now. I still wasn't sure what those ground rules were going to be, but I knew that I would need to get used to the idea of his not being guilty to upend the story I had built my entire life around.

This time, as I sat across from Roger in the visitation room on the hard plastic chairs at the small metal table surrounded by the cacophony of other visiting families, I was no longer afraid of what he wanted to tell me.

"Roger," I said as he winced a little, wanting so badly for me to call him 'Dad.' This was something I was not ready to do yet and might never be able to do. "Our last visit ended abruptly, and no, I haven't read all your letters, just bits and pieces of them, but I am ready to hear your truth from your own lips, for you to tell me in your own words exactly why you felt responsible for my mother's death, but yet you say you didn't kill her."

Roger was fragile-looking, age having stolen his formerly full head of hair and the elasticity of his face, but his eyes still twinkled, and his mouth was set in a soft smile meant only for me. He clasped his hands around his sagging belly and began with a soft, calm delivery meant to get the story out as fast as possible before the visit ended, but at the same time, trying not to sound too rushed.

"I was in a real bad way when your mom, Patty, left me. I was sad, confused, and *angry*. I knew it was my fault, that I had trouble controlling my rage, that I took it out on her. But I still couldn't bear losing her. So, I decided to come up here from New Jersey and win her back. I needed some liquid courage and stopped at this dive bar near your grandparents' house called the Blue Moon. Just a hole in the wall, a cinder block place with a neon sign and tiny windows that let no light in."

As I listened, I pictured the rundown, abandoned bar I had seen on my jog.

"So, I had a few beers with this guy named Clifton. He was a junkie, a drug addict. I occasionally bought pot from him when I was in town, and we'd share a few drinks. Not a friend, just someone I barely knew. But that day, I was really down, and I needed to talk to someone, *anyone*, and Clifton was there. I told him how upset I was, how mad I was at your mother, that I wanted her back more than anything, and that if I couldn't have her, I wanted her to disappear. That's what I said to him, *disappear*."

He stopped for a second to check my reaction to what he was saying. I sat stone-faced and nodded for him to continue.

"I was so tore out of the frame and so drunk, I was afraid I might do something off the wall, something crazy, like hurt her. I always carried a gun, a pistol—I had a concealed carry permit. And so, I asked Clifton to hold it for me; I told him I would come back and get it in a few days but that I couldn't have it near me right now. And then I got into my car and drove shit-faced to a crummy hotel nearby and passed out. The next morning, at the crack of dawn, I hightailed it back to New Jersey and passed out again in my bed there. The next thing I knew, I got a call from the police telling me that Patty had been shot and I needed to come right away, that you were all alone, that your grandparents were away at the time. I jumped in the car and headed right to you."

I sat quietly for a moment, taking his words in, words I could have heard so many years earlier if I had just taken the time to listen.

"So, that's it. You gave your gun to a drug addict, made a passing remark about wanting my mother to disappear, and he then goes to the house and kills her for no apparent reason?"

"I think in his compromised state, he thought he was doing it for me. He thought that's what I wanted. It was some weird, misguided loyalty fueled by drugs. I was a big old drunk, but I never did major drugs, hallucinogens. I can't begin to understand what it does to someone's mind, but I do know from the guys I've met in here that they can really mess up your judgment. Apparently, Clifton was taking LSD that night."

"So, why did you go down for him? Why didn't you rat him out?"

"First of all, I didn't think there was any court in America that would, believe me, believe that I just happened to give my gun to a guy who killed my wife after she had just left me. Secondly, I felt like it was truly my fault. *I gave him the gun. I gave him the idea.* I decided I had to pay the price, and that price was losing you. But I've changed. I've done a lot of work on myself in here. I know it's late, and it may be too late for us, but I'm hopeful that you might see fit to give me another chance if I get out. I'd love to get to know my grandchildren."

I didn't even know I was crying until I felt the tears stinging my cheeks. I could tell Roger wanted to hold my hand as he put his on the table and reached tentatively in my direction. I kept mine in my lap. He couldn't just undo all the pain with one conversation, but it was a start.

"I can't make you any promises, Roger," I said after a minute of silence hung between us. "But I am listening now. I am listening."

When I got to Zack's house, he pulled me into a bear hug. We stood that way on his porch for a long time, swaying to some mysterious song that wasn't playing.

"How did it go?"

"It went."

"That bad?"

"No, actually a little bit of good. I let him tell me his story."

Zack, of course, had known the story all along because he had Esther's files. But Zack wanted me to hear the rest of it from Roger, not from him.

"Good. I have a surprise for you."

"Wow, not sure I have the emotional bandwidth for surprises right now."

"This is a good one. So, you remember how Clifton ended up with your mother's rings, her wedding band and engagement ring, and he pawned them because he got scared?"

"Yes."

"Well, I knew it was a longshot, but I decided to try and track them down. As it turned out, the lady who donated her house to the state police department when she died, Zelda Ergon, bought them at a local auction. Coincidentally, Esther worked for her as a house manager when Zelda got older. She saw Esther admiring the rings on her dressing table one day, and so when she died, she left them to Esther. Of course, Esther knew they were your mother's rings. She had seen them on your mother's hand, and she had seen them at the pawnshop. She admired them only because she knew where they came from, not because she coveted them. So, she put them in her safety deposit box with a note to her husband, Pete, to find you after her death and make sure they got to you. The note had no explanation, but Pete reached out to us to see if 'We had kept track of Patty's daughter.'"

For the second time that day, tears were welling up in my eyes. He opened his hand to reveal the rings: a thin gold band and a beautiful emerald-cut diamond engagement ring. He put them into my palm and folded my hand closed. I stared down at my closed hand and then opened it again to look at the rings, to make sure they were real. I had seen them on my mother's hand in so many photographs.

"Thank you," I said barely above a whisper, tears filling my breath.

"No need. I had nothing to do with it. This just fell into my lap while I was looking for them and getting nowhere. Thank your mother. I believe it's her energy that brought these back to you, that she always intended for you to have them. It just took a little while."

"Like thirty-some years."

"True. But maybe things don't happen to us until we are truly ready for them."

"I've never thought of it that way."

Suddenly, the dwindling sunlight beaming down on the porch caught the diamond in my hand, sending a row of sparkles across the wooden slats beneath my feet. Just as quickly, they were gone.

Okay, mom, I'm ready for what comes next.

ACKNOWLEDGMENTS

I WANT TO THANK my family for once again putting up with me during what can be a long and tedious journey from writing to publishing. I would especially like to thank my husband, Grif, for introducing me to the beautiful North Carolina coast and boating, which has become a passion for both of us. I want to thank my editor, Elizabeth Turnbull, for always making me better, my publisher, Light Messages, for keeping me relevant, my friend, Kelly for his excellent work on my website, my friend Liza for continually encouraging me to promote my work, and my friend Cliff for seamlessly engineering my audiobooks.

ABOUT THE AUTHOR

AMANDA LAMB IS A TELEVISION NEWS REPORTER covering the crime beat for an award-winning NBC affiliate in the southeast with more than three decades of experience. She also appears regularly on true crime shows as an expert for national networks. Recently, she wrote, hosted, and co-produced a successful podcast called Follow the Truth, which re-examines the 1993 murder of Michael Jordan's father. She has another podcast in production about connecting unidentified remains to missing and murdered people. She has published 12 books in multiple genres, including the popular Maddie Arnette mystery series. She is the mother of two girls and makes her home with her husband in North Carolina.

Connect with Amanda:
www.alambauthor.com
Twitter @alamb
Instagram @wral_amanda_lamb
Facebook:/wralAmandaLamb

OTHER *MADDIE ARNETTE NOVELS*

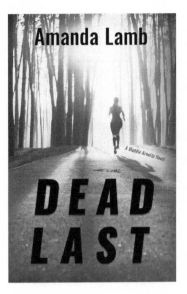

Maddie Arnette traded in her hard-news crime reporting hat for a simpler and gentler life. Yet, she cannot let go of her lifelong addiction to the dark side of journalism.

In *Dead Last* Suzanne Parker falls to the pavement in front of Maddie during the Oak City Marathon in her small North Carolina city. Maddie assumes it's an accident. But then Suzanne whispers words that make Maddie's skin go cold and sends her crime-fighting antenna into high gear—"my husband is trying to kill me."

Maddie's past is about to catch up to her in *Lies that Bind*.

Maddie Arnette has built her whole life around the narrative that her father murdered her mother. When a woman in the grocery store claims that Maddie's father did not kill her mother, the revelation forces the journalist toward a reckoning.

Is it possible that her father has sat in prison for almost forty years for a crime he did not commit? And if he didn't do it, who did?

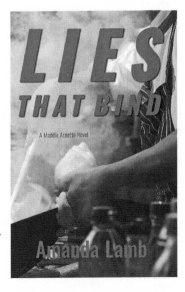